The Goatman

By

Wallace Martin, MD

First Edition
ISBN (paperback): 979-8-9899175-0-1
ISBN (hardcover): 979-8-9899175-1-8

The Goatman is available in the following formats:
hardback, paperback, e-book, & audiobook

Cover Design: Fab Bozzolo Fabia
Publisher: Tesart818, LLC
Author Contact: Goatman1953@yahoo.com
Website: TheGoatmanBook.com

This book is dedicated
to
Tyler, Elise, & my wife, Tammie, for her support and
encouragement throughout this process

ACKNOWLEDGEMENTS

I want to acknowledge the following for their encouragement, input, and support throughout the process of writing The Goatman. Thanks to Clyde Martin, Michelle Clarke, Tyler & Elise Martin, Tammie Barthen, John & Anne & Susan Searles, Andy Lawrence, Paul Stiefel, Zack Martin, & Patsy Martin.

Editors: Richard Krevolin & Nancy Cohen

Audio produced by: **SUNNY PICTURES, INC.**

Audio narrated by: Jayne Amelia Larson & Jake Eberle

Website design by: Danielle Eckerle

Table of Contents

Deep in the Shadows

The Goatman Lies

When he Creeps Out

One of us Dies

Chapter One

Death at Freeman's Mill

Though only fourteen, Zeb Barton knew many ways to die and had seen most of them. From the top of the hill, the rutted serpentine trail to Freeman's Mill looked deceptively calm, almost peaceful. Thickets and brambles underneath dense pines threatened to swallow the rocky, uneven passage. Except for the occasional abandoned shack, the encircling miles held nothing. But still, within that emptiness, the road was filled with sharp turns that mocked Zeb at every curve. Only a frenzied, death-defying descent down this trail and over the rickety wooden bridge crossing the Alcovy River would silence the voices. Drown the terrifying visions that had consumed his sleepless nights for the past three months. Or so it seemed.

Zeb raised his gangly, disjointed-looking frame from the grumbling, dilapidated World War II vintage motorcycle discarded by his next oldest brother, Clayton Barton. The Barton boys were all tall. Zeb already showed signs that he would soon surpass his older brothers in height. As he stood upright, his yellow-speckled, pale blue eyes peered through the trees into the valley below. Down by the Alcovy River. Killing the motor, he could hear sirens echoing across the silence. Leaning forward, still straddling the faded Army-green motorcycle he controlled with large, growing hands, he made out Hobbleton police cars as well as a Timms Funeral Home hearse which doubled as the town ambulance.

As Zeb studied the scene, a red-tailed hawk descended to a nearby Oak, landing softly on the smallest of top branches without a sound. Fading freckles from boyhood were still visible on Zeb's strong, maturing face — which appeared aged beyond his years. The hairs on the back of Zeb's neck tingled when he heard a noise in the thicket of briars not twenty feet away, pulling him back to the heat of the day. For a moment he thought he saw a grizzled, bearded, hunched over old man about to lunge at him. He pulled back, struggling to breathe. Then he heard a growl as a shadowy figure jumped out of the thicket and tackled him.

As Zeb hit the ground, he was paralyzed with fear. Just as suddenly, he recognized a familiar face. It was his friend Jake who had ambushed him from the scrambled brush.

Zeb gasped then let out a huge sigh of relief. "What the heck are you doing here?" he asked, as Jake released him from a death grip and they stood up. "Almost scared the life out of me! For a minute I thought you were the Goatman," Zeb finished, shaking his head.

"I bet you never even seen the Goatman," Jake said, a grin growing as he brushed the red dust from his worn jeans. "I got you good. Jolted ya right out of one of those daydreams of yours."

Jake lived in a one-room shack nearby. Rumor had it that he lived with his mother, but Zeb had never seen her and Jake had never mentioned her. He was older than Zeb, but he had missed school frequently and had been held back for more than a few years, landing him in one of Zeb's classes. Jake Stubblefield was plenty smart, but no one had expected him to finish grade school.

Clearly pleased with himself for having fooled Zeb into thinking he was the Goatman, Jake juggled pebbles in the palm of his hand, continuing, "Knew I had you when I saw that faraway look on your face. Been watching you eye that stretch of dirt for some time. It's just red clay and gravel. Ain't a livin', breathin' thing slithering about to strike!" In response, Zeb feigned a punch at Jake's midsection which Jake ignored.

"Well," Zeb began. "I've been trying to work out the best way down. Thinking about how Clayton maneuvered his way through these twists and turns the last time I saw him in the spring. At full throttle on this very motorcycle, accelerating as if he were the howling wind itself. He was laughing away when he crossed the bridge. Nobody else has ever been able to get over the bridge without crashing. I'm sure you remember my attempt last summer. I hardly got to the bridge before I panicked and took the nasty spill that broke my arm.

"Clayton is strong. After he crossed the Alcovy, he tipped his cap, as if taking a bow, then pitched me up in the air and said, 'Zeb, you little troublemaker, if you can survive that ride, you can follow me anywhere.' Then he just took off that same day, probably gone early on his yearly summer trek over the Appalachian Trail. Odd he didn't let me know he was leaving or even wait to see me make it over the bridge. Don't know when he'll be back. No one seems to know. But he does what he wants on his own time. If I make it, I'll bet he finally takes me with him when he goes trekking next year."

Zeb didn't let on that soon after Clayton left, he began to be plagued by headaches and nightmares. Zeb felt an emptiness inside him. A black hole pulling words from the inescapable air trying to fill the void. Began talking to himself or hearing voices, not sure which and maybe a bit of both. Words appeared and disappeared in an instant, like a stone tossed into a turbulent river creating ripples that were drowned. Swallowed. Leaving only the doubt. Mostly nonsensical. Nothing he wanted to share with anyone.

Instead, he continued, saying, "Clayton didn't think I could make it across the bridge, but I'm going to this time. Nothing is going to stop me. I'm going to prove to him I can make it. Got distracted by the sirens and commotion at the Mill just now is all. I can't wait to see the look on Clayton's face when I tell him. I bet he gets back home as soon as he finds out I made it down across the bridge and he'll be mad he missed it."

Zeb brushed a tangled shock of brown, sunburned hair away from his mischievous, pale blue eyes. He seemed more concerned about conquering the hill and proving to Clayton he could do it than about the significant risk of a fatal ending to this quest. Too many had ended up in the Alcovy River and never returned.

As he spoke to Jake, Zeb sensed low, distant rumbling like thunder clouds gathering, but looking around, he saw clear blue skies that held nothing ominous. Maybe he'd just heard the low, indecipherable chords of an approaching train in the distance? Zeb secretly hoped Clayton's return would stop these unpredictable sounds of impending danger, invisible echoes. The unwelcome thoughts that had begun in the last few months.

Clayton would not be returning.

Jake's eyebrows narrowed with confusion. Zeb's resolve, shown on his face, bordered on suicidal. Jake had tackled Zeb and joked around with him to jolt him out of his faraway stare, a look that showed Zeb was somewhere distant in his mind. A stare Jake had only noticed since the spring. Since Clayton left. Jake knew Zeb was close to Clayton and desperately wanted him to return, but Zeb's determination and thought that crossing the bridge over the Alcovy River would get his brother to return sooner made no sense.

Jake scratched his head. Looking at his worn shoe, he said, "There ain't but one way down, and it has nothing to do with what's in your head. Anyway, even if you make it, the climb out is rough. There's nothing down there much except the abandoned Mill. I hear it used to be a decent swimming hole back in the day, where the water was backed up feeding the waterwheel. They say snake beds are all over the place now. Can't see 'um. Jump in and they strike all at once holdin' you under. Fangs and slimy scales in cold blackness. Not for me."

This surprised Zeb, for he thought nothing much frightened Jake. He had seen Jake take on grown men and make them back down. Jake was not small and much stronger than you would have thought looking at his youthful face. A scar that jutted from below his left ear across his neck seemed to hold his head in place and screamed scarlet red when Jake got angry.

"Jake, you're not worried about snakes. I know you can't swim. You never want to go to the Mill. I think you're just scared the Goatman might be lurking around down there. Pa says it's just a silly, old fairy tale. That I should leave thoughts about a Goatman alone. But I think he's real, even though no one that I know of has ever seen him — except maybe Thelka. She said he rode in a cart pulled by twenty goats. Lived on roots, lizards, snakes, and goat meat. She said he got messed up in World War II and looks like he hasn't bathed since. Has a beard three feet long. I don't know that I believe her either, though. You know she'll spin you sometimes."

Zeb looked toward the valley below noticing the red-tailed hawk, motionless, flashing his steely eyes in search of unsuspecting prey.

"By the way, what happened at the Mill?" Zeb asked, lowering his voice as if someone else besides Jake was listening.

"Don't know. They won't let anyone nearby. Probably your Goatman." Jake smirked then playfully jabbed Zeb in the ribs with a glint holding trouble in his deep green eyes.

"Well, I've heard he is as real as the scar on my neck," Jake said, as his thin smile disappeared. He ran a dirty finger along the thick, raised, reddening line across his neck as if it would lead them to the Goatman. Jake looked around cautiously, adding, "And dangerous. Just like the nursery rhyme says... 'Deep in the shadows the Goatman lies. When he creeps out, one of us dies.' As I hear it told, he creeps about mostly at night. Moves from town to town until someone sees him. Then disappears into the shadows again. Wherever he goes, people disappear. Or die in awful ways. I heard in Chatsworth, a few months back, they found a whole family butchered like you would a pig or a goat. Thought it was the Goatman but couldn't prove nuthin'."

"According to Thelka," Zeb piped in, "the Goatman roams around North Georgia. He has been seen around here from time to time. She claims he stays near graveyards when he's skulking about. She didn't say where. Steals away little defenseless kids. They evaporate into the night. Some folks say he digs up corpses and steals from them — or worse. I'm not worried, though. Clayton says that as long as he is around, no Goatman will ever get to me or take me away.

"I asked Thelka if she knew when Clayton would be back, but she was too busy to answer. She probably doesn't know, anyway, since he just runs off whenever he wants."

Jake uneasily shifted his weight, and his deep green eyes widened. Puzzled. He reached for an old dry branch caught up in the thicket and began breaking it into smaller and smaller pieces. Seeing a smirk creeping across Zeb's face when he mentioned 'corpses,' Jake sensed Zeb was about to reveal some disturbingly graphic medical information he had gleaned while helping his father, Dr. Clyde Barton. He hoped the noise of breaking branches would drown out whatever Zeb was about to divulge. While Jake liked Dr. Barton just fine, he'd had need of Doc's services more than once in the past, the result of a violent youth. The most traumatic of these events resulted in the scar on his neck. Though it would serve as a relentless reminder of one terrible hazy night, he had been too young to remember much of what happened. Fewer gory details suited Jake.

Zeb, on the other hand, couldn't resist these moments when he could torment Jake. It was the only time he seemed braver than his friend. Trying to contain a smile, Zeb spoke louder, competing with the methodical snapping of the branch. "Some ancient Italian by the name of DaVinci dug up dead folks to figure out how a person was put together, according to some of my pa's medical books. Cut them all to pieces. Heck if I'd be carving up dead folks. No doubt they'd be haunting you in little parts. One night an eyeball. The next a nose. Then an ear. Good thing, though, is I'd probably be able to outrun them, they being all disjointed, mangily pieces and such."

Jake half-heartedly laughed. "I'm not so sure. Way you run, looks like you ain't figured out which part is to land where. Slows you down."

Jake, envisioning more of Zeb's morbid descriptions, changed the subject. "Do you s'pose Goat Hill got its name from the Goatman? Should be called Freeman's Hill, it being by Freeman's Mill and all. Never seen goat one on that hill," he said, as he snapped the last of the branch and tossed a stray piece of bark back into the thicket where it disappeared as if it had been devoured.

Zeb replied, "Well that makes sense. Just because we haven't seen the Goatman doesn't mean he doesn't exist. I'm guessin' Goat Hill is where he captures goats to pull his cart. Ones he doesn't eat anyway. Just because they're wild and elusive, doesn't mean they don't exist either. But no graveyards down there. Maybe a few unmarked graves, that's all."

Jake noticed Zeb staring intensely back down the hill and knew he would not be deterred from his "mission." That's what Zeb called these adventures that usually ended up in a bad way — and he seemed more determined than ever to accomplish this one crossing the bridge. Zeb leaned the motorcycle from side to side, checking the tires one last time. Then he balanced himself upright on the frame, readying for the descent.

"I figure if I crash, the ambulance or hearse, depending on which would be more appropriate, is already at the bottom of the hill. No better time. Anyway, seems like most times we could skip over the ambulance stage, as most bad injuries we see in the Emergency Room are fatal," he said, bemused.

Suddenly, the hawk — which had been silently perched on the Oak — dropped onto unsuspecting prey which succumbed without protest to the enormous crush of the tightening talons.

Simultaneously, a white Chevy sedan skidded around the blind corner, scattering gravel on the red clay bank. It was Joe Scully, the bald, good-natured mailman, who yelled out to Zeb, "Zeb, Thelka said you might be over here. Your dad's lookin' for you. Got somebody in the office who's in bad shape. Think he said you might know him. He said to be quick!"

The ride downhill would have to wait for another day.

Chapter Two

Death By Venom

The back alley leading to Dr. Barton's office was dark day and night. Only rarely did shafts of light force their way through the steel support frames which no one ever thought to brick over. Like Doc Barton, they stood on their own, relying on nothing except their immutable strength and resolve to hold vigilant at all hours. Though never acknowledged, fatigue was a constant enemy in this old brick building.

As Zeb rushed through the alley to the back entrance of his father's office, Ike, the tall, muscular, Black caretaker opened the door. With a vacant stare, Ike said, "Zeb, boy, best be quick. It's bad. Brought him out of the river. Neva' seen nuthin' like it."

"Like what?" Zeb asked. He'd seen drowning victims and broken necks from dives into deceptive, shallow waters — not much you could do for them. Most died, mercifully, at the scene, never regaining consciousness. Others were not so fortunate.

"They was hanging all over him," said Ike. "Had to use a rope to pull him out. It's a wonder nobody else got hurt," he said, as he continued through the door, watching every step as if some demon had set precise fatal traps. "Watch where ya step, Zeb," were his last words.

Zeb knew his father, Dr. Clyde Barton, had been up all night. Usually this resulted in a glum, damnable disposition. Today was no exception.

"Goddamn it, I said hold him still! I can't do a damn thing with him twisting all over the place. If you can't get the job done, I'll go out to the street and find someone who will!" boomed the voice Zeb could recognize in his sleep.

As Zeb stepped into the hallway, he saw nothing familiar though he'd been here hundreds of times. Utter chaos. Blood splattered on the floor, the walls, the ceiling, and all over anyone near the exam room. In the shadows lay small slithering ropes with little discernable movement.

"Look out, boy! I think we killed 'em all, but even dead they still might bite. Some kinda' reflex, they say. Hell, I say they are possessed. Not natural to kill when you're already dead," shouted a deep voice from somewhere in the melee. The voice unquestionably belonged to Sheriff Hudlow. The local law. A stout, unbending man with ruddy cheeks wearing his impeccably pressed, dark blue uniform. He stood off to the side watching.

Just as Zeb looked down to make sure he had put on the lost shoes Thelka had found for him that morning, a small copper-headed snake bit into the sole. The calluses on his feet were so thick from being barefoot most of the time, he felt nothing. Reflexively, Zeb yanked his foot upward as he jumped away from the snake, but the snake wrapped around Zeb's leg tightly, refusing to let go. As the snake coiled for a second strike, Zeb yanked it off his leg. He narrowly missed a second bite as the open jaws with protruding fangs flew by his face, spraying venom, and crashed into the wall. Ike pounced quicker than the snake's third strike. He crushed its head with the heel of his boot.

Ike asked, "You okay, Zeb? Did it get you?"

"No, I don't think so," responded Zeb. *No time to worry about that just yet,* thought Zeb to himself as he stared at the scene before him. Zeb avoided looking at the boy's face for fear he would recognize him. For fear he would freeze and be unable to assist. A thought flashed before him. *Could it be Clayton?*

"Zeb, get in here. Hold this boy's legs. And damnit-all-to-hell, don't let one of these little bastards bite you!" demanded Dr. Barton. His rugged features stood out as he sprayed the walls, emptying a suction syringe of blood not six inches from where Zeb stood. Zeb had been in these situations before. He immediately did as told by his father.

Relief clamored in his head. It was not Clayton, but the boy in some way resembled Zeb. *He must have known he was dead from the moment he jumped into that peaceful reflective pool of water in the shoal,* thought Zeb. Hundreds of fangs had punctured his youthful white skin. Right now, Zeb needed to focus on saving an innocent life.

Zeb was born to this, or at least felt he was. Did Zeb know this boy? Whose son, brother, or friend, was he? Could he feel the frantic scalpel cuts into the punctures as Dr. Barton attempted to drain away the fatal poison? All this would have to wait. Only later could he acknowledge the horror in the young man's frantic, terrified eyes that lay before him.

Draping himself over the young man's violently twitching legs took all Zeb's weight and strength. It was as if the boy's legs had become giant serpents battling Zeb for the victim's life. No, his very soul. Zeb focused on this image and, imagined or real, it blunted a sadness he held within.

"Damn it, Zeb! I said hold him still! Damn fool boy jumping into a snake bed. About your age too. Sounds like something you would have done!" shouted Dr. Barton, both reprimanding and somehow sounding grateful all at once. Doc Barton was small in stature but powerful. Doc was right. If he and Clayton had been playing together, they could just as easily been the ones challenging each other's courage and ending up in a pool of snakes. Zeb knew to remain silent. He felt like in some strange way this boy had sacrificed himself for Zeb. As he imagined the moment of sacrifice, remote whispers of thunder began to creep in. At first, it was a faint rumbling, as if someone was calling from the depths of a well. Incremental, incoherent echoes. Distant. Then, faintly, Zeb imagined a faceless voice in his head resembling his voice, only older. Resembling Clayton Barton's voice:

CLICK. Should have saved him. Should have been there by the Mill. Should have been you. If you had finished your mission to the depths of the hill, this could have been avoided. Look at the boy. CLICK.

Zeb felt the tightening in his left temple as he tried to shut out the voice that penetrated his thoughts like a knife. He knew there would be other voices too. He just never knew when they'd come. No stopping them once begun. Only one chance to alter their echoes. *Look at the boy.* This was no man; but it was a boy maybe even younger than Zeb and certainly more innocent. Zeb had seen things helping his father that most — at any age — would never imagine. Even with all he'd seen, watching this boy near his age dying so painfully filled him with a new fear.

Zeb slowly allowed his eyes to open, though he had not realized they were shut. The boy lay naked before him with hundreds of twin punctures enveloping him. Vipers' marks. Many were oozing. Trickles of blood wept from precise, surgical cross-shaped cuts into the punctures: Dr. Barton's seemingly futile attempts to release the evil serpents' venom. The boy was white from shock and bleeding but did in fact bear a striking resemblance to Zeb under the harsh lights. The boy's strength was remarkable considering his almost frail appearance. Then the shaking and convulsions began.

"Hell, I think he is seizing," alerted Zeb's father. "Not a good sign. Turn him sideways and get a tongue blade in his mouth so he can breathe and not bite his tongue off!"

Ike, who had been silently holding the boy down by the shoulders, did as instructed. Mechanically, he flipped the boy sideways in one effortless, smooth motion.

It came on like a storm. Gradual rhythmic contractions increasing in intensity until the lightning exploded through the boy's body jolting his extremities. It was no use. Only now did Zeb realize a nurse and three men were also assisting. They could not contain the desperate attempts with which this boy seemed to plead for life. Foam bubbled up into his mouth, and as the storm of convulsions receded, he shrieked like a baby rabbit being gutted in the jaws of a hunting dog. "Don't throw me in! I didn't mean anything by it! Wasn't hurtin' anybody. Goatman! Not now!" screamed the boy in the midst of otherwise incoherent muttering. His pleading became mumbles. His mumbles became silence. He was gone.

His now-hollow eyes stared straight ahead seeing nothing. Only then did Zeb allow himself to recognize the boy. He was a year younger, and Zeb had only seen him across the school yard once or twice. Zeb didn't know his name.

Zeb looked around the room. As suddenly as the chaos had begun, it ceased. In slow motion, blurry forms began to pick up syringes and bloodied towels from the floor, careful to avoid the motionless snakes. The Undead.

Zeb studied his father, who slumped over the child as if praying. He was drenched. Sweat. Blood. His muscular arms and strong hands quivered from what had been two hours of facing the demons and losing. To Zeb, it had felt like two minutes.

"Damn it all to hell," muttered his father. "How many patients out there? Start putting them back. Not a thing we can do for this poor son of a bitch. Delivered him thirteen or fourteen years ago. Good kid, good parents. Poor as dirt but thanked me any way they could. When they get here, let me know. Call Pastor Arp. Let him know so he can counsel the family and make preparations for another funeral."

Dr. Barton gave the lifeless body one more glance. Then he splashed water over his arms and face. He stepped out of the exam room, his face weathered by storm but not defeated. Dr. Barton had chiseled features. Dark olive skin with deep-set, penetrating, dark brown eyes. Handsome, despite a slightly crooked and flattened nose from years of boxing in the Navy. As Doc turned to leave the room, Zeb admired his father's strength and resolve. His capricious, uncontrollable bouts of rage were another matter. Zeb feared those almost as much as he feared the Goatman. Maybe more.

"Next time it will be different. I'll beat the bastard next time," Doc Barton mumbled as he walked down the long, darkening hallway alone. Zeb knew he was referring to Death, but Dr. Barton's face had already transmitted that message without uttering a word.

Then the throbbing in Zeb's foot began.

Chapter Three

Venom Creeps

The venom stealthily made its way from the unconscious to the undeniable as the demon seed insidiously made its way from capillaries to veins. From veins to the pulsating waves of his heart. Each beat propelled the immobilizing venom, paralyzing Zeb's vital organs.

Much as he had for the faceless shadows that haunted his dreams and hid in the edges of his vision for months, Zeb refused to acknowledge this intrusion into the first day of summer. He admitted to the pain and numbness only when Ike, who protected his father like a brother, noted Zeb trying to hide a limp after returning home that night. Ike knew its meaning from venomous jungle snakebites he'd seen during WWII in the Pacific. He also knew Zeb didn't want to add more work and worry for his father. And Doc Barton would not be pleased.

"Zeb, best tell your pa about that bite. Probably be okay with most of the poison used up on that dead boy on the table. Your pa's going to be mad for sure, but he's going to be lots madder if you up and die on him than he is about you getting bit by that little nuthin' snake," said Ike.

Ike had known Clyde Barton from childhood growing up in Maysville, a small speck of a nowhere town in the North Georgia woods. Ike had an easy smile despite several prominent scars across his forehead and massive, strong, calloused hands. He stood above Zeb like a colossus. Ike had followed Dr. Barton when he enlisted in the Navy in World War II, and, for reasons unknown to Zeb, had been with him ever since.

"Ike, you know I'll be fine. Like you said, he is in no mood for more to take care of today. He is way behind time with office patients," said Zeb, eyeing his foot as if it were a friend who had, in an instant, become a mortal enemy — an appendage that belonged to someone else. A betrayal.

"Besides," added Zeb. "Nothing he can do. Cutting into that callous won't help because it isn't going to bleed, and we don't have any medicines to treat such a thing."

"That's right." Thelka, the maid, boomed into the kitchen startling Zeb and Ike. "That poison prob'lee comes straight from the devil's mouth, and tryin' to combat the devil with his own bile is like throwin' water on a grease fire."

Thelka had been listening behind the pillars on the front porch of the Barton's brick house. She had been shielded from their view. If not for Thelka and Jake, Zeb would mostly be alone. His father was seldom around. His oldest brothers were in college and infrequently returned. Clayton had been the closest in age to Zeb, but now he was gone. Clayton was a good brother, but a little on the wild side, preferring fast cars and faster brunettes. He had a knack for finding trouble. Seemed to seek it out, but he was fiercely protective of Zeb.

Doctor Barton had been talking about sending Clayton off to military boarding school for his senior year to teach him discipline. But no one, not even Doc, was going to keep him from roaming free.

And despite wanting him to follow his directives more, Doc was clearly proud of Clayton's self-sufficiency and ability to get by in any scrape. He didn't have to worry about that boy.

Zeb was told his mother had died during childbirth when he was four. Zeb had little recollection of her. Oddly, no one ever spoke about her either. Since then, Thelka had done her best to nurture Zeb and keep him out of trouble.

Thelka was easily concealed in the shadows. She was dark as a moonless night. Like Ike, she had been with Dr. Barton long as Zeb could recall. Unlike Ike, she was short and round with an ever-present lump of snuff bulging beneath her lower lip. Best anyone could guess, she was in her early forties, but her parents were sharecroppers and her grandfather an emancipated slave. No records existed. She was superstitious and feared the night shadows, "haints" as she called them, but no flesh and blood man or woman worried her in the least. She carried a pearl-handled pistol in case the need of it arose, but the gun had recently been confiscated by the Hobbleton police.

Thelka held a wrinkle of worry on her forehead. "Boy, what did I tell you about stayin' away from them snakes? I bet ya quit hidin' yo' shoes so's ya don't hafta go ta church. If I hadn't found them for ya, you'd be in a worse way. You ain't nuthin' but trouble. Sometimes I believe you are the devil hisself."

"That'd be most of the time," agreed Ike. "But this time, it wasn't his doing."

Ike crossed his muscular, sculptured forearms while standing directly before Zeb and continued, "Now, we can sit here like most folks and worry over this a hundred times or move on and live it just once. Me, I prefer the once; but if you would like to tack on the other ninety-nine, being as you're full of stubbornness and all, I'll sit here 'til you are done counting. But one thing is for sure, your pa puts up with delaying what needs doing about as much as he does with alibis and excuses."

"Boy, you listen to Ike and git on down there back to the office. You too mean and ornery to git sick, but no use in takin' chances," chastised Thelka. She went outside to the porch, more concerned than she let on. A deeper frown spread across her forehead.

Zeb knew they were right. They always were when it came to understanding Doc Barton. Zeb took a step toward the car to make the inevitable trip to his father's office. His ankle had started to swell and ache even worse. A rolling thunder began making its way into his head. Thoughts he tried desperately to avoid gathered like smoky mists encircling mountain tops, strangling them on a sweltering, hot, humid summer afternoon. Invisible, distorted words hung before Zeb:

Could have saved him. CLACK. Should have saved him. Look now. There will be others. You don't have time for this. You can change this. Look away from yourself.

Zeb progressively appeared lost in thought. Incurable murmuring drifted through vacillating fog tormenting him.

Ike chose not to notice the faraway stare which made Zeb look more like a statue frozen in time under an inexplicable spell. Unreachable. Ike tightened his jaw in preparation to lift the boy, whose tremulous gait had shown he was beginning to struggle. To weaken. Ike was determined to carry Zeb to the car, but Zeb would have no part of that. Instead, he wriggled away saying, "Ike, do you think he suffered much? My foot doesn't feel so good, and I only got one secondary bite from a baby snake that was already pretty much dead. I can see him jumping into that cool clear water only to be attacked. Fangs everywhere. Defenseless."

Zeb visualized the dead boy's body while trying not to, unable to force the vision from his thoughts — a recurrent, inexplicable curse he fought to overcome. Then Zeb shuddered as he sensed clattered chanting. It could be threatening. Irrational. Not his voice. Not Clayton's. Unrecognizable. Yet, again, it came:

If only you had been there sooner. CLICKITY. Listen.

Unable to fully focus while also attempting to subdue the voice, Zeb continued turning his attention to the snake-bit victim. "Must be over a hundred bites, Ike. Looked like he was praying after they cleaned him up and turned him on his side. Wouldn't close his eyes neither. They'd push his eyelids shut, and they'd just spring back open. Didn't he scream something about the Goatman?"

Ike had noticed the boy's pulseless body and hollow stare. It was a look he had seen during the war. A look that he had been unable to escape even though it had been over twenty years since Japan surrendered in 1945 on the battleship *USS Missouri*. Lifeless, black-eyed faces continued to haunt Ike. Voiceless, but they spoke to him all the same. Incoherent, sporadic pleas. Unbearable suffering.

During World War II, Ike and Dr. Barton, then a medic, had been stationed in the Pacific. Ike served primarily as support for the initial waves of assault troops as the Marines launched attacks from island to murderous island against the Japanese. On burial duty, it was Ike who retrieved unrecognizable human forms and body parts. This gruesome task still gave him nightmares.

"Ike! Did you hear me?" Zeb asked, loudly. Ike jumped when Zeb spoke. "You went traveling again. Don't always know where your mind takes you, but you're not here. Being as I might be moving on to the hither yonder myself, I would appreciate your acting like you were worried."

"Now, boy, don't you start with your nonsense. That sympathy thing may work with Thelka but not with me," responded

Ike. "Yes, seems like he mumbled, 'Goatman', but all you boys 'round here say that name for anyone you don't understand. Always easier to hate and fear. Anyways, I couldn't make out half of what he said, he bein' delirious and all," continued Ike, with a blank stare at Zeb's leg. This time, Zeb didn't fight back when Ike picked him up like he was lifting a bale of hay to store in the barn.

As Ike gingerly slid Zeb into the car and started driving, he began one of his many stories to keep Zeb focused. Each held intent. Zeb had to hear them repeatedly to decipher their meaning. This one he'd never heard.

Ike began, "I am thinking about a young fella from the war about your age when I first met him in Maysville. Went to the Pacific around the time your pa and me was there. Both was medics. This fellow was an unusual sort. Smart, but couldn't tell the difference between Japs and us. Treated both the same. Probably saved as many of theirs as ours. Didn't stop the Japs from trying to kill him though. Medics were a prime target."

Zeb leaned in closer. Even though he was sitting next to him, Ike's voice was farther away somehow, and Zeb didn't want to miss a word. Ike wasn't one to explain what he had said. It seemed an odd time for a story that had nothing to do with Zeb's perilous condition, but he knew Ike dwelled in his own time — one that fused past and present. It was his way of facing the unthinkable. And the possibility of Zeb being lost with Clayton gone was more than Ike could fathom. Probably more than even Doc Barton could face alone.

Ike continued, "First met him, he treated me like I was White folk, which happened from time to time. Like your pa does. But that medic fellow really thought I was White. More than that, he couldn't see the scars on my face. People say they sees him round here from time to time. War messed him up bad."

Zeb tried not to look at Ike's scars though he couldn't help it. His recollection would not carry him back to the first encounter he had with Ike, but he did remember being told not to stare on more than one instance. Zeb had never asked what caused the multiple linear slices all over Ike's face, and Ike never offered an explanation. Didn't seem to matter to either one. Ike was still Ike. The mosaic punctures that looked as if they had been made by a scalpel didn't change that. He was like a second father to Zeb.

Zeb could sense he was becoming more confused. Ike's voice was beginning to fade in and out. But he continued to listen to Ike, as there was nothing that could be done about it until they reached his father's office.

"Odd, him being a medic and all. Most doctor-types ask me about what kind of surgeon did this and why," said Ike, unaware Zeb's condition was quickly worsening. Touching his scars lightly, he added, "Weren't no doctor did this anyway. I was just a kid. Enough of that though. And the war is over." Ike's own fading words seemed to convince himself of this.

Despite the progressive numbness and pain continuing its journey up his leg and some tingling in his hands, Zeb focused all of his attention on Ike's every gesticulation. Ike choreographed his tale in the air, like a conductor, as if driven by some overwhelming divinity. A chorus of disjointed voices concealed in one damaged war survivor. Zeb was listening so intently he hadn't noticed the numbness around his mouth or the progressive difficulty he was having breathing. Zeb refused to acknowledge fear about his own deteriorating condition. He could only imagine the horrible death that Ike had seen.

Between suddenly labored breaths, Zeb asked, "Ike, how could the Japs try to kill someone who saved some of them? This medic guy that you knew from Maysville. Doesn't seem fair. He should have killed all those Japs."

Ike noticed Zeb slurring his words and pushed harder on the gas pedal before continuing. "Not that simple, boy. We had monsters of our own. Devil uses war to creep into the soul of men. Fear and anger, they be fertile ground. Kinda' like the black dirt in that low land over by the Alcovy River. You know. Where we get worms for fishin'. From under that toppled over dead Oak tree. Anyways, that medic wasn't killed. Much worse," responded Ike.

"Wh… What did they do to him, Ike? Mmm… Must have been awful. Who found him? S… Saved him? Do you think he comes around here l… like some people told you?" stammered Zeb. Neither he nor Ike noticed the marked weakening in Zeb's voice.

As they pulled into the back of Dr. Barton's office, Ike took a deep breath as if to purge himself from what he was hesitantly about to tell Zeb. Speaking for those who no longer could. Those who banged about in his head. As Ike began, though, Zeb toppled over in the car seat next to him, motionless. Ike looked around, wide-eyed, as if trying to crawl out of the Pacific jungles. He cradled the boy, only now realizing how much Zeb had rapidly deteriorated. He swept Zeb up and, in a single motion, crashed through the back door of Dr. Barton's office.

"Doc, come quick! Zeb's hurt bad!" Ike shouted.

Chapter Four

Chaos

As Zeb regained consciousness, he sensed the crowd and activity around him. Shadows that stood at the edge of his clouded recognition seemed familiar. He sensed he had seen them before, that they were the same apparitions which had haunted his dreams. Only now they were less transparent, less gray, and less dimensionless than at the edge of the woods and field at nightfall. No one else seemed to notice them. In a low rumble, and in unison, they began to chant:

Now you've done it. You should be out there. You should stop them. CLACK. Or maybe you don't want to stop them. Maybe you are them.

Zeb was startled when a voice much like his own implored, "Zeb, can you hear me?

"Start intravenous fluids with normal saline and add some bicarbonate," his father said. "From the look of that leg, he is going to lose some muscle from the pressure caused by the swelling. Damn it all to hell! May have to cut into the compartments of his lower leg to relieve the pressure. I've got to save his leg."

Even though chaos was a frequent visitor at Dr. Barton's office — with car accidents, tractor injuries, precipitous childbirth, and the like — this was more frenzied than usual. Zeb's father and Ike seemed off-kilter, which never happened.

Dr. Barton exhaled loudly. "At least his blood pressure is coming up, and he is starting to regain consciousness. I think he should be okay if we keep giving him fluids and oxygen. That antivenom should be here shortly. I got Joe Scully to stop his mail route. He's headed over to Emory to get what we need." Dr. Barton tried to convince himself more than communicate with the somber staff. His tone was serious, but his words seemed oddly remote — as if he couldn't acknowledge that this was Zeb who helplessly lay before him. No time for that. He needed unfettered focus to save his son. Emotions were a hindrance to a surgeon most any day, but especially today.

"Add some more bicarbonate to the intravenous fluids. Need to alkalinize his blood and urine. If we don't, the acid buildup from the dying muscle in his leg could cause arrhythmias of his heart. And we need to give a lot of IV fluids to wash the myoglobin from the dying muscle. We've got to keep the kidneys from shutting down," he added, taking a draw from a Chesterfield cigarette he picked up that hung over a nearby table — a habit he acquired while in the Navy.

"Renal failure is the last thing we need. Opening the compartments of the leg so the muscle damage is mitigated is a damnable business," he said, recalling an episode from his childhood that almost took his own life.

Dr. Barton's words were noticeably void of the usual litany of curses. His face, which was always full of forced energy, even in the darkest of nights, suddenly appeared drained and overwhelmed.

For the moment, he refused to fully acknowledge Zeb's condition by focusing on recollections of himself surviving being bit by a Rattlesnake as a child. He had been running through a field outside his childhood home in Maysville when it occurred. He recalled the crushing burn and sharp sting. He remembered the enormity of pain while he shook with sweat in his family's scorching hovel of a home. The pain from his own tremendous swollen leg crashed over him like a rogue wave. The venom from a Timber Rattler was much more potent than the Copperhead that bit Zeb.

Back then, Clyde Barton was expected to die, as there was no medical care in the remote mountains of North Georgia in the years just before and after WWI. There was no money to pay for it regardless. Relatives had come and gone saying their tearful prayers over him like he'd already been tucked in the ground. Not wanting to fall behind in his work, the undertaker had even begun constructing the young Clyde Barton's pine coffin.

"Raise the IV bags up. Ike, you squeeze on both bags. We need to get those fluids in faster!" snapped Dr. Barton, as he began to think back to his having survived, trying to distance his thoughts from those of Zeb possibly dying.

As a surgeon who had to remain focused in order to successfully complete each operation, Doc had trained himself to feel nothing at the most stressful times. While this was best for his patients in dire need, it confused many of those around him and made him appear harsh, uncaring. But not Ike. Ike understood Doc. And now, with Zeb's life at stake, he understood the need for Doc to momentarily escape. Paradoxically, at times, distraction through humor in the face of death seemed the only way to continue.

"Ike," Doc began, "Don't think I ever told you about my encounter with a Timber Rattler back in the day, did I? It was before I saw you beat up and bloodied on the ground that day we first met."

"No, Doc, I don't think I heard about the Rattler," responded Ike, raising the IV bags awkwardly, as he was unaccustomed to assisting in Doc's office.

Sensing Ike twisting about uneasily at the mention of the day their lives intersected, Dr. Barton began the story surrounding the Rattler bite. He recalled how one-armed Uncle Prather, a kind, patient man, who spoke in even, level tones, told him the details after he awoke from a coma.

"Apparently, I was extremely ill to the point that the undertaker had taken it upon himself to measure my dimensions. Built me a fine-tailored pine coffin. An Ark to hoist me to the heavens," said Dr. Barton.

Doc Barton smirked at the thought. "My Uncle Prather had other ideas that conflicted with those of the undertaker. Prather raised hogs and bird dogs which often got bit by Rattlers during hunting season. It was a season that remained active throughout the year, as did the moonshine stills by clear water creeks that provided the only real money the Prather family saw. Over the years, Prather had mixed different combinations of roots, bark, boneset, and mud until he saved an occasional animal by cutting a long gash from the fang puncture up the limb. Then he packed the cut with his salve."

Zeb rolled over and seemed to breathe easier. Upon observing this, Doc Barton relaxed slightly and continued, as if telling his own story removed the venom from his son's body.

Doc continued, "Uncle Prather grinned as he told me of the events, saying, 'Now your mother thought if God wanted her son, that being you, He could come on and get you. She saw no use in me cutting you up and stuffing you with mud prior to such time. Besides, the undertaker had made such a fine box for you and all the neighbors were looking forward to a good funeral. Such an occasion meant getting all dressed up, lots of food, and perhaps more than one courtship might begin or even be consummated by some of the more adventuresome'."

"Crazy times back then, Doc," said Ike. "What did Prather say he did next?"

Dr. Barton responded, "Uncle Prather laughed and said he had taken a liking to me, that I was delirious enough, and he figured I wouldn't notice him whittling away at my leg. I remember exactly how Prather had told me.

"Uncle Prather had said, hesitantly, 'I was a bit wrong about that. But I knew you were stubborn and had an aversion to being stuck anywhere that was not in the great outdoors, much less a hole in the ground. Hell, most times you wouldn't even come inside to the supper table because you thought you'd miss something. Anyways, you gradually came around with my rudimentary surgical skills and salve, much to the ire of the caretaker who soon enough found a suitable replacement for his handiwork. Lots of ways to get dead back then, you know.' Uncle Prather had said as he finished telling me what had happened."

Plenty of ways now, thought Doc Barton to himself as he stared back at his last-born son, who was beginning to show signs of delirium slowly abating.

Zeb was his favorite son, and while he would deny this if asked, no one asked. Dr. Barton called Zeb his "privileged character" or his "cap pistol," among a multitude of other appellations. And Zeb knew he was the favorite, or at least thought he was, but he didn't understand why exactly. Several of his older brothers were smarter, more physically attractive, or more athletic, attributes his father nurtured. Zeb didn't think about the "whys" of this very often. Right now, he was not thinking about anything rational, regardless.

"Ike, you can ease off compressing those IV bags. I think we are giving him plenty to hydrate his kidneys. We'll just keep a fixed rate at 200 cc per hour of normal saline," Dr. Barton said, before changing his attention from Ike to his office nurse. "We don't want to put him in pulmonary edema. Might as well drown him if we give too much. Always trying to balance," he continued, taking another long drag from a cigarette.

A heavy rain had begun to fall. Drops hammered the tin roof in the alley like a submachine gun. The cinder block walls of the office did little to impede the resultant pounding, but Dr. Barton had spoken more loudly, drowning out the rain as it continued.

Ike walked up to Dr. Barton silently. He lowered his eyes and asked, "What now Doc?"

Dr. Barton gently brushed a fly from Zeb's face, which appeared frozen in a death mask as if it belonged to someone else. In a purposeful, calm voice, he replied, "The antivenom should be here shortly. This rain won't hinder old bald-headed Joe. He drove a jeep under General Patton in the Big Red One. That group of crazies was in the legendary 1st infantry division fighting the Germans during the European invasion. After that hell, he can drive through anything. He'll be here any minute."

As if he had been waiting on an introduction, Joe walked in with a box full of antivenom. "Doc, I got what you need," he started, as he looked around nervously. "The nurses gave me a hard time about getting the antivenom until I mentioned you were friends with Doc Emerson. They called him to confirm this. When they did, Doc Emerson told the surgical resident to finish up taking out somebody's gallbladder. He came right over. The nurses were surprised that he'd leave the OR. They'd never seen that before."

Dr. Barton smiled at the thought of his old friend from medical school at Emory and residency days at Grady Hospital in Atlanta. As he listened, he began unpacking the antivenom, noticing the first two vials were cracked. "Damn it, Joe, some of these vials are broken! They're useless. What the hell?"

Joe glanced furtively from side to side and lowered his head, stammering, "Sorry, Doc, I drove back a little fast and at one point slid into the ditch. Didn't get stuck though. Just popped right out. Like my old WWII days. Go fast enough, won't get stuck. Anyways, I peeked in the box, and I think most of them vials are okay. Dr. Emerson said he gave me enough to treat most of Hobbleton as if there was an epidemic of snake bites. Pretty sure he was kiddin' about the epidemic part."

The remainder of the vials were, in fact, fine. Doc calculated the dose to give based on Zeb's weight, a mere 145 pounds on his unruly, near-six-foot frame. The nurse began administering the antivenom as instructed by Dr. Barton. After what seemed to be hours, Zeb lifted his head and mumbled, "Where am I? What am I doing here?" Zeb's leg was throbbing painfully, and his head felt as if it was floating around the room. He couldn't tell whether he was dreaming or having a nightmare that came to life.

Joe sensed the improvement and attempted to alleviate some of Dr. Barton's worry. "Doc," he said, "Dr. Emerson was not one bit worried about Zeb. Said Zeb was in good hands. That you were about the smartest doc he knew. Also, about the craziest. Told me that in anatomy lab, if someone irritated you, that you would fling some random cadaver organ at them. Said the anatomy professor frightened the medical students on the first day by telling them to look on each side of them. That he would flunk out two of the three before the year ended."

Joe noticed Dr. Barton relax at hearing his words and continued. "Dr. Emerson said you stood up and told the professor that he may intimidate some of these lightweight tenderfoots but not you. Said your curse words had been honed in the Navy. They were different words but meant the same thing — words Dr. Emerson and most of the class had never heard before and would not forget."

Dr. Barton watched his cigarette smolder while Joe continued.

"Dr. Emerson recalled you challenging the professor. 'Bring it on.' I think that is what he recalled. Said you became good friends with the professor after you finished at the top of the class. All that true, Doc?"

Dr. Barton, with the cigarette now dangling from the corner of his mouth, looked up slowly, squinting his eyes in the plume of smoke he exhaled, and replied, "Damn it all to hell, Joe. I don't remember much of that, and my kids don't need to hear any of it. I don't want them getting any notions. They're hard enough to handle as is. Dr. Emerson is a good friend and a fine surgeon. Best there is.

"The part about the anatomy professor flunking out two thirds of the class is true though. He was a mean son of a bitch. Merciless, regardless of how close a student was to making the grade needed to stay in the program, he'd wash them out. One or two classmates couldn't take it. They'd go nuts, start beating their heads against a wall trying to make their brains retain volumes of information," continued Dr. Barton while refocusing on Zeb's clinical improvement.

The rains began to quiet, like the sky was depleted of bullets.

Zeb suddenly sat up and looked at all the IV tubes in his arms while pulling the oxygen mask off his face and proclaimed, "I'm fine. I don't need all this stuff. And get those folks out of here. I don't know any of them. Goatman there. Kinda' spooky looking," he said, as he gestured to the darker corners of the room.

Ike, noting the corners were empty, said, "Doc, must be he's getting better, getting bossy and all, but ain't anything over there in the corner. What's he seeing? He ain't been the same since Clayton's gone. Been talkin' about that Goatman stuff more often."

While easing Zeb back down on the stretcher, Dr. Barton, despite the quizzical look on his face, responded, "He's still a bit delirious, Ike. Wouldn't make anything of it."

Ike noted Dr. Barton's deep draw of the cigarette he now held more tightly. His prolonged inhale suggested Dr. Barton suspected there was more to it.

Standing in the doorway, having stayed to make certain his services were no longer necessary, Joe Scully piped in. "Doc, I best be going. Looks like you and Ike and whoever Zeb is imagining have it under control. I got to finish delivering my route before dark. Some of those country folks will shoot at any movement they can't make out. See what they killed the next morning. I dodged too many German bullets in the Ardennes to get killed by some superstitious, drunk-up, old idiot. See ya'll tomorrow." With a quick twist, Joe departed toward the back door, an ever-present, crooked, toothy smile on his face.

Abruptly, Dr. Barton faced his nurse and said, "How many patients out there? We're way behind again. Get them back in the rooms, and we'll get going. Ike, you stay in here with Zeb and let me know if anything comes up."

Dr. Barton's eyes focused on Zeb. "Damn it all to hell," he mumbled to himself. "If it's not one thing it's another." He crushed the cigarette he'd been smoking on the concrete floor of the office leaving behind a mangled corpse of tobacco and ashes.

With every passing hour, Zeb became increasingly more coherent, and the swelling in his leg stabilized. Dr. Barton finished with the last patient as midnight was approaching. He looked at Ike and proclaimed, "Let's get him home where I can watch him tonight. I think we are out of the woods, but the next few hours will be crucial. I can keep a closer eye on him at the house. Nurse, get up the supplies I'll need. Mostly IV fluids, antivenom, and an oxygen tank with tubing and a mask. I'll see what you got together before we leave."

As Ike and the nurse began collecting the supplies requested, he glanced over at Zeb who seemed to be motioning to some nefarious foe in the shadows. Ike just shook his head and continued loading up the car.

Dr. Barton packed up his well-worn, ragged, black medical bag holding the scent of betadine and chloroform with a hint of penicillin. He then slipped his .38 snub-nosed special revolver into his trouser pocket. His strong-minded, irascible personality had made him some enemies over the years.

Doc Barton started out the back door into the darkness of the alley leading to his car. He grasped his revolver when Sheriff Hudlow suddenly appeared around the corner. The Sheriff bellowed, "Doc, I saw your lights were on in the office. Figured you were here. I just got a call that someone else was found down at the Mill while that boy's family was gathering up his things by the Alcovy River. That's all I know. I'll let you know if we need you."

Dr. Barton's grasp on the pistol relaxed but not entirely. He never made eye contact with the Sheriff. The Alcovy had claimed another life. With heaviness, he continued up the alley smoking another Chesterfield cigarette and fighting the fatigue of the long day and night. Exhaustion was a constant, unwanted companion that he had long since hesitantly embraced and, ofttimes, forgotten why. A never-ending struggle that Dr. Barton refused to acknowledge or, at least, vocalize.

And now, Zeb, the son who most reminded Doc of himself, was in danger — and not only from the viper's venom. Doc knew a good deal more about the family murdered in Chatsworth, as he had treated several of their relatives. He knew no one in the vicinity was safe from the evil that committed those atrocities. And Zeb's mental state and safety, especially with Clayton not around, troubled Doc even more.

As he opened the car door, he tossed his latest lit cigarette into a nearby puddle of water from the summer rain. It hissed as the tobacco embers died out, leaving only cold wet darkness and a long night ahead.

Chapter Five

Awakening

Even though Zeb survived the night under the watchful eyes of Doc Barton and Ike, the next day remained critical. While the antivenom was effective, it had several side effects including the need for rapid infusion of fluid to maintain Zeb's blood pressure. At one point, this put Zeb into pulmonary edema as Doc Barton had feared. Zeb couldn't breathe. He was drowning in his own fluids. The change was sudden.

"Ike, pick him up and put him in my car! Call the hospital and tell them we're on our way back," Doc shouted, while gathering his black bag. "Tell them we may need to perform an emergency tracheostomy if we have to intubate him and can't."

Ike rushed Zeb to Doc's car, placing him on the front seat. Then he ran back inside and called the Intensive Care as instructed.

When the ICU nurse sleepily answered, Ike said, "You best wake up. Doc is headed your way with Zeb. He just took a turn for the worse. Can't hardly breathe. You need to get the staff ready to put an airway tube in him. If Doc can't get the airway tube placed through Zeb's mouth, Zeb won't have much time. Doc will need to cut a hole in his neck and trachea to put in a tube. Doc said to have surgical instruments opened for that tracheostomy."

Ike dropped the phone and rushed to his car, muttering to himself, "Doc almost lost Zeb to drowning once. If it hadn't been for Clayton, he would have lost him. That sorrowful Alcovy don't give up its dead."

Ike skidded into the hospital parking lot. He stopped and jumped out, taking a now-purple-complected, motionless Zeb from Doc's car.

Doc Barton followed, coughing as he hurried up the stairs. "Ike, put him in the first bay in the ICU! They'll be ready. I'm right behind you."

The staff stood prepared for the worst. As soon as Zeb was on the stretcher, they placed an oxygen mask on his face attempting to deliver 100 percent oxygen with a non-rebreather mask.

"Damn it all to hell!" exclaimed Doc Barton, noting Zeb's chest was completely motionless. He positioned himself at the head of the bed saying, "He has developed laryngospasm — his vocal cords are closed shut. That goddamn oxygen mask is doing nothing. Give me a size #8 intubation tube and an insertion blade."

Doc deftly inserted the metal device into Zeb's mouth, swept Zeb's tongue out of the way with the blade, and simultaneously lifted Zeb's jaw to visualize his vocal cords leading to the trachea. The vocal cords were swollen, obscuring Doc's ability to see where the tube needed to be placed. His first attempt at passing the tube was unsuccessful and traumatized the back of Zeb's throat causing bleeding which made visualization even more difficult. Zeb's color radiated a worsening deep bluish hue. Doc mumbled something under his breath that seemed to fuse an epitaph and a curse with a prayer.

Doc's hands, which were unfailingly steady, gave the slightest hint of a tremor. He realized another unsuccessful attempt would necessitate an emergent tracheostomy with an exponential increase in risk and uncertainties. Not to mention prolongation of the lack of oxygen which may already have caused irreversible brain damage. He fought to remain calm as visions of Zeb never regaining consciousness sliced through his mind threatening an intensified need for his complete concentration. Taking a deep breath, Doc blindly slid the tube into the back of Zeb's hemorrhaging throat. As if driven by an unseen force, the tube found its way through Zeb's vocal cords into his trachea. Doc quickly inflated the balloon that sealed the tube in place. The charge nurse connected the tube to a bag and squeezed it, delivering 100 percent oxygen directly to the lungs. By now, Doc was breathing heavily and sweating.

Zeb's darkened color hesitated at first but gave way to a methodical pink tint — a certain sign the tube was properly positioned. Then a stronger pulse followed with Zeb progressively moving. Then wrestling to the point he had to be restrained.

Zeb was unaware of anything happening to or around him. While intubated, his mind was consumed by horrid visions and dreams, which, to Zeb, were very real. A delirious amalgam of disparate, haunting images:

Low-lying clouds raced over a hovering moon that peered at Zeb's every move, a crushing weight of judgment. Zeb felt vulnerable but protected by a willowy, gray, gossamer lady in the edge of drifting darkness. She was made of mists obscuring the clarity of the night. A lady he had sometimes sensed in his waking moments. His mother? Zeb drifted further away from her. She dropped out of his vision, and in the haunting nightmarish terror stood the Goatman.

Zeb listened: A song called him back from Death's sweet, horrible draw. The Viper's poison gradually diminished flowing through his veins. A mockingbird sitting in the top of a crabapple tree spoke of hope, longing, and confusion. A cacophony of flighted creatures sang in unison from this sole, gray-winged avian who refused to acknowledge Zeb's presence. In the edge of the pine, vacillating between light and darkness, was the horrid Goatman. He crouched, expressionless, stalking. Untouchable. The Viper his scribe.

"I will not be ignored," Zeb said to himself as he slowly shifted a rifle, that had appeared, from his left hand to his right. "Now will be the Redemption and the Revelation."

Zeb envisioned hand-painted signs with threats of the coming Rapture strewn along pine-tree-lined highways ribboned through the mountains in North Georgia. Signs scrawled in the mists, in blood of innocents: tears frozen on clapboard paintings as a red ooze weighed heavily on each encrypted letter. Scrawled by faceless, featureless visages cloaked in piety that spoke of hatred. Blurred images floated across, not touching the ground. All orchestrated by the snarling Goatman, monstrously ripping his way through briars that clawed at him at every turn.

As he placed his index finger on the trigger, Zeb began to feel a strengthening in his pulse: Control the Viper had stolen would soon end if only one pure, clean shot of powder and lead directly pierced the heart of the Goatman, the Deceiver, who sang in a multitude of voices claiming none.

"Remember to steady the pounding fear. Gently strangle the trigger to lifelessness." Zeb spoke to himself as he slowly exhaled. And then, the twirling bullet exploded from the barrel without making a sound. Drilling through thick, motionless air, it struck without warning and burrowed its death message into the beautiful plumage of the gray Mockingbird. Zeb was entranced by the red blood trail of matted feathers.

In that instance, the Mockingbird began a terminal spiral down to the harsh, hardened, red clay. As the ground took him with a jolt, the pounding ceased as

the Goatman smothered this innocent winged sacrifice,
snarling as his eyes devoured the death of yet another.

Zeb felt a sharp, piercing pain in his chest and sat straight up in bed. Pounding heart. Sweating. The delirium lifted as the innocence was lost.

The Goatman melted into the darkness as daylight prodded Zeb to consciousness.

Zeb had a rough, slow recovery. It had taken several days to wean him off the ventilator. Each day seemed endless to Dr. Barton, as he was not certain Zeb would regain consciousness. Even if Zeb did, how much brain damage had the prolonged lack of oxygen caused? After several sleepless nights for Doc, Zeb did begin to show signs of purposeful movements. His condition progressed to the point he could breathe without assistance from the ventilator. Subsequently, he was extubated.

It took another week before he could leave the hospital. Zeb remembered none of this. After returning home, Zeb's health continued to improve. During the first three days, Thelka watched over him as he twisted and turned in bed as if wrestling an ancient enemy.

"Well, boy, where you been for the past three days?" boomed Thelka, startling Zeb awake. "Ya wuz wrestlin' like ya took on the Devil his own wicked self. Not sho' who won, but I know'd you'd make a good showin', 'cause ain't no doubt ya stole some of his devilment along the way. I'se thinkin' we might need to call on Pastor Arp to pull that devil right outta ya." She laughed, glad to see him sitting up for the first time since he lost consciousness.

Zeb's head felt as if it was swirling. He wasn't sure what was real and what was a dream and shook his head trying to stop the spinning and overwhelming sense of loss. "Thelka, what happened? What day is it? How did I get here?" Zeb choked.

"Boy, it's Wednesday. Ya been fightin' off the devil's swill from a Viper's fang for near three weeks now. Some bad things have raised their evil heads since ya been nappin'. Them polize been askin' a lotta questions 'bout most everyone's whereabouts these last few days. Seems somebody else was kilt' other than that boy. And this one not by them snakes," said Thelka, as she shook at the thought.

"They's sayin' whoever it was got kilt' several days before the boy died. They haven't found all the parts, like they wuz all cut up." Thelka stared out between the partially drawn curtains of the window into the morning light, as if trying to ward off the unspeakable monster that carved up that poor soul.

Zeb looked down at his now-slightly-swollen, mottled leg while listening to Thelka phone his father, who was already back in the office this bright morning. He had stayed up most of the night after removing an inflamed appendix from a golden-haired, four-year-old girl. Dr. Barton had a hard time leaving the bedside of this "youngster," a name he used for addressing some of his favorite patients regardless of age. He had lost a three-year-old girl due to overwhelming sepsis from a ruptured appendix years prior and, right or wrong, he felt he could have done something differently. Something more. Could have saved her.

On the rare occasion when things slowed down, Dr. Barton would relive each decision he had made during her treatment. He could see the deep pain buried in the eyes of the parents, who thanked him for his efforts despite her death. Her lifeless, small body. All vividly. And there were others. Some accidental, traumatic injuries. Some abused children. It was best not to slow down. Not to think. Not to sleep.

Zeb craned his neck and listened while Thelka phoned in an update to his father.

"Yessir, he woke up jus'a few minutes ago. Yup, still mean as eva' I s'pose. Think he's gonna be all right. I'll fix him somethin' to eat when he's full woke up and quits shakin' his head around like a bug done crawled up in his ear. Guess he still ain't seein' straight jus' yet.

"Ain't all bad 'cause I sho' ain't much to look at no mo'," she chuckled.

As he continued to wake up, Zeb laughed to himself for the first time in what felt like a different lifetime. Though his leg throbbed slightly, much of the swelling had abated, and the tingling and numbness that crawled over him before he had lost consciousness was entirely resolved. Thelka hung up the phone, and his stupor continued to wane. Zeb grinned, thinking about what Thelka had said regarding her aging appearance, and decided to continue joking.

"So, Thelka. Two things. One, I was thinkin' maybe God got one thing right when he made old folks like you lose their sight. Otherwise, that first look in the mirror in the morning might spoil the rest of the day." Thelka, for her part, did not look amused as she pretended not to hear Zeb by opening the curtains with a snap.

"The other is I bet I know who did it, who killed that person they found." Zeb recalled his conversation with Jake Stubblefield before Joe Scully had interrupted them that first day of summer.

"Must have been the Goatman," Zeb blurted out his conviction. "He's dangerous. Why, Jake was telling me all about him. Said he butchered an entire family in Chatsworth. Said people had seen him skulking around these parts at night. Said he hung out around old grave sites. Spooky-like."

"Boy, I ain't payin' you no neva' mind," Thelka responded, shaking her head as she headed to the kitchen to make breakfast and feeling certain that the Goatman would have had nothing to do with these murders.

"Thelka, for once, you crazy old woman, come back in here and stay on what you were saying," Zeb called after her. "What else do you know? You said once you'd seen the Goatman yourself," Zeb recalled, as he also remembered Ike acting uncomfortable upon hearing that name.

Thelka clearly did not want to continue discussion about the Goatman. Zeb didn't understand why. Zeb slowly sat up, and Thelka turned around, taking a few measured steps in his direction. Then she abruptly changed the subject.

"If ya quit botherin' me, and quit all this murder talk, I'll learn ya some things ya ain't gonna git from those silly books yo' pa's got ya readin'. And don't ya dare tell him I said that, but I don't know why he got a young'un like you readin' 'bout some old dead folks' sayins'. I opened those books 'bout those fellas' Plates Slow and Sockrats. Didn' make much sense. Used a lotta words ta say somethin' that was a lot mo' simple. Least seemed that ways ta me. But I only peeked at a page or two.

" 'Fraid I'd turn to stone iffen I'd reads any mo'. Sockrats —
what kinda' name is that anyways?" Thelka laughed, knowing full
well the philosopher's real name but simply delighting in the fact
that Zeb was awake and able to joke and laugh again.

Zeb held back a smile. "We already talked about this. You
know their names are Sock-ruh-tees and Play-toe." He phonetically
pronounced each name with reverence.

"At least they had better sense than the one who walked
around talking with rocks in his mouth to improve his enunciation,
like that Demosthenes guy."

Thelka stared at Zeb with a stitch forming between her
eyebrows, responding, "Boy, what I done told ya 'bout messin' with
me with yo' silly little words that don't add nuthin'?"

She spun around now and laughed. "Yeah, I could see ya
with a buncha rocks in yo' mouth like yo' pa said ya oughta try. I'da
quit mumblin' 'afore I got them rocks stuck 'tween ma' teeth."

Zeb could no longer hold back his laughter even though his
head was a bit shaky. His leg still throbbed slightly. While the
thought of Demosthenes with rocks in his mouth amused Zeb, his

mind drifted back to the dismembered murder victim. He wondered if the Goatman had been sighted again and if Clayton and Jake were okay. Jake's hovel of a shack was just up the hill from the Mill where the murder had occurred.

"Thelka," he said. "Have you seen Jake since I got bit? I was with him Saturday before Joe Scully came across us up the road from Freeman's Mill. I think Jake may know more about the Goatman than he's letting on. And I haven't seen Clayton since we were at the Mill. Is he back from hiking yet?"

Thelka looked troubled and ignored the part about Clayton. Best for all not to talk about Clayton she'd been told.

"That ole fool boy, Jake, came by ta make sho' ya wuz all right. Said he had some things he'd found out about and wanted to tell ya. He ain't got much sense, fightin' anybody who looks at him sideways. He sho' does watch ova' yo' little skinny tail.

"Ain't seen Jake's ma in years. Heard she wuz kilt'. Real purty she was when she was a young girl. From near Ringold. Seen her at the County Fair before the war. Coulda' had any boy she wanted. Golden green eyes that sparkled like they wuz lit up with fireflies dancin' in 'em. And dance she did. Move like a Black girl but mo' graceful like. Golden hair too. One of those boys finally tamed her down, but that didn' turn out so good." Her voice trailed off to a place she clearly didn't want to take Zeb. Not just yet anyway.

After feeding Zeb, Thelka continued her chores and began to iron Dr. Barton's shirts. She did this in the room at the end of the house where Zeb would listen to her stories, not knowing which were real and which were imagined. She meticulously pressed each crease with a surgeon's precision, touching her moistened finger to the plate of the iron to make certain it was hot enough. The resultant sizzling hissed across the room. For the life of him, Zeb could not understand how she didn't get burned each time. He had tried to lightly touch the iron only once, with the result being he could not throw a baseball for a week, a disaster in a summer of endless daylight and no other organized sports.

Thelka put a dip of snuff inside her lower lip and rolled it around with her tongue until she had found just the perfect spot. The resulting bulge in her left lower lip was as much a part of her profile as her nose or forehead.

She began humming some spiritual song Zeb did not recognize. Then she turned over the shirt she was pressing and started rambling.

"I 'specially don't want ya drivin' me home nowadays in yo' condition. They's been some bad 'uns comin' down out of Atlanta that I don't knows. They be sellin' they drugs and ruckusatin'. Real dangerous doper N--."

"Thelka, you know that's not a word you ought to toss around casual-like," Zeb said, interrupting Thelka.

He contorted his face, trying to erase what Thelka had been about to say. The N-word was a word his father had never spoken. Zeb had never spoken. Neither had much use for it. Plus, he'd seen way too many patients who'd landed in Doc's office with a busted lip and short a few teeth over that one word.

"Well, it's why I'se always tryin' ta git ya ta drop me off on the main highway, so's them outsider druggy dopers won't do ya no harm. The locals won't hurt ya. Helped raise most of 'em. If they's sellin' anythin', it'd be that Mary Wanna. Stinkin' stuff smells like skunk. In the country back when, we called it 'Boneset.' Used it to numb up when somebody got they broken bone fixed. Just makes ya stupid and play tha fool. Them dopers out of Atlanta, now they be sellin' heroin. Hard stuff."

Thelka nonchalantly flipped Doc's white shirt, slightly stained with cigarette smoke, coffee, blood, and whiskey. Stubborn remnants and reminders of Dr. Barton's relentless nights in the office. The Jack Daniel's whiskey stains defined his darkest moments.

She continued ironing repeatedly over each side with the scorching steam of starch. Thelka made sure to cover each inch of the shirt as if to burn out any of a myriad of potential diseases concealed in the fibers. Steam hissed as Thelka spoke. "Well, boy, ya ought not git on yo' high horse at me. I been knowin' that word ya so partic'lar 'bout since way before you wuz hatched out. Married me one once that ain't no word would tell 'bout him no better. Went on 'til he hit me one time too many, and I shot his ass. Last I saw of him he wuz runnin' like a scared jack rabbit across the corn field.

His shiny Black butt with the fall moon lightin' it up so's ta make a better target for me."

She grinned at the thought, as if she still stood on the rickety porch on a scorching summer night in the middle of nowhere. She imagined her sixteen-year-old-self sighting up and pulling that trigger over and over, trying to erase the harm her first — and last — husband had caused her and her two young children.

"Anyways," she continued, through a cloud of steam, "I've knowed white 'uns and red 'uns and some blue-lookin' 'uns when they got what they were deservin' of. The N-word ain't got a preference on color. That was made up by folks got nuthin' better ta do."

Zeb understood what she meant but responded, "Be that as it may, it's a good idea to watch where you say that. Lots of people take offense."

"People don't pay me no neva' mind. Most think I'm crazy as hell except yo' pa, 'cause he's crazy hisself, and you 'cause ya don't know no better," she cackled.

Thelka was right about the Hobbleton projects. She knew the dangers and she tried to protect Zeb as much as her own children. While Zeb acted older than he was, he was still a young teenage boy. Too young to be legally driving. Because his dad took care of most of the folks in the county, no one said anything. Regardless, the projects were not the place for a White boy, primarily due to the outsiders from Atlanta. They were unpredictable and answered to no one.

Thelka looked up momentarily, continuing, "Boy, even that hussy Sheriff Hudlow knows you ain't nearly ole enough ta drive. And it ain't 'cause yo' purty face and pleasin' disposition that he don't pull ya ova'. Only reason he don't stop the car is 'cause yo' pa birthed all his kids and saved his ma when she had a terrible bout of pneumonia. And they's been more than one time the honorable Sheriff needed a shot of pen'cillin for thangs he ought not been doin'."

Zeb didn't comprehend the penicillin comment but acted like he did, because he learned early on that most older people — Thelka included — could not keep secrets and mysteries that eluded a young boy's mind. He'd find out what she meant soon enough, but he wanted to get her back to what she knew about the murder at Freeman's Mill. More about the Goatman's involvement. He felt that capturing the Goatman would stop the murders. Stop his night terrors. Stop the smothering voices drowning him in blackness in the night and day. Stop the very thing that threatened them all. Then maybe they would focus on Clayton's whereabouts.

Thelka could talk for hours telling a story — with several more tossed in — so that by the time she was done mixing times and places and people, neither she nor Zeb had any idea where they had started, were headed, or where they had been.

"Anyways, boy, I don't want yo' pasty little ole White self drivin' in the projects no more. Ya got that?" she huffed more emphatically than usual.

As she finished, Zeb heard Dr. Barton's dogs barking in the front yard. Most of them were bird dogs, a combination of English Setter and Springer Spaniel and any other dog that happened to come around at an opportune breeding moment. Quail hunters didn't worry too much about registered thoroughbreds with papers. If someone did happen to have a registered, bred hunting dog with papers, most hunters looked at the animal with disdain and suspicion. Like they would a politician or a priest. Closest most of the hunters had come to any kind of papers was when they were served for a repossessed car or a previous wife who had realized the error of her ways by marrying the miscreant in the first place. Most quail hunters would rather hunt than work — or most anything else for that matter. While many a divorce paper proclaimed "incompatibility," this was just a legal term for too many hunting seasons.

"Who are they barking at?" Zeb asked, as he stood on wobbly legs to get a look for himself. Only rarely did anyone venture down the dirt road into the woods where he lived. To Zeb, anything out of the ordinary was a threat.

Thelka squinted her eyes as she studied a white car in the distance coming up the drive. "Boy, way them dogs are carryin' on, you'd a thought the devil hisself wuz comin' ta visit. I knows one thing. Iffen whoever that is runs ova' one a them dogs, he'll wish he'd brought his business elsewhere. Yo' pa might be on one a his bad days and not just use his pistol on 'em. He may pull out that cannon he calls a rifle," Thelka said, as her squint turned into an odd-shaped frown distorted by the snuff inside her lower lip.

Zeb relaxed, seeing the car.

"Thelka, I know my dad watches over those dogs as much as us kids. Maybe more. We've seen him when he gets that dark-eyed look like some evil thing is peering out, but I don't think he'd shoot anybody, much less use that 44 Magnum rifle?" Zeb more questioned than stated. "I've seen that rifle blow a good size pine tree half in two. I'm with you. It's more like a cannon than a rifle," he added.

"Well, I don't know what he might do. He got a wicked bad temper, as you know," Thelka responded, keeping an eye on the white car in the drive.

"I remember one day right before yo' pa was headin' into the office for the evenin' ta see patients, he got a call from the 'mergency room 'bout somethin'. The somethin' don't matter. But the 'mergency room doc musta' got uppity with yo' pa. Musta' thought just 'cause yo' pa wuz older he didn't have much fight in him. But he's like them ole bird dogs that can't hardly walk 'lessen ya bring out a shotgun. Then it's like they wuz possessed by a young pup, jumpin' up then landin' on they side or they head, anywhere 'cept on they feet."

Despite his leg, as she spoke, Zeb began to mimic her description and jumped in the air landing on his head on the mattress howling like old Major, his dad's favorite dog.

"Ya stop that, ya fool boy. I guess ya must be feelin' better. Ya prob'lee gonna be wantin' ta go out and find Jake. Or is you thinkin' maybe you'll run into the Sheriff's daughter ridin' around town on yo' motorcycle? And don't think I hadn't noticed you eyein' her at the County Fair. Her name Wanda? I will say she's mighty purty. Seems she smiled back at you, but I can't say I sees why," Thelka mused.

Zeb started to blush but turned away and tried to change the subject. "Once again, you old crazy woman, you got no idea what you're talking about!"

Zeb had last seen Wanda from a distance walking out of church after one of Reverend Paul Arp's Sunday sermons. She had been wearing a long, tapered, blue dress that unsuccessfully attempted to conceal newly developing curves around her hips and the small of her back. Zeb couldn't help but stare when she walked away, the silky dress clinging to her. All of her was a mystery to Zeb. She was the sole reason he ever went to church, but her father, Sheriff Hudlow, kept her a good distance from all boys. This frustrated Zeb to no end. This and the fact that she most likely had no interest in him.

Thelka gave Zeb a lingering, knowing look before returning to her story. "Yo' pa went straight ta the Emergency Room. Told me ta go ta the hospital kitchen and see if they wuz any left ova' food from the day to feed his dogs. When I came out with a bucket full, I could hear a awful commotion with ole Doc givin' this fella mo' than a little bit of his attention. Guess this younger doc said a couple mo' things than yo' pa would allow. Next I see is this fella, who was a sight bigger than yo' pa, layin' on his back holdin' his nose, bleedin' all ova' the place.

"Doubt he knew yo' pa was a boxer in the Navy. Heck, he still goes into that wet stinkin' basement most every day and pummels that mildewed sandbag," Thelka added.

"Sometimes so much that his hands bleed," added Zeb, as he stood up. He straightened his back and assumed the boxing stance his dad had taught him. "Probably wants to be ready if he is cornered by the Goatman."

"Now, boy, don't be gittin' no ideas. Leave the fightin' to yo' pa and Jake and maybe old Ike. Ya ain't built for such as that. Now where wuz I? Oh yeah, this is tha' best part," Thelka said, grinning. "That younger doc got up slow. Hollerin' 'bout how he wuz gonna sue ole Doc. Know what yo' crazy ole pa did then? With nurses hollerin' and patients scatterin', he reaches up with his hands and grabs this fella, whose bout a head taller. Tells him, 'Now damn it, hold still!' and yanks his nose back straight. Truth is, he overdone it one way and had to march it back the other. All the while, that young fool doc screamin' an' hollerin 'bout suin' and such. Well worth carryin' the bucket of food for them dogs," Thelka finished, with a howl of her own.

"Well, I still don't think he'd shoot somebody for accidentally running over one of those dogs. Must be eight of them out there now if you include that mangy, brown stray that he claims crawled up in his car to get out of the cold last winter. Said it wouldn't get out," Zeb argued, while he watched the white sedan come out of the trees at the far end of the long driveway about a half mile from the main dirt road.

"Don't act like you'd a done no different boy. I see'd how ya bury them newborn bird dog puppies that die every spring 'cause they jus' too little ta make it. Wrappin' 'em up in white cloth and placin' 'em in a shoebox for buryin'. And not jus' anywhere, but down by the creek under the big Oak when ya thought I wasn't watchin'. See'd ya more than once plantin' moss or flowers or somethin' over 'em. Looked like you was keepin' 'em company. Talkin' to 'em and such," Thelka added with a smile.

"Don't know what you thought you saw," Zeb countered. "But more than once your blind old eyes have tricked you. You should mind your own business."

Suddenly the smile that wouldn't leave Thelka's face dissolved like the first frost of fall melting from the windowpane after the sun burst through the morning mist. She peered down the driveway watching the driver bring the white police car to a halt.

"I'll be darned," she snapped, as she looked down at her finger which smoked from the burn of the iron. "Neva' done that 'afore," she said, more as a distant observation than an immediate reaction to any pain.

Zeb looked out the window and saw the Chief of Police, Hank Bullock, struggling to pull himself out of the car. The Chief of Police was Sheriff Hudlow's subservient crime investigator. He was a round, ruddy-faced man who wore an ill-fitted uniform and seemed suspicious of anyone and everyone. Zeb mostly knew him from the doctor's office when gunshot victims were brought to be treated by Dr. Barton. Bullock had always been good to Zeb and his brothers. Like Joe Scully had been.

Zeb recalled the night Bullock had pulled over Clayton for speeding through Hobbleton, running the only red light in town in the process. Zeb was in the passenger seat, trying to make himself disappear, listening as Bullock asked Clayton why he was speeding. Clayton's response, " 'Cause I like to go fast."

Bullock had laughed and waved them on. No lecture. No ticket.

Strangely, Zeb had recently noticed that when Bullock would interrogate victims in the office who were injured, Zeb's hands would start to sweat as if he had been the culprit involved in the crime. Or that he should have stopped it. All too often he felt he had been there.

Assuming that Chief Bullock had come to get Doc to help with someone shot or cut up as he did when the home telephone wasn't working, Thelka walked to the screen door and hollered out, "Doc's not here!"

As Bullock wrestled to exit the car, he sharply responded, "I'm not here to see Doc."

Chapter Six

Pearl-Handled Pistol

Z eb tried for days to get Thelka to tell him what the Chief of Police wanted that morning. She had more sense than just about anyone he knew. She loved to talk, and he loved to listen. This time was different. She would tell him very little, which was unheard of for Thelka. He had been forced to stay in bed while Thelka and Bullock conversed in the front yard. Zeb watched through the window, but they spoke in such low whispers that he couldn't hear a word. Bullock talked and Thelka listened. Her head cocked to one side. She rolled her eyes, mixing a reaction of shocked disbelief with an equally placid, blank, wide-eyed stare in reaction to what appeared to be Bullock's accusations.

Later, from Thelka's gloomy demeanor and what little information he obtained, Zeb was fairly certain of one thing: the Goatman was the one who had committed another heinous crime, and for some reason, Bullock thought Thelka knew something about it. Bullock didn't like Thelka, and Zeb thought he may accuse her just out of spite. Without a rational explanation, Zeb had a feeling he was the only one who could stop the monstrous Goatman. Protect Thelka. Even more strange was that he felt in some way responsible for the Goatman's deeds, as if he was the one who was causing harm to a victim, even though he wasn't involved at all. Since he wasn't allowed to leave the house until he recovered fully, he waited anxiously to talk to Jake about finding the Goatman.

Several days later, as Zeb attempted to emerge from a deep sleep, he tried to force out the horrid visions, which seemed to come from the past while simultaneously portending a crushing inevitability.

> *Shapes in the darkness that transformed into chaos frozen in twisted metal. Fatal screams and pulseless, misshapen forms thrown into a red clay embankment laced with wild roses clinging to the hillside. Zeb gasped for meaning in the deafening silence.*

> *Heavy, starless Georgia air held no promise as he desperately attempted to crawl through thick, thorny vines of wild red roses that slashed at him. The shadowy, demonic figure of the Goatman hovered*

overhead cloaked in robes of disheveled goatskins. Though it was dark, he could sense that in the distance was the brightness of morning. In the awakening light, blood — barely discernible at first — began a slow trickle from the mouth of the roses, seemingly obscuring his vision. In the night, senseless rage had altered and held captive the sweet scent of spring roses transformed into the sweet sickening smell of death.

Zeb woke up, covered in sweat.

"Boy, you are the sleepin'est boy I ever know'd of. I got eight, and none are harder ta git goin' than you are," Thelka boomed. " Yo' pa's left a while ago. Had a baby to deliver. Said you'd be fine. Swellin's all gone in yo' skinny little leg.

"Now git outta that bed before I take a switch to ya. I got lots of chores to do. I don't want to be here late when there ain't no people around," Thelka added in a serious tone.

Zeb's nearest neighbor lived a mile away down the dirt road. Thelka didn't want to be out in the countryside in the dark. She had no problem living in the projects with drug dealers from Atlanta paying visits and the like, but in the isolated darkness every sound was a haint. Only later would Zeb find out why.

Zeb sat up and looked around as if to be certain he was awake. Then he started in on Thelka right away. Zeb wanted to know more about the Goatman who, to this point, was still little more than a childhood nursery rhyme that haunted his dreams. "Thelka," he began with a yawn, "what did that weasel-eyed Chief of Police want anyway?"

Thelka put her hands on her hips when she didn't want to talk about something. This was inevitably followed by a furrowed brow and a look of consternation mixed with concern as she rerouted the conversation with her answer. "I 'specially don't want to be out here in the middle of nowhere since them polize took ma' favorite pearl-handled pistol and all. Don't know why they took it 'zactly. Didn't leave nobody dead or nuthin, and yo' pa got they polize car fixed up and all after I shot a couple a three holes in it. Still mad at him though, 'cause he wouldn't come git me outta jail that night. Sho' 'nuff got me the next mornin' just to cook for you chilluns."

Zeb recalled the Saturday night a few months prior when his father answered the phone. It was around midnight, and Zeb and another brother were eating steak with Dr. Barton as he "philosophized." That is what he called the times when he would teach life lessons. These interludes consisted primarily of stories about interactions with patients. Zeb looked forward to the late nights, as his father would drink two or three cups of coffee while he gave the children that were still awake the best pieces of steak. Zeb was always hungry.

Dr. Barton usually relaxed a little and seemed almost human as he talked about some of his crazier patients. If he'd had a shot of Jack Daniel's before he left the office, all the better. Zeb recalled his father slowly standing up from the old pine dinner table to answer the phone, which seemed to ring all night every night. He took a draw from the cigarette he'd lit up as it rang.

He muttered in his usual after-midnight tone, "This is Dr. Barton." Zeb watched as a look of amusement transformed into a look of concern. Dr. Barton listened intently to the voice on the other end of the line. After several seconds, Dr Barton responded, "Well, I'll be damned. Did she kill anybody?" followed quickly by, "That's good. And hell no. I'm not coming to get her. You keep her there.

Maybe it'll teach her she can't be shooting at folks. Yes, I'll pay to get the car fixed.

"She's got to come feed these kids in the morning. Ike will be over to get her then," he added, as if he were speaking to a child.

Dr. Barton hung up the phone muttering to himself, "Crazy as hell. Her and most all women for that matter."

Once Dr. Barton appeared more agitated than amused, everyone scattered from the room. Zeb's father had a temper that would blow in like a tempest. Anything or anyone in its path would encounter the full fury — intended or not. Guilty or not. Dr. Barton picked up his coffee as he walked down the hallway. He crumpled into bed where he fell asleep moments later while listening to his favorite music, Beethoven's *Moonlight Sonata*. Dr. Barton never said another word about what had transpired. And while Zeb could eventually pry it out of Thelka, he certainly would never purposely bring up a sore topic with his father. Nothing to be gained by that.

Thelka knew Zeb wanted details from whatever happened that night months ago. Now was as good a time as ever to tell the story. She needed to move Zeb away from the discussion of the

Chief's interrogation from a few days before. That she did not want to discuss.

Zeb shook his head, dislodging the final visions from his nightmares. Now fully awake, he returned his focus on what came to be known as the "Dollbaby Encounter."

Zeb said, "I heard it wasn't for lack of trying to kill somebody. They say you shot at Dollbaby five times then reloaded twice and missed every time, though you did manage to wing an unfortunate squirrel that was probably watching in amusement at what a poor shot you were." Zeb thought the world of Thelka, but he couldn't give up an opportunity to give her a hard time.

Dollbaby was Thelka's nemesis, competing for what Thelka called her "mens." Thelka saw no use for marriage now because of her failed attempt at marriage as a teenager. Consequently, she had a new man out of wedlock for each of her additional six children. Though she'd joke with Zeb about the night her ill-fated marriage ended, Zeb had always been suspicious she was hiding something about that. Zeb had never even seen Dollbaby, but, according to

Thelka, Dollbaby was always flirting with her "mens." That's all that mattered.

Irritated by the insult about her shooting skills, Thelka said, "I'm not studyin' 'bout you, boy. Maybe you should sleep all the time, so I don't hafta listen ta all yo' nonsense. Anyways, if them polize men stayed away, I'da got Dollbaby's Black ass for sho'. And they put me in that jail, for what?" Thelka tutted.

"How's that leg of yours?" She asked, changing the subject as she began tidying up the room. "Don't look too bad today."

Zeb, noting his leg pain was gone and feeling back to himself, continued to goad her. "Probably locked you up 'cause you are such a bad shot, embarrassing yourself in front of all those reputable drug dealers and addicts in the projects. Giving them a bad name," Zeb said, trying to make Thelka laugh and amusing himself in the process.

Those were words for all-out war. Thelka pulled the sheets off the bed with remarkable ease sending Zeb tumbling off the bed. He landed on his back. This seemed harsh, but Thelka knew the boy well, and he'd be fine.

Hardly able to breathe for a moment, much less to speak, Zeb used his last bit of air trying to act as if nothing had happened. He coughed then cleared his throat. "So what occurred that night with your buddy Dollbaby?" Zeb knew this would get Thelka even more riled up. Even more talkative.

"Well, boy. Let me tell ya what happened on tha' other end of that phone call." Thelka took the bait.

"After I got home from work that Sataday and fed my young'uns, I go'd out to Jack's Bar at the project lookin' for my man."

Zeb laughed and asked, "Thelka, which man now? You switch them out whenever you want. Like you put a hex on them." Then Zeb channeled Thelka back to Dollbaby. "You were telling me about going to Jack's Bar looking for your man. I didn't even know there was a bar in the projects. Where is it?"

"It's tha' place ya knows as J.T. Washington's Funeral Home. That place on the main highway where I makes ya let me out when things are a little lively in the projects," Thelka responded and put the bed together now that Zeb was on the floor.

"Anyways, since ya didn't know, J.T. Washington's dead folks' parlor — Funeral Home what you'd call it in the daylight — is Jack's Bar on Sataday night. Drinkin' and dancin', ain't woke no dead'uns boxed up in the back rooms yet. And for my part, I'd order up dancin' 'afore I'd be wantin' a buncha stiff Sunda' schoolers wailin' and all tha' while plottin' ta toss dirt on me stuffed in some box. Dead is dead. Gone is gone. Burn me up and toss my ashes in the flower beds. Iffen God wants me, he'll find me either place jus' fine."

She rolled her eyes again and continued, "As I walked into ole Jack's Bar, I see'd Dollbaby sidlin' up ta one of ma' men folks with her hair all stuck straight up on her head like she wuz somethin'. She wuz workin' that fat ass of hers, and my ole fool man was grinnin' like a brook trout.

"Next thing I know'd is I had her by the hair pullin' her outta tha' door. Jack don't mind carousing, but fights and killins' inside is bad for his nighttime business. S'pose it would be good for his daytime business though. Anyways, out we go. She's squawkin'. That fool man a mine be runnin' outta the back door trippin' ova a couple of corpses ain't been embalmed yet. They bein' just dead and all. And me, who long been ova' this hussy bitch, tended ta let her join up with the two of them dead'uns waitin' in line for ole JT's services."

Thelka's face changed now. Zeb had seen the same look when Thelka told of the beatings she took at the hands of her first and last husband in the shanty of a house they lived in as sharecroppers years before. An anger she had no control over oozed from every pore.

"I didn't want ta beat her ta death," she continued. "Too messy. As I went to pull ma' gun from ma' purse, the heifer escaped ma' hold and took off down tha' road just a hollerin'. She kept on sayin' 'Hep' me Jesus!' And I wuz tendin' ta help her meet up with Him. Jus' helpin' her out."

She rolled around the snuff in her lower lip. "Things wuz goin' purty good up ta this point. I'se aimin' up my pearl-handled pistol and shootin' away. Then them polize ruin't all ma' fun, but not before I shot their noisy siren car all to hell when Dollbaby dove in it headfirst." As she spoke, Thelka raised an invisible pistol over her head and pulled a silent trigger repeatedly.

Then Thelka's face relaxed, and she smiled proudly. "Boy, ya shoulda' seen her big ole butt stickin' outta that winda' where she got stuck. Funny as hell. Them polize, they wuz laughin' once they checked theyselves ova ta make sho' they kept all they parts and didn't have no holes in 'em."

Zeb was a little angry himself now. " Thelka," he scolded, "you old she-devil witch. You're lucky the police didn't shoot you!"

"Ah, boy, they wasn't gonna shoot me. They know'd me. Yo' pa birthed 'em both, and they knows they'd a had hell ta pay if they hadda' shot me. Sides, what you worried 'bout? Other Black folks makes biscuits and fried chicken 'bout good as me. And for my part, I wouldn't hafta put up with yo' silly little self," she mused.

"They wuz nice and all but said I couldn't be shootin' up the polize car. If it hadn't been for that, I think they'd a let me go. They put me in a cell but left the door unlocked aft'a I told 'em I'se afraid of tha' dark and would it be okay if I came out now and then ta make sho' someone wuz there. I knows folks who hung theyselves in there. Some bad ones. Haints is in there for sho'," she said, as she looked at a spider crawling over her torn old shoes. Thelka, like Doc, had no use for concern about external appearances. In fact, she mostly distrusted anyone who did. Shoes were shoes. Nothing more.

"They kept me there after they called yo' pa that night. Said he'd send Ike to git me in the mornin'. Said they woulda' asked him to come sooner, but they know'd how he could be. Especially afta' he wuz up all night after seein' patients and deliverin' babies and such. Not to mention havin' a drink of whiskey or two hisself. Then they may a had lots a shootins ta sort out," she said, grinning, as she ignored the spider now crawling up the side of her leg.

"Yo' pa didn't say nuthin' ta me. Not then and not since. Guessin' he know'd I didn't have no control ova' myself. Looked at me like he did when I wuz sixteen and he took me and ma' two little'uns in after I ran ma' no good husband off. Whelps from his beatin's all ova' me. Yo' pa wuz took ova' by a mighty sadness that day, and I don't think it wuz just 'bout me," she spoke, as she gazed out the window at several purple morning glories that had closed up tightly in the daylight.

Then she came back, "Worst wuz them polize took ma' pistol. But I'll be gettin' that back soon as I promise them polize I won't shoot they car no mo'. Sides, iffen I'da meant ta kill ole Dollbaby, she'd a done been bleached out bones." Thelka's voice drifted away as she firmly, but without lethal intent, flicked the spider from her leg.

Zeb now stood up, unwinding his gangly limbs and trying not to hurt himself in the process. He was never certain which way each appendage might be traveling at any moment. Thelka watched the awkwardness of youth knowing this young colt would eventually manage a coordinated movement. Trouble was, she wasn't sure she had enough lifetimes to be there for an event that seemed nowhere close to occurring.

"Thelka, I think I'm going to restart the summer by taking that motorcycle down the hill to the old grist Mill full throttle. I know I can make it over the bridge. I was about to the other day, but those Copperheads got in my way by biting that boy. Tried last summer but I didn't quite make it. That's not altogether right. I did make it, but as I crossed that wooden bridge over the Alcovy River, my front tire found its way between the wooden slats. Got me a busted arm and good scars up and down my leg," he finished, with a smile. "Remember that?"

Proudly, he raised a long bony leg with islands of corrugated scar that clung to him like kudzu along a riverbank.

"At that point, I remember thinking to myself I could die quickly by staying the course and flipping onto the red dirt road at bridge's end or swerve to dislodge the tire and plunge over the rail into the Alcovy River," Zeb continued, as he watched Thelka's face, not certain why he was watching so intently.

She seemed disturbed and a bit confused by what he said. She didn't know what to make of some of his thoughts. Was this his dreams or his imagination that drove him to do some of the things she couldn't comprehend? To say some of the things he said in the face of the events that had occurred at the Alcovy. He didn't seem right.

"Now, boy, you jus' settle yo'self down. I done had enough 'citement ta last all the summer without you adding more. Don't you be gittin' no more ideas 'bout going back down that hill," said Thelka, in her most demonstrative voice.

Zeb may have heard her, but he wasn't listening. He jumped up and ran as best as he could down the creaky hallway. He almost tripped over his baseball bat and was tempted to give it a swing. That would have to wait. He hurdled and dodged shadowy concealed and imagined adversaries. After grabbing a biscuit from the table, he burst through the screen door into the cool, misty morning of another summer day. The screen door slammed shut behind him and sent shock waves that propelled him forward.

He had a mission before him, and no one would dissuade him from the inevitable. This time he'd track down the Goatman surely hiding around the Mill. He would be the master of all that haunted him when he made it across the bridge without falling into the Alcovy and dying. He'd check on Jake first to make sure he was okay and see if he'd spied the Goatman. Then he planned to conquer the Alcovy and find out what the Goatman had been up to.

Just as he cranked the old motorcycle, Sheriff Hudlow pulled in the driveway. His route through the pines kicked up dust that had piled on the back of his car. Sheriff Hudlow put on his hat and sunglasses. He stepped out of the police car gingerly holding a pearl-handled pistol.

"Where's Thelka?" he demanded, turning his head to look at Zeb. "I need some questions answered. I know Bullock was here, but I haven't been able to match up with him since he spoke with her. He can be hard to find. Pretty much the whole town knows we found a body where that boy got all those snakebites down by Freeman's Mill. Was cut up pretty bad and disfigured. Had been there for a while decomposing. Not for sure who it is yet, but I got my suspicions."

Thelka shook her head overhearing the conversation. She motioned Zeb to move on, as she didn't want him to hear anything Sheriff Hudlow had to say or wanted to know. She already knew who they'd found.

Chapter Seven

The Autopsy

Zeb rode the motorcycle down the driveway leaving Thelka and Sheriff Hudlow in the house. He inched out onto to the main dirt road, planning to search for Jake, as a second police car arrived. It was driven by the Chief of Police, portly old Hank Bullock. He managed an uneasy smile at Zeb as he pulled his patrol car into the driveway.

Hank slowly lifted himself out of the police car and ambled toward the front door. A pack of dogs rushed to jump all over him, leaving a trail of ubiquitous red-clay paw prints. He advanced to the front porch preceded by an abdomen that protruded forth as if he had a miniaturized version of Stone Mountain hidden under his uniform shirt that could hardly be contained. Hank spotted Sheriff Hudlow's car parked around the side.

"Thelka," Hank called out, knowing the windows were

always open at Doc's house in the summer. "I need to show you and the Sheriff somethin' we found behind the old burned-out schoolhouse."

Thelka had immediately recognized her pearl-handled pistol, but the bloody, bright-orange shirt with brown frills Bullock held in his hand, while familiar, would not let itself slip into her consciousness. She opened the front door slightly while Zeb hid in the shadows. He had doubled back, leaving the motorcycle at the end of the drive so as not to be detected by the rumble of the motor. He always felt protected there in the shadows and did not want to be seen regardless. He knew Thelka would run him off again if she saw him.

While Thelka tolerated Sheriff Hudlow's questions, she had no patience for Hank Bullock's inane inquisition. She had already tolerated him once. "Hank, ya knows better than ta come out here 'lessen ya need ole Doc fo' some 'mergency. I done reminded ya 'bout that the other day ya came out here without no invite," said Thelka through the crack around the back door.

"Iffen he don't shoot ya thinkin' you is a prowler or someone he's riled up, one a these boys is shootin' guns in the woods all the time. 'Bout the only thing they don't hit no mo' is the house. Doc done cured 'em of that when Zeb blew out all the windas in the garage with that twelve-gauge shotgun shootin' at somethin' he tossed in the air. Little fool told on hisself, which made Doc pull off his bein' angry and started him ta laughin'and cussin' at the same time. Ole Doc just muttered, 'Damn little fool. More like me all the time.' But them boys got the message."

The steamy summer heat was rising up early today. The sun reflected off Chief Bullock's forehead as he lifted his sweat-stained police cap. Zeb noticed his fingernails were broken and stained with what appeared to be old blood and dirt. But then, Hank had never had clean high on his priority list. In contrast, Sheriff Hudlow was impeccably dressed, with perfect creases announcing his dark blue uniform.

The Chief of Police Bullock entered through the creaking kitchen door. He cleared his throat and said, "Well, I am here to talk to you on police business. I had a woman brought to the morgue a little ways back. She had been cut all to pieces and tossed in a thicket by Bramblett Shoals. She didn't have any connected parts that would identify her and no clothes to speak of, and her face was gone. Before she gets buried, I at least gotta confirm who she is. She is a Black-skinned woman, and some drugged up man came by the morgue saying it's a woman by the name of Dollbaby. Said she was pregnant and that he was the father. I, being tuned in to such things, asked if she had anything about her that would identify her from any other Black, dead woman that might be walking around."

Bullock seemed to be trying to impress Sheriff Hudlow with this recitation.

Thelka gave a sideways glance in Zeb's direction in a gesture of consternation as she listened to Hank. She had noticed Zeb partially hidden in shade down the road but within earshot. He had already heard most of what she wanted kept away from him before she spotted him. Zeb was forced to stay in bed when Bullock had previously discussed many of these details with Thelka, so he had been shielded from their conversation. Now she couldn't stop him from hearing without drawing attention to his spying. Zeb tended to dwell on death way too much, and Thelka didn't want to add fuel to that flame. For his part, Zeb found one phrase both curious and disturbing. He'd never seen a 'walking around Black, dead woman.'

Thelka, impatient to find out what her gun had to do with this, said, "Hank, we's done talked about this. I'se know'd ya since you and my son Thomas played football together ova' at Central. You'se a little different sort and I got nuthin' 'gainst ya, but my time is beginnin' to evaporate in this heat and formin' up some thunderin' clouds in ma' head. So, are ya here ta arrest me again, 'cause ya'll done that once already and it didn't work out so good for nobody. Cost ya to feed me, ma' kids at home didn't get fed much a nuthin', and Ole Doc wuz late to his office seein' patients all evenin'. Not to mention I'se still missin' ma' pistol, which I see y'all took a likin' to."

Sheriff Hudlow hid a smirk as he watched Thelka lecture Hank Bullock about the error of his ways.

Though he tried to conceal it, Hank's beefy face reddened and then ever so slightly twitched. "Thelka, I'm here as the Coroner as much as I am a police officer. And I'm just trying to figure out who this dead woman is."

Thelka nodded her head knowingly as she muttered to herself, "Most everybody in the projects knows it's Dollbaby." She'd been missing since the night Thelka took to shooting at her.

What Bullock said was in fact true. The Coroner was a politically driven position. He had been appointed by his first cousin, the Mayor. Hank had no special training and got paid next to nothing to look at dead people at all hours of the day and night. This included young and old. Some dead by natural means. Some dead by not so natural means. Odd thing was he volunteered for the job when the previous Coroner, who was perpetually drunk, disappeared. He probably drowned in a nearby river while in a drunken stupor, at least that's what most folks said.

Hank continued in a bizarre staccato-patterned voice. "I didn't recognize this druggy fella, and he disappeared soon as I turned my back. Thought he might have had something to do with it even though he said she was carrying his baby. Probably out from Atlanta coming here, so he won't be recognized by anybody while he is up to no good. Seeing lots of that nowadays. Anyway, he says she got this scorpion tattoo on her left breast. Well, he's right on both counts. First, I verified the tattoo. Then, when I cut into her insides to establish a cause of death, this baby's hand comes reaching out at me. Seemed like it was trying to grab me and pull me in. Spooky. But I guess I was just jumpy because that little thing was long dead."

Zeb shook his head. It seemed everyone in Hobbleton knew it was Dollbaby except this bumbler Bullock. Since she had been cut to pieces, the cause of death seemed apparent to Zeb. He'd seen patients bleed to death in his dad's office. Worst was a farmer who had been run over by a harrower with rotating plates of steel rows cutting him all to pieces. *Blood finds its escape leaving behind only a corpse in short order*, thought Zeb.

Thelka had a confused look about her, as well as a sadness. Hank never had made much sense to her, but his absurd remarks about a walking around dead woman seemed almost normal coming from him.

"Hank, iffen it is Dollbaby and you polize is thinkin' it be me that kilt' her, you'd be wrong on that count. I want my pistol back. If they be some monster out here, I needs to protect these chilluns and my own," Thelka demanded.

Hank narrowed his beady eyes.

"Thelka, you got a good alibi, since we found that she went missing the morning after you were locked up. Apparently, she was plenty alive last time the officers saw her stuck in the window of one of my police cars. Dollbaby is the same person you were shooting at that night. Least that's according to the officers that arrested you. What I want to know is do you recognize this shirt? We think it belonged to the victim. She may have been killed next to the projects then brought to Bramblett Shoals down by Freeman's Mill later that night."

In her mind, Thelka could see Dollbaby running and diving into the police car from that night. She could see that ugly orange, brown-frilled shirt stuck in the window.

"That's Dollbaby's all right. Neva' hated her. She jus' kept on messin' with ma' men folks. Didn't know she wuz havin' no baby," Thelka said, her voice trailing off, almost apologetic.

"Well, that ought to do it then," declared Hank Bullock, looking for affirmation from Sheriff Hudlow. No one said anything, so he continued in a tone that sounded as if he had rehearsed this moment repeatedly. "We got a body, least most of one, plus all of an unborn one, confirmation on clothing, and a motive. Think we can put this one to rest. Had her on cold storage since the day we found her."

"What is the motive, Chief?" asked Zeb, now too curious to remain in the shadows and wondering if he was speaking to the Coroner or the policeman or both.

Hank said, "Well, hey Zeb. I didn't know you were back there. I thought you were headed out on your motorcycle when I drove up. Good to see you are getting better. Motive is obvious. The Black man that disappeared on me probably killed her, not wanting her to birth his child. Didn't want to pay child support or something like that. Not sure why he came to the morgue, maybe remorse or maybe just wanted to see his handiwork in the daylight," Hank continued, as a calm settled over his face like the reflective surface of a sea after a pounding rain beats down the waves. Dollbaby, or at least parts of her, would be buried with an uneasy explanation.

Sheriff Hudlow then shifted his gaze to Thelka and, in an authoritative, deep voice, interjected, "All that may be true Thelka, but I don't want you going anywhere until we complete our investigation. Sometimes Hank and I look at things a little differently. If you try to leave, you may find yourself back in jail."

With that, Hank and Sheriff Hudlow exited in silence until the ever-vigilant dogs began their concoction of barks and yelps and howls. The men walked toward their cars under the dogs' — and Zeb and Thelka's — watchful eyes. When they thought they were far enough away not to be heard, they stopped briefly, talking in low voices.

Zeb thought he heard Sheriff Hudlow reprimanding Bullock for not sharing information about the case with him.

The only thing he heard clearly were the disturbing words from Hudlow to Bullock as he said, "You watch her close. I'm not so sure she isn't the culprit. She tried to kill Dollbaby that night and could have succeeded later that next day after she was released from jail. If it weren't for Doc, I'd arrest her. She has a nasty temper. Doc protects her, but Doc doesn't get to be the judge and jury. I've still got half a mind to arrest her today."

Sheriff Hudlow added, "We've got three recent violent

deaths in the county. Several more in the surrounding counties. Most victims getting cut up, which makes me think they may well be related. Could well be a serial killer."

Bullock dropped his gaze and started picking at his fingers.

Zeb moved closer to the house when both white cars pulled away. Thelka was too far away to have heard their threatening conversation. Zeb knew Thelka couldn't survive in the isolated darkness of a jail cell. As Zeb walked up the stairs to the porch, Thelka said. "Boy, that don't make no sense. Nobody pays no alimony 'round here 'lessen it be some White fool got caught with his pants 'round his bony knees. And usually, a fake gold bracelet and a nice dinner out will cure that problem. Most of tha' men I knows be braggin' 'bout they populatin' the neighborhood. And the mo' they 'pregnated the better."

Zeb didn't fully understand all that, but he nodded in agreement with her as he took off into the daylight.

As he jumped off the porch, Zeb yelled back at Thelka, "Going to find Jake and see what he knows. We spent lots of time sliding down those rocks at Bramblett Shoals not far from the Mill last summer. It's close to where Jake lives. I bet he can find the spot she was cut up quickly. Those woods are his." Zeb was excited at the prospect of proving what had happened. More importantly, he needed to protect Thelka. She wouldn't do well in jail. He was even more certain he knew who the killer was.

"Boy, you need to eat!" Thelka shouted after him, adding, "And you stay away from that Goatman. Ya got no idea what you be stirrin' up!"

"I'll eat when I get back!" he yelled. "And get your gun back. You might need it."

Thelka hoped he was wrong and that the suggestion to get her pearl-handled pistol was simply his own anxiety, something which was heightened since Clayton had gone. First, Hank wouldn't leave her pistol, saying it was evidence. When Sheriff Hudlow showed up with it, she hadn't insisted, because she was distracted by Bullock's nonsensical motive for Dollbaby's killer and, even more so, by the thought of the unborn innocent child. Thelka's attention was drawn to her now-throbbing finger. She had forgotten she burned it. The scars on her hands numbed most of the pain. This time there was something unfamiliar, almost insidious, about the sensation.

And outside, the dogs began their warning howls.

Chapter Eight

Search Begins

As Zeb cranked up the motorcycle and headed out to find Jake, he was anxious to hear what information he had discovered about the Goatman. He arrived quickly, turning into the short, uneven, partially graveled drive leading to Jake's dwelling. It was a leaning, ramshackle plywood structure with a tin roof that seemed on the verge of collapse.

Zeb called out, "Jake, where are you? Thelka said you were looking for me."

Jake stepped out from behind the well with a grin that spread with each long stride he took, saying, "There you are. I figured it would take more than one nibble on your foot to do you in."

"Yep, I'm fine. For such a small wiggle worm, that snake bite had a punch. How have you been? What did you find out?" Zeb asked, as he throttled down the motorcycle and sprang toward Jake.

"Crazy things been going on around here," responded Jake, as he leaned from one foot to the other in a measured pattern. "As soon as you left to go help your pa before you up and got bit, I kept an eye on the goings on we were watching down the road toward the Mill. After the ambulance tore off with what must have been that boy that was killed, there was another commotion nearby. Seems they come across something else in the woods that got their attention."

Zeb, certain this would have been Dollbaby's remains, jumped in abruptly, "Jake, I know what they found. It was a Black woman named Dollbaby. Thelka and she had ongoing warfare about the men that hung out with them. That chubby old Chief, Hank Bullock, and Sheriff Hudlow came by the house this morning and told us what was found. Sheriff Hudlow is trying to implicate Thelka, but he can't fabricate enough evidence to make that stick. She was locked up that night anyway. I'm worried Bullock might make something up just to get on Sheriff Hudlow's good side."

This got Jake's attention as he shifted rhythmically back and forth. "They ought to leave Thelka alone. She's a good woman. Goes out of her way to be nice to me. Always has."

He stopped swaying and reached down to pick up a sparkling rock. Then he tossed it down the hill, watching it until it came to rest in the ditch.

Jake continued, "Well, that explains all the commotion that morning by the Mill. What it don't explain is the wild-eyed Black man that came running through the woods up from the Mill. He looked like he was being chased by the devil hisself or at least a near relative. Maybe a Demon."

Zeb leaned in, as he was certain he would get the clues he needed to confirm it was the Goatman that killed the boy in the river who'd been bitten by snakes — and probably Dollbaby too. Zeb had heard the boy call out the Goatman's name in fear as he was gasping in his final breaths. The Goatman had probably cut up Dollbaby. And probably, this unfortunate boy had happened upon the scene. The Goatman drowned him to shut him up. The snakes just finished him off.

Zeb excitedly asked Jake, "I bet you saw the Goatman chasing that old Black man, didn't you?"

"Thought I would," responded Jake. "I heard rustling through the trees. Sounded like a herd of deer tromping up the hill, but strangely enough, I couldn't make out a blame thing."

"What happened to the Black man?" Zeb inquired, scratching at his foot where he'd been bit.

"Don't know," Jake responded. "He was fast runnin' through the woods. Limbs was fallin' all around him. All I could see was he was plenty scared. Must have got beat up pretty bad with scratches and all. If the Goatman caught him, those scratches would be the least of his problems."

As Jake continued, the scar on his neck began to darken. "What did the Goatman do to that Black woman they found? Dollbaby, funny name. I don't want no details. Was it same as they found in Chatsworth with that family all cut up?"

"Well, Jake, it was the same, only worse. The woman was pregnant and pretty far along as best I can tell. The Coroner or Police Chief, depending on what Bullock wants to call himself, said when he was doing the autopsy on Dollbaby's trunk that the unborn child spooked him."

Jake no longer methodically rocked from side to side. His movement was now uneven. He stopped Zeb short, asking, "Why did you say 'trunk'? I don't know all your fancy medical names."

Zeb grinned as he saw the uneasiness in Jake, who had begun stroking his neck as if the scar consoled him in some way. Zeb found it amusing that Jake, who was so powerful physically, could be so vulnerable to mere words. It somehow kept a sense of balance between them to Zeb's way of thinking.

"Jake, the 'trunk' is not a medical term. They found her with her appendages — her arms and legs — cut off. Think of it like the trunk of a tree after harvesting the branches. Bullock said part of her face is still missing too. Anyway, when old Bullock cut her open for the autopsy, he said a small hand reached out as if to grab him. It was the unborn child. Far enough along to identify parts, but maybe early enough that she didn't even know she was pregnant," explained Zeb.

Incredulous, Jake narrowed his eyes. "That's not possible. Is it?" Jake's rocking morphed into an unpredictable jerking as he reached down to pick up irregularly shaped rocks lining the red clay twisting road.

"Apparently, Dollbaby was a big girl," Zeb said, chuckling, as he noticed Jake getting a little woozy. "I have seen my pa deliver babies when some big women didn't even realize they were pregnant. They came in with cramping stomach pain thinking they had eaten something bad. I thought one had appendicitis. My pa got a kick out of that. Seems crazy, but it's true. Some didn't know they were having a baby."

Zeb now recentered on his reason for finding Jake as he shaded his eyes from the patches of sun creeping through the canopy of pines. First, he had confirmed Jake was okay. This was not a given with the Goatman on the prowl. Especially now that they were talking about a serial killer. Maybe Thelka was right about Jake's mother, a person Zeb had never seen, being killed years prior. Could it have been the Goatman who killed her? Jake lived out here alone, as far as Zeb knew. If she was killed, Zeb needed to protect Jake as well as Thelka.

He knew Thelka was innocent and now was the time to go to the Mill and find evidence implicating the Goatman. At least that might shift the focus of the police investigation on the Goatman and away from Thelka. Halt the uncontrollable rumbling in Zeb's head. The inexplicable guilt.

That old fool Bullock had already decided it was someone from Atlanta that would clearly never be pursued. No interest and not much way to find a Black drug dealer from Atlanta. Any informant would be killed, and Bullock wasn't particularly interested in a Black woman's death regardless.

"Jake, it's time we went down there to see what we can. The Goatman does his deeds in the dark, not the light of day," declared Zeb. "If we go now, we should be safe," he added less confidently.

Jake, now sporadically rocking back and forth, said, "Probably not a good idea. If he sees us snooping around, we'll be next. Doubt he knows where you live even. But he sure knows where I live being as the Mill is so close by."

"Come on. I'm going to check it out either way. Jump on the back!" Zeb cranked up the motorcycle which lurched forward seeming to have a mind of its own. After hesitating briefly, Jake ceased his indecisive rocking and jumped on the back, hanging on to Zeb tightly. Ahead lay a steep descent.

Chapter Nine

Freeman's Mill

As Zeb and Jake hurtled down the gravel road to Freeman's Mill, rocks flew in all directions. The motorcycle was unsteady. More than once it seemed to Jake a crash was imminent. Though Zeb applied the brakes to slow their descent, the brush that hung over the road still slapped them in the face. As they went deeper into the abyss, wild pink rose bushes became briars that clawed at them. Fragmented streams of blood crept down their arms. They approached the Mill quickly, and before Zeb was ready, the wooden slab bridge crossing the Alcovy River lunged out in front of them.

Zeb tightened his grip on the handles and yelled out to Jake. "Hold on! This is where I crashed last summer!"

Jake only heard 'crashed' over the rumble of the motorcycle as Zeb throttled down. The muffler spat out exhaust, seemingly warning of dangers ahead. Zeb knew that the gaps between the bridge's aligned, rotting boards could catch the wheels, which would either lead to a bad spill or toss them over the rusted-out metal rails right into the Alcovy River. Neither of the options seemed tenable, and Zeb knowing Jake couldn't swim didn't help matters.

Zeb remembered crashing last summer, then a brief mental flash of a second descent. *CLICK*. One he refused to acknowledge. Blocked out. Then he panicked. *CLACK*. It was as if the barren Oak was ripped from the dirt and turned upside down. The cracking, delicate roots crawling into the sky. Grasping. Taking hold. And then nothingness.

Zeb slammed on the brakes, sending both boys skidding sideways into thick underbrush just a few feet before the bridge. They rolled toward the riverbank until a tangled jungle of wild roses clawed them into submission. All went silent except for the water rushing over the rocky shoals of the Alcovy. It seemed oddly tranquil. Both boys looked around to make certain they were not seriously injured.

Jake looked at Zeb's arms, which were streaked with blood, exclaiming, "Dammit Zeb! I thought it was the Goatman that I needed to worry about. You coulda' killed us!"

Zeb tried to conceal the tremorous pounding of his heart as he stammered back, "Wasn't that bad!" However, Zeb could not contain the low rumble in his mind mocking him for his failure to complete the descent across the river:

Couldn't do it. Failed again. CLICK. Coward you are. You'll pay. They'll pay.

Zeb almost seemed in a trance as he wondered about whether he had been here earlier this year. Before summer. Seemed like the same terrifying ride, but maybe in the spring. When the flowers were just beginning to bloom. And freezing cold water. Frozen recall. Water? Why water? Or was his imagination taking over. He couldn't tell the difference.

Jake poked Zeb in the ribs playfully to try and get Zeb to stop his deep stare, a look which had started when Clayton had gone and which spooked Jake.

"Well, you cut us all to hell with them briars. Not sure the Goatman could do as nice a job," joked Jake, breathing more slowly, happy to be breathing at all. Both boys' arms were lashed with similar streaks of blood. They pulled themselves out of the thicket, which was holding them like a spider web, and took their first steps toward the darkened Mill.

Freeman's Mill had long ago ceased operation. The water wheel, which pre-dated the Civil War, had become obsolete at the turn of the century. It stood frozen, rusting as water poured over the paddles which momentarily held the life and energy of the water only to feel it slip away. Motionless, it remained now only as a reflection of the history that had passed by.

Zeb and Jake knew the Mill had been boarded up, but there were several hidden entryways built through the decades. Ancient, hand-carved slabs of wood made up the walls.

Zeb rubbed his head as he approached the Mill. Trying to look around in all directions at once, he outlined a plan to Jake saying, "No need to go inside the Mill. Goatman is too crafty to be cornered. I say we circle about so we don't miss anything."

Jake was fine with this. He liked exploring the woods near his shack where the boys often played and hunted but had no interest in entering that dark, old, musty building. Even in the daytime, stories he had heard about Confederate apparitions rattling their sabers inside the hidden passageways during the night caused him to shiver.

Side by side they advanced, glancing around with every break of a twig or rustling of a dry, crisp leaf. The boys started their search at the water wheel and marched around the water intake canals to the irregular board walls of the back of the Mill.

Seeing nothing unusual, Jake starting to calm a little then asked Zeb, "How many times you been down here? I watch it from above, but I only vaguely remember being here this close once. I was little. I don't remember much. I think I was with my ma before she got gone."

Zeb found it curious that Thelka thought Jake's mom had been killed. The "how," Thelka had not offered. He did not feel Jake would welcome any discussion about her possible demise. Still, he couldn't help but wonder how she may have died and why Jake would have said she just left. Zeb studied the green moss softly nestled into the bank of the drive and decided that Jake's mother's death likely had something to do with the Goatman.

Zeb sensed Jake's stare while he waited for an answer and said, "Been here only a few times myself, Jake. Thelka brought me here when I was little to fish a time or two. I don't count the time last summer when I tried to make it all the way down on my cycle full out and lost control. My arm was broken up pretty good. Didn't hang around long. My pa took care of it more quickly than usual because of the exposed bone. The longer the exposure, the more likelihood of a bad infection. If not for that, I'd have waited until after the last patient of the night was seen."

"I remember. You was hollerin' at me as soon as you rode out of here. You had done broke it, so the bone stuck through the skin. 'Bout made me sick," Jake said, twisting his face.

Zeb wasn't listening to Jake's response about his broken arm. He was much more intrigued that Jake had made mention of his dead mother. Zeb had never heard anything from Jake to suggest that he had much memory of her. Jake had avoided the subject. Zeb had never asked about her, as he figured the whereabouts of Jake's parents and the cause of that scar on his neck might get him riled into one of his fits.

This time was different. Since Jake had brought it up, Zeb thought now might be as good a time as any. He figured the search for the Goatman held most of Jake's attention and they had both nearly been killed or mangled. Bringing up the subject of Jake's mother couldn't be much more dangerous than that. It may even give more clues about the Goatman, which could help him protect Jake and save Thelka from the Sheriff. He slowly raised his head toward Jake and spoke quietly, as if he were holding dynamite that might explode at the slightest ill-timed movement. "Jake, what happened with your mother?"

Jake turned his head as if it hung on a creaky, broken hinge. "That ain't none of your business. Was a long time ago, and I don't remember much anyways. Some things best not be remembered."

Zeb knew better than to push Jake any further. Plus, as he thought about it, he didn't want Jake asking the whereabouts of his mother as no one talked about her either. He hesitantly changed the subject back to their investigation of the Mill. "It gets colder back here where there isn't much light," he said. "Smells like the cold earth is all up on you. Wants to cover you up." They both shivered at the thought.

"I haven't seen the smallest thing yet to shed light on what happened down here. Have you?" Jake asked, still a bit annoyed at Zeb conjuring up painful questions.

Turning the far corner of the Mill, the scene was concealed by even deeper shading. Little light could penetrate between the ominous decaying structure and the adjacent bank leading up Goat Hill. Suddenly Jake stopped. Then, as he crept forward silently, Jake pointed to something in the dirt. Crouching down, Zeb could see the clear imprints of several hooves. Some were large and deep. Others shallow and much smaller.

"I bet anything those are goat prints! I knew the Goatman was here! That he is real. Can you tell how long ago these prints were made?" Zeb could hardly contain himself.

"I'm not sure, Zeb. These could have been here for weeks or only a day or two. Not much direct rain hits this spot with the Mill blocking one side and the hill the other. Nothin' much to wear down these prints," said Jake, absorbing what lay around — a rusty old harrower, a couple of broken-down wagon wheels, a curled-up leather harness. A gray, seemingly lifeless lizard clung to rotted lumber next to the stone base of the Mill.

"Let's get out of here," Jake continued. "I don't like this much. Feels like somethin' dead movin' through me when that cold air gets to swirlin' with the wind channeled through here," he whispered. Zeb knew what he meant. They ran back out into the sun, which was straining to filter through the pine needles as the prehistoric-looking lizard crept between the slats of decaying wood.

Continuing their search, they found the spot where the young boy had died of snake bites. There were unmistakable yellow tapes which had been used by the police to mark off the scene. Not far away, deeper in the woods, was a second set of tapes. Undoubtedly, the site of Dollbaby's demise.

Zeb observed the first scene. "Jake, this is where the Goatman tried to finish off that young boy that got all bit up."

The pine needles and leaves covering the ground by the Alcovy River were in disarray with marks of a struggle. The Alcovy was dark, enigmatic. Unfathomable. Water crashed over shallow shoals then calmed in enticing, deceptive, deep pools. It held life and death. Zeb could imagine the Goatman repeatedly pushing the boy, who had resembled Zeb, back under the darkness. Over and over. Drowning him. That is until the Copperheads took over.

Engrossed by the scene and his imaginings, Zeb sensed a sudden silence. He glanced around. Jake had noticed something far up Goat Hill, and he had started in that direction. Zeb followed Jake's line of sight. The sun had momentarily lit up a small clearing below a large, ancient tree. Zeb couldn't make out the type of tree. He didn't think he'd ever seen a similar one.

Zeb called out, "Jake, wait up! What is that? How did you happen to see that? There ain't nothing but briars and thicket and trees around here otherwise."

At that precise moment, slivers of sunlight burst through angles in the tree limbs and underbrush that would otherwise have concealed the area. Zeb ran by the site of what he thought was

Dollbaby's murder in his haste to catch up with Jake. He noticed the sagging yellow tapes marking the area and felt a thick heaviness in the air. He figured the rains had washed away evidence that the police hadn't bagged. Zeb caught up with Jake, who was now on his hands and knees approaching the dense, clinging underbrush.

After rapidly crawling through the tangled thicket on their hands and knees, the boys arrived at the clearing, unnerved by what lay before them.

Chapter Ten

The Clearing

"What are we looking at Jake?" asked Zeb, shading his eyes from the sun which seemed even brighter after they had crawled out of the surrounding darkness. Superimposed rays amplified the light like a magnifying glass.

"I'm not sure, Zeb," Jake said, squinting as he looked over several scattered stones. Some had flat surfaces and were leaning over or fully toppled on the ground. These appeared to line up somewhat. Others were more rounded or irregular, appearing hastily and haphazardly placed.

"Some of these stones have inscriptions on them," said Zeb, moving closer. "Here's one I can make out. Says 'Confederate Private Josiah Simmons.' And below says 'Departed this Earth July 1864'. Least that's what I think it says."

"We found us a graveyard, Zeb!" Jake exclaimed. "And an old one at that. I'd heard rumor there was a graveyard dating back to the Civil War down here. I thought it was just part of made-up ghost stories about the Mill we've been hearing since we were kids."

"Unusual that the area is cleared out from the briars and such," said Zeb, lowering his voice, half expecting the Goatman to jump out of one of the graves and seize them. Zeb had never much liked to be in any graveyard, much less one so isolated and mysteriously concealed. Zeb wasn't concerned about The Departure, necessarily, but he wanted that to be on his terms. Oddly, the shadows and unknowns were much more terrifying than the acceptance of death. Peering into the briars, Zeb imagined the Goatman creeping up on him in the night as he slept. Dragging him off as he tried to scream for help but no words would come out.

"I done figured that one out, Zeb. That Goatman fella, he must tidy this place up pretty regular," chuckled Jake, pulling Zeb out of another one of his vacuous stares.

"Not so funny," admonished Zeb. "The Goatman could well be exactly who keeps it cleared. Clayton never said anything about a graveyard down here, and he used to come down here to get away sometimes. Wonder if he knows it's here. All Clayton ever said about a graveyard is that he never wanted to end up in one. Being buried in a box was not for him."

Jake's scar across his neck appeared to mottle. "Zeb," he began, "I agree we got to find somethin' to stop the Goatman from all these awful killings. Bet there's lots nobody even knows about. Poor folks around here disappear all the time. Most say they moved out. Me, I ain't so sure. That said, unlessen the Goatman planted that Black Walnut tree over there, he got nuthin' to do with this clearin'. And I doubt it. That tree is well over a couple hundred years old. My grandpa told me, before he died, that Black Walnut trees give out a poison which kills off any growth beneath."

Zeb continued to look around, muttering, "That may be true, but I've never seen or heard of a Black Walnut tree around here." Zeb didn't doubt Jake, as Jake knew his trees and he knew more about the woods in the surrounding hills than anybody else Zeb had met. Yet Jake's explanation did not help in discovering more about the goings on of the Goatman.

Jake continued explaining the reason for the paucity of Black Walnut trees, despite Zeb's objections. "Reason is not only are those trees bad on plants, they are also bad on horses. Makes them lame. Nobody exactly knows how. When most all this land was in corn and cotton farmed by sharecroppers, the Black Walnut trees were cut down and burned," explained Jake. "Least that's what my grandpa said."

Zeb seemed satisfied by this clarification but also frustrated. He wanted evidence, not explanations. Plus, Zeb didn't want another of Jake's revelations at this moment. He wanted to find the Goatman.

As he was standing still listening to Jake, Zeb felt Jake's stature growing. He seemed to be getting taller. Jake was looking down at Zeb. Suddenly, Zeb noticed it was he who was sinking into the ground. Startled, Zeb jumped forward leaving deep imprints in recently turned, soft soil.

"Explain that away, Mr. Jake Stubblefield! I bet this is where the Goatman buries his prey! Who'd look in an old Confederate gravesite hidden away here? Perfect spot for concealing his deeds.

133

Dollbaby's parts would be in the ground hidden here rotting if that boy hadn't come across the Goatman cutting her up. We best get out of here before the same happens to us!" Zeb yelled, as he backed away — only to step in another sinking plot, then another.

Pointing to the ground, Zeb excitedly added, "And look over here. More hoof prints. Animal hair entangled in the brush. Goats been here too."

"I'm with you," agreed Jake. "Let's get outta here! You better go it alone and tell them police. I don't like them much, and they're not too particular fond of me."

After forcing their way back through the briars and underbrush which grasped them at every turn, the boys found themselves back on the road by the bridge. Hurrying onto the motorcycle and cranking it up, Zeb failed to notice Joe Scully tearing down the hill in his car on his daily route delivering the mail. Fortunately, Joe had seen the motorcycle and slammed on his brakes, stopping short of the boys.

Joe leaned out the window grinning and called out to the boys, "What are you two doing down here? Probably not the safest place what with those Copperheads around here. And that dead woman. Least they figured out who killed her. Seems was some Black drug dealer from Atlanta knew her and had a reason, she being pregnant by him and all."

Zeb throttled down the cycle and yelled back over the noise of the muffler, "Joe, I think they got it wrong. It was the Goatman. No doubt about it. We found goat tracks hidden behind the Mill and then at an old Confederate gravesite up Goat Hill with fresh dug graves. I'm headed to tell Sheriff Hudlow so he can dig up those graves. Not wasting time with that incompetent Chief Bullock."

Joe cocked his head at Zeb, noticing the scrapes on him. "Zeb, what happened to you boys' arms?"

Before Zeb could answer, Joe added, "You best leave all this up to the police. Not safe down here. I had a delivery to make; otherwise, you wouldn't see me around here. Let's go see what you boys think you have found. I got a minute. I have most of the mail delivered for today."

As the boys turned toward the Mill, Joe added, "Let's get that motorcycle off the main road before someone runs into it or steals it. Follow me and we'll park it up that side trail."

Zeb was not surprised that Joe Scully knew about a side trail. Joe knew pretty much every navigable route in the county. Since the war, Joe had been delivering mail to every dwelling that existed in the county and knew the whereabouts of most everybody at any one time. That said, he did find Joe's concern about anything getting stolen unusual for two reasons. One being nothing they had was worth stealing, and two being nobody ever came down here much anymore. Certainly, with the recent murders, nobody would venture down the hill unless they had a strong reason.

Still, the boys were relieved to have Joe with them. Joe was smart and seemed to know pretty much something about everything. Even though Joe was small in stature, he was wiry and quick as a Rattlesnake strike.

As Joe exited his car, he asked again about the scratches on the boy's arms. Zeb looked at his bloodied arms, surprised they were not more painful. "We were crawling through the underbrush and briars as we investigated the area looking for clues about the murders."

Zeb purposely left out the part about them crashing before crossing the bridge. Dr. Barton would not be pleased if he heard about this. He'd already had to patch up Zeb's arm once because of that rickety bridge and had warned him not to go there again. Doc tried to take the motorcycle away at one point. Zeb couldn't remember what had stopped him. But Doc was emphatic that Zeb was never to barrel down the hill over the Alcovy to Freeman's Mill again.

Joe had been looking at his watch as if he were calculating something. Suddenly he looked up in response to Zeb's answer. "Zeb, what do you mean murders? I know about Dollbaby. You know about others?"

Zeb was a bit startled himself at Joe's coiled questioning. "Joe, I know the Goatman was trying to kill that snake-bit boy. When the boy was dying, he kept saying something about the Goatman. Sounded like the Goatman was drowning him until the

Copperheads took over. The Goatman probably took off not wanting to get bit or else someone or something scared him off."

Joe appeared relieved by the answer. "Now listen here you two. Maybe there is something to what you boys have found. I am not interested in fighting that underbrush. Let's find an easier way."

The boys began looking for an opening to the clearing, as wrestling through the briars again did not appeal to them either. They pointed in the general direction, and Joe quickly plotted a path to follow. Zeb and Jake mindfully followed as Joe, like most of the men his age who had survived WWII, had a good sense of his surroundings and knew how to handle himself. With Joe nimbly leading the way, they arrived at the clearing surprisingly fast.

Too fast.

Chapter Eleven

Back Home

"Thelka, where did Zeb run off to? I need to check on that foot to make sure it doesn't get infected. If he treats it like he does most of the times he gets hurt, I'll probably have to clean it out later. That boy won't hold still long enough to think," lectured Dr. Barton, as he picked up the daily newspaper and sat down to breakfast after returning home for a brief nap. The appendectomy "youngster" was doing well. Dr. Barton wore a cloth bathrobe and resembled a boxer warming up for a fight.

Without looking up from the bacon she was frying in an old cast iron pan, Thelka nodded in agreement. "He is full of mo' devilment than most. Maybe mo' than any I knows of anyway. He tore outta here this mornin' with next to nuthin' to eat. Said somethin' 'bout Jake Stubblefield and the Goatman and his 'mission'. Some other such nonsense. You knows how he is."

Dr. Barton lowered the newspaper and peered over his glasses. Thelka noticed Dr. Barton's strong, weathered face had seemingly aged almost overnight. While he still had muscular arms for a man in his late sixties, he was not the same energetic man who had taken in Thelka and her kids years before when they had no place to go.

Not only had Dr. Barton been a boxer in the Navy, but before that, he was an undersized running back in college. This was the only way he could attend school after a political appointment to West Point fell through. Seems he arrived on the main campus on the Hudson River ready to start his plebe year only to be told his right eye had betrayed him. Left 20/20. Right 20/200.

Clyde Barton had returned to Maysville. Having no prospects, he used massive metal tongs to deliver fifty-pound block ice from home to home. Back-breaking work. This was the cheapest form of refrigeration at the time in this small forgotten town. Fortunately, a football coach by the name of Red Barron knew about Clyde's playing abilities from his senior year in high school. Learning of his predicament, Coach Barron reached out to him, offering Clyde a spot on the Winder Barrow High School football team for a *bonus* senior year. He promised a college scholarship if Clyde played well.

Clyde reminded Coach Barron that he had already graduated high school in Maysville. Coach Barron liked to win and needed a running back who could also play defensive back. His cursory response would entirely change the trajectory of Clyde's future. He simply said, "They don't know that around here."

Subsequently, Red Barron made good on his promise. Clyde Barton received a full scholarship to play football at Furman University in South Carolina. Unfortunately, Furman's football coaches tried to run him off the team when he arrived on campus, as he was much smaller than his high school accolades suggested. Under the steamy hot sun on clay-baked, rocky soil, the Furman coaches repeatedly had him run against the varsity's older, much larger players.

According to Clyde Barton, the coaches would grab his helmet and yank his head around demanding he quit. He had only one response. "You'll have to kill me first. I've got no place to go," he said, as tears streamed down his face mixing with blood and dirt. He graduated with honors four years later, having become starting quarterback on a team that defeated the University of Georgia his senior year. Fortunately, it was a year before one of Georgia's greatest players ever showed up and avenged the loss with a 77 to 7 trouncing of Furman.

Those years took their toll. The aching joints and muscles rebelled periodically, as was the case today. Dr. Barton slowly stood up, cursing the stiffness in his legs. Seeing Ike working in the yard, he called out the open window, "Ike, go find Zeb! If he's not at Jake's house, he's probably down at Freeman's Mill. That stubborn little fool gets more like me every day. Probably best not to be down there with all that's gone on recently. And he knows I don't want him down there and by the Alcovy. I don't think he remembers what happened down there. Don't you be bringing it up either. Last time we tried to, he ran off into the woods for three days. Came back incoherent. Took a couple of weeks before he made any sense. He'll quit running from the memory when he is able. I'd take that damn motorcycle away, but there's no use fighting about it. It's Clayton's and he won't let it go."

Thelka wiped her forehead as sweat gathered from the heat of the oven. She worried about Zeb. He wouldn't listen to her either. Nothing more she could do just yet. She tossed a towel aside, looking out the window at Ike cranking up his worn-out, rusty car. *Good man that Ike*, she thought to herself, wishing that her first and, it turned out, last husband had been like him.

"Thelka, when Zeb gets back, you tell him that I said again for him to stay away from the Mill in no uncertain terms. Then send him my way. If he's not helping me, he needs to be studying those books I gave him about the Great Philosophers. Not chasing some childhood fable that for all purposes died years ago," Doc muttered. "The Goatman! What people don't understand they come to fear and hate. They demonize. The Goatman has nothing to do with hurting anybody. Anyway, I need Zeb to help me in the office. Lots of calls last night. Several patients need to be seen. Good for him to keep his mind occupied," he added under his breath.

Thelka was taken aback by what he said about the Goatman. She knew better than to try to find out what he meant in referring to him being innocent. On mornings like these, when Dr. Barton had little sleep and a long day ahead, there was no room for anything that approached idle conversation. Anyway, if Clyde Barton knew anything more and wanted to share it, he would have.

"Doc, Ike is headed out," Thelka noted. "He'll find that little ole fool Zeb in no time. Don't you be worryin' none."

"I'm not worried about anyone hurting him. Around here, nobody would dare as long as I am living. But Zeb doesn't seem to think he is mortal. Or if he does, he isn't the least concerned about dying. I don't understand that at his age or these night terrors he's been having, but I suspect they are related. Started right after Clayton left us," said the doctor, as he peered out the back door observing several of his bird dogs and a few mongrels he had picked up along the way. He couldn't help but wonder where Clayton could be.

After emptying his third cup of coffee, Dr. Barton finished getting ready to leave, wearing the same old shoes he would wear until there were holes in them. He had two pairs of pants that he would alternate and three white shirts that Thelka would do her best to bleach out and press until they, too, had to be discarded. He had one light blue suit that was sufficient for all occasions: weddings, funerals, and the rare church service. Ultimately, Clyde Barton would be buried in that suit. The depression years had imprinted on him. Waste was not acceptable, and excess was a vise.

He walked out into the summer morning, which was already heavy with moisture as dew evaporated from the grass around the yard leaving a light, morphing mist. He paced once around the car he had driven years beyond its intended use. This ritual occurred daily, as Dr. Barton was careful not to back over any of his dogs. They napped everywhere including behind the car. Tossing a cigarette on the ground, he slid into the driver's seat, cranked up the vehicle, put the car in reverse, and then into drive. This all-in-one motion created a grinding from the gears that made the motor groan.

As he pulled away, Thelka looked out the back screen door, locking the handle as she turned back to work muttering to herself, "Done had enough 'citement for one summer already. What with

Dollbaby and all. What done happened before that in the spring. Don't need no mo'. I sho' hope them boys is okay."

Thelka had sensed something troubling about the morning and was more worried than usual. She felt a cold darkness as she envisioned the boys at the Mill. *Something's not right.* She hoped Ike would get on down there. On this occasion, Thelka's premonition was correct. The boys were in danger.

Chapter Twelve

Unknown Assailant

As the clearing opened before them, Zeb found himself watching Joe Scully study the newly dug graves mixed with the decades-old Confederate headstones. He had never noticed that Joe carried a knife on his belt, but this wasn't unusual for a WWII veteran. All the veterans he'd ever known had quirks and oddities. Most of them were damaged by what they had seen and done.

Zeb trusted Joe. He was a friend to Clyde Barton and had helped out through the years. "Doc," as Joe and most all of Hobbleton called Zeb's father, would frequently slide his car into ditches as he barreled down curving, gravelly roads making home calls for his sicker patients. Sometimes he'd pop right out of the ditch. Others not. When called at any hour, Joe would go pick up Doc, given the least information as to his likely location, and cart him around cheerily until all patients were cared for. Joe was a good man, but today he was acting strange.

"Zeb, I see what you mean. These are recently dug holes and they do line up in rows between headstones. Lots of hoof prints as well. You boys may be on to something," said Joe, as he crouched down and quietly pulled out his knife. On seeing this, the boys stepped back. Joe skillfully twirled the knife in his hand then reached forward into one of the areas of recently turned dirt and began digging with it.

"Only one way to see what's buried here, boys, and I ain't doing all the work. Get over here," Joe said, grinning away. Relieved, Jake and Zeb grabbed sticks and started pulling at the loose dirt.

As they dug, Jake stopped and turned his head as if he heard something. Zeb stopped. Jake could hear things most people couldn't. Upon seeing this, Joe laughed and said, "Now what is it? You two are spooked by every little noise. Me, I don't hear nothing. Now get back to digging. This has me more than a little curious."

They began to dig again. A limb further up Goat Hill clearly snapped. A breeze through the pines picked up as clouds overhead began to darken. The further they dug, the more difficult the task became. It was almost as if the dirt did not want to reveal the secrets it held. Jake was the first to see something. "Look here!" he exclaimed. "There's something hard and different-colored than this red clay we run into."

"It's bones," declared Zeb, none too surprised. "I thought so. Bet there's dead folks all over in here!"

"Not so fast Zeb," said Joe, picking up a grisly bone with his bare hands like he was picking up a piece of firewood. "I've seen too many human bones to count from my stint in the Ardennes. And these ain't human. Some animal. Kinda' strange they are buried here of all places, like someone didn't want them disturbed in this graveyard in the middle of nowhere."

As Joe finished inspecting the bone he held up, Jake and Zeb heard a loud crashing through the trees up the hill, headed in their direction. Simultaneously, the clouds gathering closely overhead erupted in thunder as a bolt of lightning crackled, exploding through a pine nearby, splintering the bark from its trunk which scattered and lay motionless on the ground.

Between the thunder claps a voice could be heard calling in the distance. The words were indecipherable.

"Boys, let's get out of here. Lightning down here gets fearsome for some reason. Could be the metal around the Mill. That noise uphill is probably a small herd of deer getting off the hill away from the lightning. They sense it coming. And I think I hear someone calling out for you two."

The boys had already headed away from the grave, but they had to wait for Joe Scully to lead them out. Zeb was surprised that even Jake couldn't find the trail that Joe followed like he'd been here before. Zeb was uneasy once again.

When they got to the base of the hill, the boys could hear a voice clearly calling out through the rumbling of the storm overhead, "Boys, where are ya? We gotta get out of here. Doc said it's not safe, and it don't feel right to me down here neither! Bad things find this place."

It was Ike. Zeb, for one, was relieved to see him.

"Ike, we're over here! You aren't going to believe what we found!" exclaimed Zeb.

"Get on over here! Let's get in my car. Gonna be pouring down shortly. Doc wants you back at the office!" yelled Ike over the thunder, as drops of rain landed flatly on Oak leaves nearby and crept their way into the pine-needle carpet. The boys ran to Ike's car, waving to Joe as they left. Joe Scully didn't notice. He was focused on the noise up the hill coming ever closer as he tightened his grip on the knife in his pocket.

Zeb jumped into Ike's car. He couldn't help but wonder about Joe's actions. Zeb would later have more reason to question Joe's intent as an event from Joe Scully's past surfaces.

Then an echoing thunder separated from the storm and rolled insidiously into Zeb's thoughts as they crossed over the bridge to escape the impending downpour. He twisted his head to the right and compressed the left side of his head with his hand, fighting the impulse to acknowledge these unwelcome intrusions. His left temple began to tighten like a vise:

Jake will soon be among the unliving. CLICK. Only you know this. Only you can stop this. CLICKITY CLACK.

No one noticed the shadowy, disheveled figure hidden in the nearby brush observing all that had transpired. Rain drops coursed down, dripping from a long, graying beard — a frozen sculpture tangled in a web of twisting vines.

Chapter Thirteen

Slashed

As soon as Zeb entered Dr. Barton's office, he heard the staff scurrying about, shuffling patients in and out of exam rooms with little time in between. Clyde Barton was moving through them like a harrower slicing through fertile, soft, brown dirt in the spring. Zeb was anxious to tell him about the discovery at the Mill. That would have to wait.

"Zeb, come on in here. I need some help sewing this one up," called out Dr. Barton. Zeb looked down as he walked into the exam room. Before him was a logger who had been slashed by a chainsaw across his back and down to the bone of his spinal column.

"Lucky that ole Dennis here wasn't cut in two," Dr. Barton joked. This was not the first time Dennis had been on the receiving end of a chainsaw, as evidenced by additional scars on his extremities. But none were like this time. This cut began across the back of his left hip. Its jagged course ran up diagonally to his right shoulder. Muscle bulged out of the gaping gash as if trying to escape from the depths of the wound.

Dr. Barton lit up a cigarette, drawing in the deadly smoke. Tobacco flickered as it burned. He placed the cigarette on the edge of a table nearby, "Hell, Dennis, you damn near did it this time. About another half inch through your backbone, you'd be paralyzed or worse. We got to find you another line of work."

Dennis was lying on the exam table face down with blood oozing, half congealed, around his sides. He had a strong, still face and thick, calloused hands. He looked around at Dr. Barton, raising up slightly, agreeing, "You are right Doc, but I got no trainin' to do nuthin' else. Shoulda' listened to you years ago when you told me to stay in school. I was too busy chasin' tail and makin' good money to finish out high school much less get any trade schoolin'."

Zeb watched the cigarette on the edge of the table as the ashes on the end began to accumulate.

Dr. Barton went to the sink and washed his hands while Zeb opened the sterile tray and poured betadine in a bowl to sterilize the wound. Zeb knew the routine and moved methodically initiating each step. Dr. Barton placed sterile drapes around the massive crevasse and began the process of cleaning out the wound of any clothing, bark, and other debris. Zeb found it odd that Doc rarely wore sterile gloves but never asked why he didn't. This was an education by experience and immersion not idle words.

Zeb kept a vigilant eye on the smoldering cigarette at the edge of the table. It was on the verge of dropping ashes. They would soon feather to the stark tile floor. To Zeb, the cigarettes were a daily death threat to Dr. Barton's health, as he'd already had one heart attack. Despite this, Dr. Barton chose the risk without concern for the consequence.

"Dennis, you doing okay?" asked Dr. Barton, more as a courtesy than a concern.

"Yep," replied Dennis, knowing Doc was there to repair the damage, not to hold his hand. "I guess I oughta be more careful, but that damn saw jumped around and bit me before I could get out of the way," finished Dennis, as Zeb watched the next segment of cigarette ashes slowly tumble to the floor.

"Hell, Dennis, you've slowed down in your old age. You're almost forty. It's still not too late to get some trade. Electrical work or plumbing pays well and is a good bit safer. I'm getting tired of stitching you up," laughed Dr. Barton, as he began approximating muscle over bone, skin over muscle. Dennis didn't even flinch despite a paucity of local anesthetic. Dr. Barton didn't believe in numbing the pain much. Not for himself or his own kids even. *Toughen them up*, he thought.

Dr. Barton glanced over at Zeb as he spoke to Dennis, adding, "I will say you are one tough SOB. I put a little local anesthetic in here, but if I put too much, it can get you in trouble. We could go to the OR, but I know that's costly. Plus, maybe you'll think twice before you crank up that chainsaw next time if I get your attention now."

Zeb knew he should be listening, but his mind kept taking him back to the Goatman and the graves at Freeman's Mill. He wanted to get Sheriff Hudlow to start digging up whatever had recently been buried. Joe Scully would probably have told Sheriff

Hudlow what they had found by now, but not everyone paid attention to Joe.

More ashes fell.

"Zeb, are you listening?" grumbled Dr. Barton. "I said to give me that damn nylon suture and get over here. You can do some of this. Wash your hands. I'll have you sew up the skin. Ole Dennis won't mind. He'll just punch you in the face if you hurt him," laughed Doc, only half kidding.

Dr. Barton enjoyed his work and liked most of his patients. Dennis was one of his favorites because, like Doc, he was tough and no-nonsense. Zeb could learn from him. Zeb watched from the edge of his vision as Doc leaned over to his now-smoldering remnant of a cigarette. He picked it up with his bloody, bare hands and took a drag. The final ashes flew to the ground.

As Zeb began to suture the skin meticulously, his father admired Zeb's work. "You might be worth a damn after all. Make sure you square those knots where the muscle is trying to bulge through. Otherwise, Dennis will unzip, and we'll be back tonight."

Dr. Barton's voice darkened as he spoke, "Thelka told me this morning after you left that you were headed down to the Mill. Zeb, I don't want you going down there. Let those incompetent police do their job. It's more dangerous than you think."

Zeb placed the last suture. He impulsively jumped at the opportunity to tell his dad what he and Jake had found, even though the patient was fully alert. Zeb retold the events of the morning and his pursuit of the Goatman, though in an abbreviated version given Doc's impatience for long stories.

His father crushed the remains of his cigarette unmercifully under his foot, responding harshly, "Zeb, no more of that. This Goatman business is a fairy tale that you kids have repeated so often that you've come to believe it. I don't want you down there. Understood?"

"Yes," Zeb replied, knowing full well that the Goatman was no fairy tale, and he was committed to proving it. As soon as the office work lightened up, he was off to see Sheriff Hudlow. And if he was lucky, maybe get a glimpse of Hudlow's daughter, Wanda.

Chapter Fourteen

The Girl

From a distance, Zeb could see Wanda Hudlow. Wanda had been Zeb's classmate since kindergarten. She was a dark-complected, beautiful girl with iridescent brown eyes. Like most southerners, she was an amalgam of heritages fused into one. Wanda was athletic. In their younger years, she had held her own while playing games with the boys. She tackled as well as anyone in a school yard game that resembled rugby. And she won as often as not in a wrestle and push-off-the-hill game behind the row of cinderblock classrooms, two games that resembled chaos but frequently resulted in more work for Doc Barton, usually in the form of fractures. Neither had a name.

Just in the past couple of years, Zeb had become uneasy around Wanda. She had developed curves and fullness in areas that fascinated Zeb. While he wanted to know more about her, he felt everyone around was watching as he approached her sitting on the steps of the Courthouse. His throat tightened as he got closer, thinking about what he would say.

Wanda looked up with an inviting, troublemaker smile. Zeb started up the stairs to the Courthouse in search of Sheriff Hudlow. Wanda was always friendly toward him. *But she is friendly with most everybody*, Zeb thought, as he exhaled nervously before saying, "Hi! I'm looking for your dad. I need to talk to him."

She tossed her dark-black hair over a bare shoulder partially concealed by the bright yellow strap of the flimsy sundress that clung to her, making her new curves all the more apparent. Wanda laughed, saying, "Get over here. I won't bite. I was sitting here hoping to see you. I haven't seen you since summer started. I was worried sick when I heard you got bitten by a Copperhead. My dad told me about it. Are you okay?"

As she spoke, Zeb barely heard her words. He only saw the perfect, tan skin of bare shoulder leading down her shapely arms, and a smile which he thought said more than her words. He noticed the thin strap of a black bra that revealed itself playfully whenever

Wanda moved. He tried not to stare into her enticing eyes, which he found mesmerizing, and shifted around on his clumsy feet, responding, "I'm fine. It was a little snake. I shouldn't have stepped on it anyway."

"I'm glad you're okay. I want to go for a ride on your motorcycle whenever you have time, but we'll have to go without my dad knowing. He, being Sheriff and all, has eyes everywhere, so we'll have to be sneaky," she said, lowering her voice so no one could overhear.

Zeb felt his pulse increasing and his face warming as she spoke. Did she really want to go someplace — just the two of them, away from adults — without anyone knowing about it? His heart raced as he envisioned them close on the motorcycle with her arms wrapped tightly around him pressing her chest against his back.

Suddenly, a voice came rumbling out from the Courthouse doorway, "Wanda, get on up here. I need you to file some legal papers."

The voice turned toward Zeb. "I see you are feeling better."

Towering over them from the landing, Sheriff Hudlow added, "Did you need something Zeb? We're busy. Wanda's got a job to do, and I bet Doc could use some help in the office."

Zeb rose from the steps, only now realizing he had been sitting beside Wanda. Imagining the Sheriff could read his thoughts regarding Wanda, he stepped away from her as he rose. Zeb was probably correct in his imaginings. Sheriff Hudlow was friendly with more women than his wife. Consequently, he assumed, correctly in this case, that Zeb was interested in more than youthful conversation on the steps of the Courthouse.

Zeb stammered, responding. "I, I, well I was actually here to see you, Sheriff. I found some things down at the Mill I thought you might want to know." Wanda rose while Zeb spoke. He tried not to look at the subtle curvature of her back before it disappeared into her dress which loosened as she stood. As Wanda straightened the dress, it slid lower, covering her long, bronzed legs that didn't seem to end. And another tan line.

"Go on. What did you think you found? We've been down there multiple times after the deaths. Chief Bullock has forensic evidence from every inch of the crime scene," continued the Sheriff, as he watched Zeb sneak a look toward Wanda, who was now secretly waving at Zeb behind her father's back.

"Zeb!" exclaimed Sheriff Hudlow, snapping him back into the conversation.

Zeb remembered not to mention Jake while he explained the events at the Mill. He didn't see how this was going to help keep Jake out of the local law's crosshairs, as Joe Scully liked to talk and would have mentioned Jake's name if asked about what they had found. By now, Zeb's story was well-rehearsed. He was pleased with himself at the presentation. Surely now Sheriff Hudlow had what he needed to seek out the Goatman and arrest him. Lock him up once and for all. And leave Thelka alone.

But the Sheriff was not impressed by what he heard. He straightened his suit, which needed no straightening, saying, "Zeb, I've been listening to Goatman myths and stories ever since I moved here. Joe already came by earlier. Nothing you said is hard evidence of anything other than some hooved animals left prints at Freeman's Mill. I'll have Bullock go look around that old Confederate gravesite. Nobody's got any business digging there. That's a crime but doesn't have anything to do with Dollbaby's murder.

"Chief Bullock's working on that case. Probably some drug dealer from Atlanta that we'll never see again," he said, being careful not to mention Thelka as a suspect for fear it would anger Doc Barton should Zeb repeat this suspicion. Sheriff Hudlow continued looking down at his perfectly polished shoes, focusing more on their appearance than the validity of his words. The Sheriff knew Hank Bullock was a bumbler, but he was *his* bumbler and kept Sheriff Hudlow out of the trenches. The Sheriff had secretly made the decision to arrest Thelka, but the timing needed to be right to mitigate the wrath of Doc Barton.

"Now go on, and don't be hanging around here. You should be at the ball field playing with your buddies when you're not helping Doc. Enough of this Goatman stuff," finished the Sheriff while admiring his reflection in a Courthouse window.

Zeb gave a subtle wave to Wanda and left. He was disheartened that no one listened to him or just dismissed what he knew to be true, that the Goatman was not just a character in a fairy tale or nursery rhyme and was probably the murderer. As he walked

away, he imagined Wanda wrapped around him on his fleeing

motorcycle as the landscape zipped past them, blurring his focus.

Turning the corner of the Courthouse, Zeb saw Ike stealthily exiting

Doc's office through the dark edges of the back alley with a box in

his arms. He tried to follow Ike, but Ike disappeared like he had

something to hide and didn't want to be followed.

Chapter Fifteen

Doldrums

The summer had begun with fireworks, but soon the long days and nights dragged in a monotonous routine. As Zeb suspected, the bumbling Chief Bullock found nothing further at the Mill. Joe Scully had taken Bullock to the Confederate gravesite because Dr. Barton had forbidden Bullock from taking Zeb back there. Apparently, Bullock had not even dug up any of the gravesites, saying it would have been a desecration of the dead, though he did confirm the skull they had dug up was that of an adult goat. A local farmer was consulted by Bullock, completing what Zeb saw as his shortsighted and thoroughly inadequate forensic analysis.

The fact that Zeb's father would not let him return to the Mill told Zeb at least two things: One, his father thought the killer was still out there and close by. Two, his father didn't know who the killer was.

Clayton had still not returned.

Zeb's inexplicable terrors had temporarily quieted after the Freeman's Mill murders down by the Alcovy but, especially with Clayton still missing, they soon returned. In addition to the voices about Jake possibly dying, visions of Jake held in some dark, dank hidden place permeated Zeb's latest dreams. He had warned Jake to be careful. Jake had only laughed and pushed Zeb away saying, "*You* be careful. I'll be just fine. Folks know better than to mess with me. Scrawny thing like *you* is easy pickins'."

Zeb needed answers. He continued to question Ike and Thelka, who clearly knew more about the Goatman. Today was no exception.

"Thelka, you once told me you'd seen the Goatman. Or was this one of your many imaginary friends?" goaded Zeb, as he tracked Thelka to the laundry room sorting clothes. "What does he look like? Where does he hide?"

"Boy, I done told ya that yo' pa don't want no more talk about no Goatman. Real or not, makes no neva' mind. You needs ta git readin' them books yo' pa gave ya," admonished Thelka, more serious today than usual.

Zeb would need another approach to get information about the Goatman. "Thelka, do you remember when we watched those astronauts floating around in outer space?" he asked, taking another direction.

"Course I 'member. It wuz all make believe like them movies they makes in Hollywood. Can't nobody float around in space. Next thing ya knows, the gov'ment be makin' a show claimin' they done landed on the moon. They sez that'll be next. Everybody knows can't breathe out there. And that moon is too far away and too soft. The gov'ment just tryin' to trick us the way they does," Thelka responded, as she stared out the window watching Dr. Barton's horses in a nearby pasture.

Zeb continued, "Well, I'm starting to think you are making up that you saw the Goatman. Kinda' like the government tricked us into thinking we saw someone floating in outer space."

"That don't make no sense. The gov'ment makes a show to trick us to believin' they does mo' than they does. 'Specially them commercials they does for the gov'ment sayin' they be buildin' and creatin' jobs and all. Justifies them takin' all them taxes yo' pa complains about," she objected. Zeb didn't understand all this, but at least he had her talking.

Thelka then grinned, and Zeb knew a tale was on its way.

"Zeb, I eva' tell ya about yo' pa and Mr. Taxman? I wuz helpin' yo' pa cleanin' the office, and as we wuz leavin' Mr. Taxman he shows up. He be all dressed up. One of them three pieces of suits. Fancy tie and a shiny little suitcase not good for carryin' much a nuthin'," Thelka smiled, twisting her head about as if she had a full audience in the room.

"No, Thelka. I'm surprised. I've heard most of your tall tales dozens of times. I haven't heard this one," Zeb replied.

Choosing to ignore him, Thelka continued, "This young fool Taxman was there representin' the gov'ment, wantin' ole Doc to pony up. To pay mo' taxes. He wuz gonna follow us out here in his shiny car ta see what all Doc had bought ta fix up tha' house. But ole

Doc told him it wuz too rough a drive on these dirt roads for his new car, which wuz part true. Doc leads him outta his car and shakes out that ole stinkin' dusty blanket he covers the springs where the bird dogs dug through the front seat of the car. Dog fur and dust flyin' everywheres. Tells him to have a seat." Thelka laughed, picturing the scene in her head.

Her hands, which had been folding clothes, swirled around as if the dust and dog hair were right in front of her. "We gits' goin', and it was cold in that car, there bein' no heat. Taxman asks if Doc would turn on the heater. Yo' pa, not carin' much about looks and all, tells Mr. Taxman that he hasn't had it fixed for years. And he adds that hole in the back where I wuz sittin' don't help neither."

Zeb chuckled at this point knowing one of the bird dogs had accidently stepped on a shotgun trigger in the back seat while they were out hunting. Blew a large hole in the side door. Doc didn't see much need for repairing it. Fortunately, no one was killed.

"Yo' pa half told him the story. 'Bout then we gits here and dogs is jumpin' all ova' this little fella who's lookin' at the mess you chilluns leave everywhere. Mr. Taxman don't give up, tellin' yo' pa he wants ta see home improvements. Yo' pa walks him into tha' livin' room full of old broken furniture sayin', 'Here it is.'

"Mr. Taxman, he notices a piece of furniture leanin' ova' 'bout ta collapse and asks ole Doc what happened." Thelka smiled. "I knows, then, Doc got him.

"Doc says, 'I had me a drink or two of Jack Daniel's whiskey after a long day. Got back here about midnight and happened to notice this piece of furniture I didn't like worth a damn. I pulled out this here .38 snub nose pistol and shot the hell out of it'."

Thelka was laughing out loud now, saying, "Ole Doc he up and kicks ova' that desk, which collapses, showin' five bullet holes in tha' wall. Mr. Taxman, he asks yo' pa why he shot it five times and yo' pa says, 'Cause my gun only holds five bullets,' as he pulls the .38 out of his pocket and empties the chamber, resultin' in five unspent bullets bouncing around on the floor. Way Mr. Taxman wuz jumpin' away, he thought them bullets wuz gonna shot theyselves."

Zeb, smiling, added, "I bet he did."

"Mr. Taxman got next ta nuthin' and neva' been back," Thelka finished.

Now was Zeb's opening, "That's a nice story, Thelka. Probably no different than most of your imaginings, like you thinking you see haints or the Goatman."

"Little fool. I ain't studyin' ya boy. I sees what I sees and ya ain't trickin' me, but that Goatman is real as you or me," Thelka responded. She added reluctantly, as she stared into the woods beyond the pasture, "He got an ole cart that holds whatever it is he carries. Lots a goats pulls it. Ya smells them goats and prob'lee that fearsome-looking Goatman long before ya sees 'em. Dirty ole beard must be three feet long."

"Where did you see him, Thelka?" Zeb excitedly questioned. "Do you think he killed Dollbaby and that family down in Chatsworth? Maybe more?"

As Thelka looked into the woods, she spoke hypnotically. Zeb had seen this look before. He thought she was visualizing ghosts. Maybe haints. Maybe the husband she probably killed years before as he was about to beat her teenage former self and her small children.

"Boy, theys bad folks out there. Some born that way. Others damaged that way causa' what they been through. Some a little of both, but bad jus' the same. I ain't tellin' ya no mo' about no Goatman 'cause I don't know any mo'. Iffen I thinks on it too long, don't do me no good. Evil things out there. I can't tell ya no mo' 'bout nuthin'. And you'd best stop askin' 'fore ya git yo'self into trouble ya cain't git out of."

"Well," said Zeb, "Yesterday, it was the dark woods that held demons for you. The day before, it was crows or bats or some other avian creature. Tomorrow, I'm guessing field mice, ferocious creatures that they are."

Thelka emphatically placed her hands on her hips and stared down Zeb.

"Ya mess with me all ya want, little man, but all I'm sayin' is jus' 'cause ya don't see tha' wind don't mean it's not there. And as far as haints goes, I believes if they are riled up at ya, they can hurt ya much as strong gusts of wind in a thunderin' storm.

"Now go on. Git outta here. I gots work ta do. Speakin' of trouble, I think I sees that Jake boy comin' up the drive," Thelka finished, pointing an accusing, stubby, scarred finger in the direction of the motion she had noticed.

Sure enough, it was Jake, and he was running up the drive. Out of breath, he yelled out to Zeb through the open window. His words were indiscernible, but Zeb knew their intent. Zeb's dreams had again become more violent. More deadly. His visions often portended some terrifying event, and since many of them these days were about Jake being held captive, he felt particularly nervous about something happening to his friend.

Things were about to change. A rogue, downward gust of wind bent over the pines ever closer to the house, snapping off brittle limbs.

Chapter Sixteen

Dextera Domini

O nce within earshot, Jake could hardly contain himself as he told Zeb all he knew, saying, "He's done killed someone else. Another boy about our age. I was in town and overheard Bullock yapping about it at Edge's Coffee Shop. They couldn't see me, as the hot sun had me hidden in the shade of the big Oak. Bullock said they found most of him, but they are missing his head and right hand."

Jake looked a little queasy at the thought.

"Are they going to arrest him, the Goatman?" Zeb asked. "Thelka says he's real. Sometimes she'll spin a tale, but I believe her this time. Says she's seen him with a bunch of goats pulling a cart. Scary-looking. She won't talk much 'cause my dad told her to keep quiet about him. I guess he thinks the Goatman is a myth."

"Zeb, Bullock mentioned he would be questioning the Goatman. We ain't even seen him yet. I say that is the first thing we need to do. Gotta be careful, but if we listen, I bet someone will give away his whereabouts," Jake added, as he rubbed his scar.

"I agree," Zeb answered. "Now we could use some help. I bet Wanda would spy on her dad and maybe come up with some information." Zeb scratched his chin nervously, thinking about what he might say to her the next time they met.

"What else did The Chief of Police or Coroner, or whatever he is, say?" Zeb asked.

Jake ground the dirt clods beneath his feet into progressively smaller pieces.

"Happened close to the Alcovy River again," he began slowly. "About a mile from the Mill. This time, Bullock said the boy was 'viscerated. Done had all his innards cut out of him. They were tossed all around hanging from the trees. Blood dripping everywhere. But no one could find his head or right hand."

"*Dextera Dei*," Zeb whispered to himself.

"Huh? What does that mean? Is that from one of those old-timey books your pa has you readin'?"

Zeb straightened himself as he responded. "It's Latin. Another way to say it is *Dextera Domini*. It means the right hand of God. Michael, the Archangel, was God's commander, holding a spear in his right hand. The right hand of God also lifted Christ through the clouds," Zeb finished, while imagining the horror of the sacrifice. Another murder victim.

Zeb could feel the pressure building in his left temple. He attempted to halt the unruly intrusion by rubbing his thumbs against his fingers. *A pathetically futile distraction* thought Zeb. And, Unstoppable, they came:

CLICK. Another. You could have been there and saved him. You should have been there. Maybe you were there. CLACK.

Jake looked away as the heat of the day created a haziness, obscuring his vision. "So, you think the Goatman cut off the right hand on purpose. In his twisted mind, to disarm this latest boy? If that is so, why didn't he do that with the snake-bit boy?"

Zeb momentarily pulled himself away from the accusation and guilt rumbling in the voices. "I think that boy was in the wrong place at the wrong time. He probably saw the Goatman finishing off Dollbaby. He jumped in the Alcovy to escape. While the Goatman was attempting to drown him, the Copperheads got him first. His yelling attracted someone's attention, and the Goatman had to make a quick escape, figuring the boy would die of those bites before he said much."

"I never heard who found the snake-bit boy. Did you?" asked Jake.

Zeb studied the irregular tree line as if looking for answers. "No," he said. "We need to find that out. Maybe they know more than what we've heard. Something else Wanda may be able to get from the reports. She does the filing in the Courthouse and in the Sheriff's office. I'm going to town and try to find her."

Chapter Seventeen

Spies

As Zeb throttled down his motorcycle, planning to park it out of earshot of the Courthouse, he saw Wanda. She was walking up Crogan Street, moving gracefully and singing to herself. Zeb could hear her voice and watching her every move made him worry about how he looked. He hadn't talked to her in a few days. Maybe he had imagined that she was attracted to him. Or maybe she had moved on to someone else. Zeb was mystified by girls, especially her. At least she was alone this time.

He called out, "Wanda, wait up!" as he jogged up the street to her. Wanda spun around. She wore a loose-fitting red top that danced in the breeze. Her shining black hair sparkled as it caught the sun. Her playful eyes focused on him, making Zeb blush though he tried to resist.

"Well, there you are. I've been wondering when you would come back to visit me. You still owe me a motorcycle ride," Wanda teased, with what seemed to Zeb to be a mischievous smile. He liked the idea of their having a secret only between the two of them and had begun thinking of where he could take her without anyone knowing.

Zeb slowed down to a walk as he approached, trying to control his breathing. He didn't want to seem too interested in her. By contrast, Wanda was extremely confident about everything. Trying to impress her but not to seem overly important, Zeb replied, "I've been busy helping my dad in the office with patients pretty much every day. I don't do much. I am mostly assisting him doing minor surgery and suturing people up. Every now and then he'll let me sew a big laceration, especially on repeat customers who are already all scarred up. Been riding horses some. Playing some ball at night over at the ball fields."

"I know," said Wanda. "I've been watching you play. Sometimes my dad will be policing the park, and we'll stop on the hill and watch the games. He won't let me out of the car, but I get to watch you from there. You've been playing very well. My dad doesn't want me around you — or any other boy for that matter — but he says you are the best one out there. Says if you grow into your awkward frame that you could be really good. Sorry, his words not mine. I think you look fine." She nudged him playfully. What she said next, she said with a grin, "You'll figure out where your feet are someday."

Zeb was surprised that Wanda was so straightforward and felt good about what she said — except the part about 'any other boys.' And was the 'you' only him or did she mean all the boys on the field?

Zeb suddenly noticed the murmuring, indistinct voices in his head beginning to grumble and wondered if Wanda could tell. He never knew exactly what would trigger the voices. Stress, maybe. As he rubbed his index finger into his thumb trying to erase any doubts, he replied, "I didn't know you came to any of the games. If I had known, I'd have played better."

To this Wanda replied, "I didn't come to just any games. There's a schedule that was posted at the Courthouse, so I knew when you were playing." While she spoke, Zeb was entranced by the way she uttered each word. She looked him directly in the eyes, which made Zeb uncomfortable. It seemed she could read his thoughts. Maybe Wanda knew him better than he thought.

Zeb felt a warm excitement moving up his neck at the thought that she had made a point to see him play, but he quickly changed the subject, not knowing what to say next. He felt his shaky voice become more certain. "When you are filing papers at the Courthouse, what types of reports do you see?" he asked. "Reason I ask is there's been another murder close to Freeman's Mill. Someone about our age. I didn't know if those police reports were filed by you. Jake and I know the Goatman did it, but no one wants to listen. That buffoon Hank Bullock, Chief of Police acting sometimes as Coroner, doesn't know anything about what he is doing."

Wanda shook her head in agreement. "And my dad is more interested in checking up on the single women in Hobbleton than police work," she said, looking skyward at high-drifting clouds, exposing the sleek curvature of her neck. Zeb was surprised by her response as he looked away to avoid staring at Wanda's enticing neck. He was starting to make sense of some of Thelka's comments about Sheriff Hudlow and his outside "interests."

Responding to Zeb's quizzical look, Wanda continued, "Yes, I know about my dad's escapades. My mom does too. They used to argue about it, but now they just coexist without much interaction. And yes, I see all the reports. I read them when no one is watching. I especially read the more serious crime reports. The only murders we've had in Hobbleton in several years, that weren't drug-related or from the projects, were those two boys and maybe Dollbaby. As best I can tell."

Zeb was shocked by several things she said. Understanding her was difficult, as his brain became his head's version of tongue-tied, so he just watched her more than he was able to listen to her. Instinctively responding without much deliberation, Zeb blurted out, "I had no idea you knew so much about all of this. About your dad. About the details of the killings. And that you also think both boys were murdered."

Wanda smiled. "Zeb, do you think I am just another pretty face? Another of your admirers? Of course, I know about these cases. And yes, I think both the boys were murdered. The second one they discovered two days ago was obviously murdered based on preliminary reports. Pretty gruesome. The first one I'm not quite so certain. The Copperhead-boy."

Zeb was momentarily at a loss for words. He tried to quiet the rumble of incomprehensible voices in his head while formulating a response. Most of what she said was true, but he had no idea she would be this interested in the murders. That she would read the gory details contained in these reports.

And what did she mean by "admirers"? Freckle-faced with big ears and uncoordinated, gangly limbs that didn't seem to match up with the rest of him, Zeb knew he wasn't much to look at. Maybe she was joking with him. Maybe even making fun of him, he began to think, as the incoherent voices in his head were growing louder, competing for his attention.

Zeb noticed he was rubbing both index fingers against thumbs and stopped immediately, saying, "Good. I was hoping you could look at some of those reports. Seems you already have. Who do you think did this?"

Wanda twirled her dark hair which she pulled to one side in a ponytail. She considered the question. "I know you think it was the Goatman. It is in all the reports that creepy, bumbling Bullock turned in after he interviewed Jumpin' Joe Scully regarding what you and Jake found down at Freeman's Mill. Me, I am not so sure. I do think he exists. That he is not just the fairy tale rhyme we learned as kids. Based on what I read in the police reports, he probably stays hidden in the woods close to the Mill. I don't know why they don't find him and question him. Regardless of what I think, he is still a prime suspect."

"I agree," Zeb said, nodding. "I don't get that either. Why don't they question him?" Before she could answer, he said, "Back to the reports that Bullock turned in regarding the murder... Were there any clues pointing to the Goatman? Anything unusual? Similarities to the Copperhead-bit boy?"

Wanda smiled at Zeb. Her eyes brightened. She enjoyed his rudimentary detective instincts. "Zeb, I know what you are thinking.

You have already convicted the Goatman in your mind, but we need facts, not suspicions and fairy tales, to stop these murders. I don't file records outside the county. I do overhear conversations in the Courthouse that suggest the person doing this could be responsible for multiple murders. There have been several more in Coweta County down by the Ocmulgee River. And by the Ogeechee River. The mutilations are progressively worsening. More gruesome. About the only consistent findings are that the suspect is probably using a WWII machete-type knife, based on the type of injuries and fragments of a blade that were found. He is skilled with it. One cut. Indicative of a single slice decapitating a victim. The other thing is he almost always amputates the right hand."

"That's what Jake told me about the most recent boy victim. That his head and his right hand were missing. Said everything else was scattered about in the trees," agreed Zeb, wondering if she really knew what he was thinking. She seemed to know so much about what no one else did. Did she sense the mutterings in his head? If so, could she help stop them?

"That's odd," Wanda said. "There was no mention of the right hand missing in Bullock's report about that last boy. Bumbler though he is, that is a significant oversight. He got worse at his job or jobs since he was appointed Coroner. Crazy system to have the Coroner appointed by the Mayor — who happens to be his uncle. Probably no one halfway sane would take the job. Doesn't pay much. Only good for giving you nightmares.

"Oh, one other thing I came across surprised me. I don't think it means anything. I just didn't know about it. Seems there was an accident. Joe Scully's first wife died after hitting her head on the stone hearth of their fireplace. Happened soon after he returned from the war. Joe said she tripped and fell hard. There were never any charges filed against him. Sad is all."

Zeb did not respond, but he couldn't help thinking about Joe's suspicious behavior at the Mill. He looked in the direction of the Courthouse wondering what, if anything, the police could be hiding and why. As he looked back at Wanda, he suddenly had a strong urge to see her later after she finished working. *No,* he thought, *that would be too much too soon.*

"Gotta get back to work now, Zeb. My dad will be suspicious if I am late. I'll let you know if I find out anything. That is if I see you again," she laughed, giving Zeb a backwards, furtive glance as she turned and started back towards the Courthouse. Her sleek, curved silhouette, outlined by the sun, looked to Zeb like a it was surrounded by a giant halo.

Zeb responded, "If you come this way tomorrow about this time, I'll wait for you. See what you can find."

Wanda did an about face and ambled back to Zeb. She slyly grinned, saying, "I go this way about this time every day. My dad can't spy on me all the time, and things are heating up at the Courthouse with these mysterious murders. He'll be less attentive. Maybe we can take that motorcycle ride. You keep thinking, and we'll work through this together."

Wanda then playfully tapped Zeb on the forehead and said, "I know there's lots going on in there. Slow it down. I'm certain you will get where you need to be in time."

Zeb was half listening and didn't know what she meant. Was she complimenting him or making fun of him? Whatever she felt, in his mind, he was already envisioning the two of them going on the motorcycle ride. Maybe that and something more, though Zeb was not very sure of what that something more might be. He waved as she sauntered up the steps.

Zeb observed her hips rotate enticingly with each step and suddenly felt as if someone was watching him watch her. Yet he looked in all directions and could not see anyone.

As Zeb had turned to leave, he sensed someone moving away from a window in the Courthouse. Someone who was watching intently enough that Zeb had felt his or her presence. Real or imagined, Zeb could feel Evil. This confused him. *Who in the Courthouse would have evil intent?* he wondered. He would have to remember to ask Wanda about that.

As Zeb went around the corner toward his motorcycle, he saw Ike, who called out, "Zeb, where you been? Doc needs some help in the Emergency Room. One of his patients dropped a lung. Gotta put a tube in to pull it back up. He's breathing real hard."

Chapter Eighteen

Breathing and Burning

Zeb cranked up the cycle, waving to Ike, acknowledging what he said. He sped to the ER and arrived five minutes later. Running inside the trauma room, he saw a frantic man in his twenties breathing hard with an oxygen mask strapped to his face. His face seemed swollen and purplish. The nurses were trying to calm him.

"Johnny, now lie back and hold still," Dr. Barton instructed. "You are going to be fine. Zeb and I are going to put this little chest tube in you, and you'll be able to breathe better. Won't be much worse than when I set your leg after you busted it up falling off that crazy horse you used to ride."

Johnny did as instructed. With a struggle to breathe, he let out the patient's pledge of allegiance to Clyde Barton. "Doc, I trust you. I'd let you cut off my head if you told me I needed it."

"Well Johnny, fortunately that won't be necessary today," Dr. Barton replied, without emotion. He turned toward Zeb and, pointing to an area on Johnny's chest, said, "Zeb, wash up this area with betadine and drape with sterile towels. This is the best place for a chest tube: mid axillary line, fifth intercostal space. Johnny's like other thin, young men that are prone to spontaneous pneumothorax. Can be fatal."

Doc nudged Johnny's shoulder lightly adding, "But Johnny here is going to be fine. Got here in plenty of time. Plus, he's too stubborn to let this keep him down long." Dr. Barton wore a rare smile.

Zeb, already having donned a sterile gown and gloves, began prepping as instructed. Zeb never knew how much of a procedure he would be expected to complete on his own. Johnny was clearly a long-time, loyal patient of Dr Barton. This, for whatever reason, increased the likelihood they would do well. More importantly, from Zeb's perspective, it increased the likelihood that he would do more of the procedure. That, and the appearance that Dr. Barton was in a good mood. His patients must be doing well, and maybe Doc had gotten some unbroken sleep. Zeb looked forward to working with his father, though with some reluctance as Dr. Barton could be a harsh instructor. His demeanor could be volcanic, unpredictable at best.

"Now, show me the spot you are going to numb. You've helped me do this before. Good. Now put in a syringe full of local. Johnny will appreciate that," Doc said, grinning at Johnny who had calmed at his presence. "Give it a minute, then make the incision. Johnny's tough. He'll be fine."

Zeb did as instructed but hesitated as he initiated a small incision. His father had no use for indecision. Indecision in this moment would not be harmful but in others could prove fatal.

"Damn it, Zeb," Dr. Barton cursed. "Go on. Pay attention. You know what to do. You've watched me." He turned toward a nurse. "Get me some gloves," he barked, as a dark shadow seemed to fill the room.

Zeb proceeded to make the incision longer. Then he used a curved Kelly clamp to spread the intercostal muscle fibers. This required controlled force, as the fibers were tough, but too much pressure and the clamp could plunge into the underlying lung or into the heart with catastrophic consequence.

Dr. Barton observed closely with his gloved hands at the ready, saying, "Good. Johnny, you okay? We're about there. Your breathing is about to get a lot easier."

Simultaneously, the Kelly clamp popped through the pleura lining the chest cavity which startled Zeb. Air under pressure propelled from the incision. Johnny twisted slightly as the clamp went into his chest. Then he relaxed, able to breathe more easily. Doc handed Zeb the chest tube, instructing, "Now. Almost done. Slide this toward the apex until you meet resistance, then pull back an inch and sew the tube in place."

As Zeb pushed the tube inside Johnny's chest, he couldn't help but think of all the vital structures he could injure. Oddly, this excited him as much as worried him. He didn't want to hurt Johnny, but the impulsive thoughts were not ones he could entirely control in this stressful moment. Or other moments for that matter. Challenging times when Zeb mentally fought back compulsions that could be injurious. Paradoxically, this internal friction led to a strong sense of right and wrong. Zeb *could* control his movements in this moment and completed the task.

"Johnny, we'll leave that in on wall suction to keep the lung expanded until it heals. Then Zeb will remove it in four or five days if the lung cooperates. If not, you may need surgery. Zeb let's go. Big office today."

The assistants in the room had watched Zeb's every move. They stood around, finally relaxed, pleased with Johnny's improvement and Zeb's skills. No time for admiration though.

The nurse in charge spoke up with a measured flat affect, stating, "Dr. Barton, you promised hospital administration you'd make that meeting this morning. They saw you coming into the ER and wanted me to remind you."

Dr. Barton, who routinely missed the monthly medical staff meeting, muttered, "That's a hell of a note. A bunch of incompetents that like to hear themselves talk. Silly nonsense.

"Okay. I'll see what they want. Zeb, you wait outside the door. This won't take long," Dr. Barton said, motioning Zeb to follow him as the nursing staff watched them walk down the hallway to the conference room, aware that something was up.

The conference room held about twenty physicians. Some young. Some old. Some competent. Others not so much. Generally, the incompetent ones were much nicer than those with actual medical or surgical skills. Undoubtedly, this was a survival method learned early in their training programs and carried into their medical practices but unfortunate for unsuspecting patients who were taken in by their charming demeanor. Dr. Barton had no use or patience for the incompetents.

"Good morning, Dr. Barton," welcomed Jim Blinken, the appointed Chief of Staff. Jim was a harmless, likable fellow. He always wore a bow tie and a smile. He lived for these meetings, because they gave him a sense of importance as well as a captive audience.

"Hey, Jim. I understand you've been requesting my presence. Well, here I am. I'm busy. What do you need?" Dr Barton questioned, as he lit up a Chesterfield and hung it from the corner of his mouth.

"Doc, we've been having a problem understanding your medical record documentation. We know your schedule stays full and appreciate your indefatigable skills," Jim deferentially replied. "But could you look at one of your discharge summaries? It's a patient who was hospitalized with a necrotic gallbladder requiring multiple interventions. It pretty much resembles the rest." As he spoke, Jim Blinken eased a single sheet of paper into Dr. Barton's hand and quickly backed away as if confronting a coiled Canebrake Rattler.

Dr. Barton slid on his glasses. Taking a drag on his cigarette, he studied the single sentence indecipherably scribbled on the top of the page. A wrinkle of blue ink from his fountain pen for a signature. After he completed the inspection, much as he would a newborn child for anomalies, he spoke clearly, saying, "You are correct. This is not worth a goddamn."

The room seemed to exhale with a collective sigh of relief, though perhaps prematurely. For Doc Barton, paperwork was a waste of time. He knew his patients from birth to death as well as he knew his own kids. Each medical history was well-catalogued in his mind. No need for scribblings on a page.

With a single deliberate motion, Dr. Barton reached into his pants pocket with his right hand and, with his left hand, raised the page high in disdain. He pulled his lighter out, flicked it, and precisely ignited the near corner of the paper. Zeb watched from the side of the door as the physicians stared in disbelief.

Doc admired the combustible masterpiece as the flame licked at his fingers. He seemed immune to the heat and entranced by the mutating patterns as the page was devoured. He dropped the flickering, ashen page into a nearby circular metal trash can and silently exited the room. The staff, who had been watching from the nursing station, quietly looked down at their charts to avoid Dr. Barton's wrath.

Nothing more was ever said.

Chapter Nineteen

Nursery Rhyme Lives

Z eb finished helping in the office later than usual that night. As he rode home around midnight over the empty rutted dirt road, he tried to make sense of the day. Despite other's doubts that the Goatman had something to do with the murders, Zeb still felt certain the Goatman was the culprit. Though it was late, Zeb couldn't resist the urge to swing by Jake's house and check up on him. Jake generally stayed awake late into the night, not wanting anyone to sneak up on him in the dark.

"Jake, you still up?" called out Zeb, listening to the tree frogs quiet then surge forth with a flurry of competing voices. Zeb found comfort in their calls, since they would quiet only when threatened by unusual sounds or predators. Harbingers of a sort.

"Zeb, come on in," welcomed Jake. "I was meaning to come by in the morning. You won't believe what... who... I saw. At least

I think I saw while you were visiting your lady friend at the Courthouse.

"I was on the County bus doing community service to avoid jail time because of a fight I was in a few weeks ago. That part don't matter. I was looking out the window as we were driving by the old shut-down cattle farm off Apalachee Road. In the far back corner of the fields, I could see a two-wheeled cart with junk piled high and what looked like goats pulling it. Several other goats were scattered about grazing. I watched as the shape of an old man at the front of the cart appeared. It was late afternoon. I could hardly see for the shadows changing as the bus moved along, but I am certain it was him. It was the Goatman. The shadowy creature himself. Long beard to his knees. Sort of slumped-over shoulders. Dangling arms. From where I sat, pure Evil."

"You sure it was him? That's close by. Maybe we could sneak down that way and get a better look," Zeb responded, his heart starting to pound with excitement joined with an equal injection of fear.

"Not tonight, Zeb. I feel a storm blowing in. Plus, probably safer in the daytime when we can see. Some say the Goatman works at night 'cause he can see better in the darkness than he can during the day. I don't know if that's true, but I don't plan on finding out," Jake said.

Zeb looked about Jake's hovel, which contained only a few cans of food. Some of Jake's clothes were strewn on a small cot in the corner. A single lamp shed some light in the small, quiet place. He thought about Jake's misgivings regarding a nighttime search and said, "Jake, you're probably right. Plus, I'm meeting up with Wanda Hudlow again to see if she was able to find out more about the murders. We can go after that."

"I thought you talked to her earlier. You needin' to see her again? Mighty convenient and mighty pretty. You could be out of your league with that one, Zeb," Jake chuckled. Zeb felt his face reddening.

Zeb shot back, "It's not like that. We've known each other since kindergarten. She was one of the hardest to tackle when we played in the schoolyard. Fast and strong."

"I am sure she was, but now she is awful easy on the eyes. Smart as a whip too. But best watch out for the Sheriff. If he catche's you around her, it won't be so pretty," Jake snickered. He cradled a piece of wood he'd been carving and began inspecting it.

Zeb looked at the figurine in Jake's large hands. It was far from complete, but the curvature and fine recesses already resembled the dark, scary shape of an old, bearded man. Every recess and indentation spoke of darkness and terror. Zeb never knew Jake had such skill. This surprised him given the enormity of Jake's hands for such a delicate creation. Even more, he was surprised Jake seemed to know his subject — the Goatman — much better than the glimpse from a moving bus hundreds of yards away would have allowed. *The figurine is probably as much imagined as real*, thought Zeb, not thoroughly convinced.

"Let's meet up around noon tomorrow. I'll come by here to pick you up. Don't go wandering off like you do sometimes. I want to put my eyes on the Goatman. Seems like everyone else knows more about him than me. If we follow the tracks of the goats from where you spotted him, he shouldn't be hard to find. Especially if it rains tonight. That many goats should leave plenty of prints in the soft dirt," asserted Zeb.

"Sounds like a plan, Zeb. I'll see you tomorrow provided you can get yourself away from that pretty girl you seem stuck on," kidded Jake.

Zeb cranked up the cycle to drown out Jake's last sentence, as he knew it was coming. The tree frogs silenced with the roar of Zeb's cycle but struck up their comforting chorus as he rode away. Only to become silent again, leaving Jake alone, vulnerable.

Chapter Twenty

Revelations

That night Zeb's dreams again turned to terrors.

The road spiraled downward, imperceptible at first, then undeniable. Red clay worn and rutted. Gravel thrown up the embankment laced with soft wild roses clinging to the hillside. He had been here before. In the darkness of night, shapes had begun that slow transformation into chaos frozen in twisted metal. As a car lunged forward, uncontrolled, and pulseless, misshapen forms relentlessly grasped for meaning in the silence. CLICKITY CLACK.

Zeb awoke early the next morning, startled by the bright daylight. He lay still for a few minutes to separate his nightmare from what he perceived to be real. The heavy rapid thudding in his head finally slowed. As he lay there, he could hear Thelka and Ike arguing down the hall. This was unusual, as the two seldom spoke to each other.

"Ike, I thinks he be needin' to know. I'm not sho' what Doc is thinkin', but I don't think Zeb's gonna stop lookin' 'lessen he knows mo'. He gits mo' like his pa every day, and that ain't all a good thing," whispered Thelka. Her voice, though low, traveled down the pine-floored, narrow hallway so that Zeb could understand every word.

"Now Thelka, old Doc got his reasons, and we both owe Doc. He's been mighty good to us. He wouldn't do nothing that would put Zeb in danger. Doc wants Zeb to leave the Goatman alone and doesn't want us involved. We know too much. And you know Doc said not to bring up the other," responded Ike.

Zeb was shocked. He had no idea what they could be saying. Did his father know the Goatman? What did this mean? And what was "the other"? He continued listening as he stared at the small, jagged cracks lacing an otherwise blank, empty ceiling.

"Ike, I'm gonna tell him if you ain't. It's not right. I worry 'bout that boy and these crazy dreams he has 'bout as much as anybody, but I don't see hidin' the truth 'bout things helpin' much. As ya know, one of ma' boys kilt' hisself. Had same crazy dreams.

Seemed like people was in his head sometimes talkin' ta him. Zeb ain't got it that bad, but I worries 'bout him. Maybe iffen he knows the truth 'bout the Goatman and 'bout 'the other,' he'll stop havin' them bad nightmares. Zeb thinks too much."

Ike took a few minutes before he said, "I agree that he thinks too much. Some things are best left alone. We all got our bad stuff. Hadn't been for Doc, when we were kids in Maysville, I'd probably been killed by some mighty mean White boys. They were out playing ball in a dirt lot outside of town. I couldn't have been no more than nine or ten years old. I was watching them play, hidden in the trees 'cause Black boys didn't mix in with the White ones back then." Ike halted, taking a slow breath as he rubbed his fingers over the multiple linear scars on his face like he was trying to make them fade away. They wouldn't, nor would the memories.

He winced and continued, "One of them boys hit a ball into the trees near me. I stayed hidden, but they couldn't find the ball. I don't know what I was thinking. I stepped out to show them where it was, and as I pointed, showing them, one of the older, bigger boys jumped on me. He was saying that I hid the ball and was trying to steal it."

Thelka was wide-eyed now as she listened. Ike had never confided in her. Maybe all the pain and worry about Zeb and Clayton had brought Ike back to that day. Thelka prodded Ike, and not because she was curious. She had a good idea what came next by the way Ike was staring at the rock-laden pasture, feeling every curve of the scars on his face as he spoke. She said, "Ike, you need to say out loud what happened next. Git it outta yo' insides. Not good to hold that in all these years. It'll turn to corruption."

Ike nodded his head in reluctant agreement, continuing, "They started beating me up bad. A mean boy with bloodshot, yellow eyes took off a baseball shoe with sharp metal spikes. As the others held me, he repeatedly bloodied my face with those spikes. Cut my face all to pieces. I am pretty sure they were going to take me down to the river to drown me to hide what they done, but another kid lived nearby that I knew of. Clyde Barton. He heard all the noise and somehow got them off me. I don't remember any of that. Doc got beat up pretty bad saving me from them older boys. I came to at the local hospital. There was only one country doctor and his helper. They put me back together as best they could."

Ike was visibly sweating, reliving the memory as though it were happening again. The linear cuts on his face seemed to bulge forward about to burst.

Thelka was quiet. She looked across the pasture at the horses as they grazed. "Ike, I known'd ya owed ole Doc. Now I know why. I do too. Maybe we don't say nuthin' to Zeb just yet. Doc got his reasons. Maybe it's too soon like he said."

Thelka leaned forward, speaking at a low whisper that Zeb could only partially make out, asking, "Ike, do you think he done it? Kilt' all them people that way?"

Ike looked Thelka straight in the eyes and said, "Thelka, at this point, I don't know who done it. There are a lotta folks with hidden evil. Bad things happened to them along the way that turns them into something no one would ever suspect as a mutilating killer. Turns them from an innocent person into a monster hidden right in front of your eyes in the light of day. The Goatman isn't any different. He just looks and acts different, so people point their finger in his direction. Now that doesn't make him guilty, but that doesn't make him innocent either."

Thelka added, "And the Goatman got plenty a reasons to hate. Way people be treatin' him like he wuz nuthin' all these years. What they say he done, he paid for. He done his time. I don't know nuthin' about before that. But I know somethin' changed him in the war. That's all needs to be said right now." Thelka looked out the window again. "I see Doc coming back up the driveway. He delivered a baby early. Tore outta here. He be back to shower and change for the day. He don't need to hear none of this."

Zeb was now more puzzled than ever. He knew trying to extract more information from Thelka or Ike directly would shut them up entirely. Best approach would be to watch and listen. He would have to be patient. More answers would come.

Chapter Twenty-One

The Plan

Zeb hurried out the back door to escape notice while his father came in through the garage. He had told Wanda he would be back, and he intended to keep that promise, hoping it would lead them somewhere. Not that he had any idea of where that would be. If his dad saw him, Zeb might be helping in the office for the remainder of the day. When Zeb arrived in town, Wanda saw him first. She motioned to him to come over to her in the edge of the old Oaks that lined Culver Street.

"Well, you did make it back. Come over here behind these trees so no one will see us. My dad's like yours. He's got spies everywhere," she said, smiling, getting close enough that Zeb could feel her warm, sweet breath, which made his neck tingle. She continued, "I was able to pick up some more information about your Goatman. Nothing too enlightening. Police Chief Bullock seems to have a good bit of misinformation in his reports. No surprise there. He doesn't even seem to know where he is half the time, except when he's hanging around my desk telling me how smart he is. They are focused on a Black man that came by after Dollbaby's murder, thinking he may be responsible for more. Pretty typical. Blame Blacks for everything. Leave the White folks alone even if the evidence proves otherwise."

"What did you find out about the Goatman?" inquired Zeb, unable to stop staring at Wanda's brown eyes, which sparkled with greenish emerald flashes as she listened.

"Like I said, not much, but your dad's name came up. Seems they are staying away from the Goatman because they don't want to cross Dr. Barton. Does your dad treat the Goatman as a patient?" she asked.

Zeb responded, "Not that I know of. And I think there is more to it than that. I overheard Thelka and Ike arguing this morning. They are hiding information from me about the Goatman. Apparently, my dad is making them stay quiet. I think I heard them say something about a bad thing the Goatman did years ago, and that he'd done his time. Plus, I saw Ike sneaking something out of my father's office when I was leaving last night through the back alley. Maybe that had something to do with the Goatman."

Wanda replied, "I saw that in some notes I found from years ago. He was arrested for nearly beating his wife to death. I couldn't read it all. Some was torn out. Other passages were marked through. I think there was something about a child and the wife left in a field. Some mention of grandparents. I couldn't make out his real last name, but someone had put it in a folder labeled 'The Goatman'. Who knows? May not even be the same person."

"I bet it's all the same horrid, violent person. For some reason my dad's protecting him. I have no idea why. I wasn't aware he even knew the Goatman until this morning, but I'm going to find out what's going on. I'm meeting up with Jake when I leave here. He saw the Goatman yesterday not a mile from Freeman's Mill with his cart and a bunch of goats."

Zeb stood up straighter, continuing, "Jake said the Goatman was as scary looking as he thought he would be. We're going to track him and see what he is up to," said Zeb. He was courageous in the light of day in the safety of the Oak trees trying to impress this girl he admired.

"You be safe," Wanda said, as she gave Zeb a hug. "I wouldn't do well without you around."

Zeb couldn't stop the smile that spread across his face as he stood awkwardly immobile in that moment. Wanda seemed to be saying she wanted him around. Did she mean all the time or maybe only to talk to sometimes? Zeb didn't understand what she meant. Too many variables. She was too pretty to look at and be rational at the same time. But she had hugged him, so he knew she must at least like him somewhat.

"I'll let you know what we find. Keep looking through those files. You're coming up with helpful information," Zeb instructed, emboldened by her hug and their shared secrecy. Wanda turned to go. Hesitated briefly. Then ran back, hugging Zeb once more. This time adding a brief kiss on his cheek lightly brushing against his lips. This time, not so innocently.

Later that morning, when Zeb arrived at Jake's shack, he could see Jake pushing his way through the underbrush. Jake was more disheveled than usual. His shirt was torn and, there were streaks of blood on his arms and scratches across his face. He had been up all night. Zeb stopped in his tracks, wincing at Jake's condition.

"Jake, what happened to you?" gasped Zeb. "You look like you've been wrestling a wildcat."

Jake looked up, exposing dark circles under his eyes. "I heard a terrible commotion in the woods last night and couldn't sleep. I figured whatever or whoever it was knew where I was. That I'd be better sneaking up on them than them on me. I left the shack and crawled through the thicket. As I listened, I could make out two men fighting with each other. I didn't recognize their voices, and it was too dark to make out any features. I thought I heard one of them say something like, 'If you've got anything to do with this, it must stop. You need to leave.' They heard me, I think, because they suddenly looked around and took off running. A car with its lights turned off came up the hill from down where they were. Close to the Mill. Whoever was driving ran into the ditch and crashed pretty hard.

They were going fast and popped right out. As soon as the car got to the main road, it sped off," Jake said, exhaling deeply.

"Did you recognize the car or have any idea who was driving? It wasn't Joe Scully, was it? Sounds like the way he drives." Zeb asked, with a dour look creeping across his face.

"No. Like I said, it was dark, and I couldn't see much of anything. The left front of that car should be beat up pretty bad though," Jake continued. "I looked around where they were arguing and didn't find anything this morning except this tattered, worn grey cloth that smells awful."

Zeb reached out and took the cloth. "You are correct. It smells awful. Smells like rotten milk. I don't recognize it from anywhere. It looks like something the Goatman would wear though. Let's track him from where you saw him yesterday by the old farm and see if we can get a closer look. See if that was him you heard last night."

"Zeb, I'm tired out. I don't think I'd be of much help. Let's go tomorrow," Jake suggested, taking a deep sigh. This was the second time Jake had dissuaded Zeb from directly pursuing the

Goatman. But Zeb was feeling more invincible after seeing Wanda, and he would not be stopped today.

"Tracks will be too hard to follow by then. I'll go see what I can find. Goatman doesn't kill in the light of day. If I'm not back by nightfall, let Ike know where I am. He'll come find me," Zeb responded, as he headed out to where Jake had last seen the Goatman off Apalachee Road.

Unbeknownst to him, Zeb was about to be closer to the Goatman than he ever intended.

Chapter Twenty-Two

Death at the Graveyard

When Zeb arrived at the dilapidated farm, he easily found the hoof tracks of several goats scattered all around the collapsing farmhouse and barn behind it. These were similar to the ones Jake and he had found by the Mill and Confederate Graveyard. In addition, there were bare footprints mixed with the goats' and a pair of wheel tracks. After looking around, it was clear the Goatman and his congregation had long since departed. The cart tracks were easy to follow. Leaving his cycle hidden behind the barn, Zeb began to search.

There was not a discernable trail from a distance. Yet, once Zeb started following the cart imprint, a path wide enough to let the cart pass appeared before him. The trail was well-worn, suggesting the Goatman had travelled this way many times. And it circuitously wended in the direction of Freeman's Mill, which was about a mile away. Zeb had travelled the main road adjacent the trail many times. He had never seen anything in this direction, but the thick underbrush would have concealed the Goatman, the cart, and dozens of goats.

As Zeb crossed over a narrow ridge, he could make out the top of the paddle wheel at Freeman's Mill in the hollow below. He was on the top of Goat Hill. He'd never been up this far previously. No one he knew had. Zeb was surprised at the panoramic view. He could see Jake's shack particularly well from a clearing at the rim of the ridge. Looking around, he found trampled vegetation throughout, with goat prints and a few stray goat hairs clinging to underbrush. No doubt that the Goatman often concealed himself here.

Zeb surveyed the scene below looking for any movement. After about ten minutes, he noticed a slight tremor of briars in the general vicinity of the Confederate Graveyard. A breeze had picked up, with clouds gathering overhead.

"Could be just the wind picking up causing the brush to waver," Zeb whispered to himself and started down the trail hoping to finally find the mythical creature he'd heard about as early as he could remember. Approaching the Mill, Zeb noticed a strange silence. No musical tree frogs. Only an occasional distant rumble from a late morning summer storm organizing over the hills.

Zeb suddenly felt entirely vulnerable. What was he thinking? The Goatman had every advantage in this desolate place. Zeb had no protection, and no one would hear his pleas for help. He crawled up behind the stone wall that had funneled water to the paddle wheels. He sat motionless. The rumbling of distant thunder seemed to be nearing as it grew louder.

From his vantage point, he could make out the clearing at the graveyard. Odd that it had been there all these years and no one much knew that it existed. If it weren't for the Black Walnut tree killing off the vegetation underneath, most likely it would have remained part of a ghost story. As he watched, a goat walked into the clearing followed by several others. *No doubt the Goatman is here,* thought Zeb, as he shivered.

Gathering himself up from the ground, Zeb crawled quietly up the opposite hill to the graveyard. Every pine needle giving way beneath him might betray his location. The slightest snap would announce his presence. He slowed every few feet, ready to run if detected. About twenty yards away from the clearing, he stopped and watched. This was close enough. The sky continued to darken as an occasional high bolt of lightning coursed across it.

Then suddenly, there he was — the Goatman.

Scraggly matted hair hung over his face as he leaned over to pick up something. His clothes were tattered, grayish brown, and clearly hadn't been washed recently, if ever. He was stooped over at the shoulders with a stained, gray beard that touched the ground when he leaned forward. Zeb could hardly see the Goatman's weathered face beneath the unkempt hair. A crumpled, round-brimmed hat sat askew on his head. He held a crooked, knobby cane which anchored his every movement. A Demon.

Remaining paralytically still, Zeb watched as the Goatman cleared an area of underbrush encroaching on the graveyard with a razor-sharp machete. He began digging in the graveyard with what appeared to be an old WWII collapsible shovel. *These are the instruments that he uses to kill and mutilate his prey,* thought Zeb. He inched forward to see what the Goatman was burying, expecting to see the missing right hand or maybe the missing head from his kill of two days before. He was ready to run if detected. Surely, he could outrun this old man who relied on stealth and dark shadows to entrap his victims.

The Goatman's face appeared as an ancient frozen sculpture. Not human. Dimensionless. *He's like some supernatural creature*, thought Zeb. The furrows on his brow crept down his face, meandering across his neck. He seemed to growl, snarling as he moved. Every joint groaning, creaking, resisting his intended movements. Goats encircled him as if entranced by some forbidden spell.

Zeb could feel the pulsations in his neck rise and become almost audible when the Goatman lifted a small limp object wrapped in cloth and lowered it into the grave. As he did, the goats surrounding him moved in closer. With the ever-nearing storm and darkening skies, Zeb was terrified by this apparition. Progressively ill-defined shapes hovered above the graves. Despite this and his increasing fear, Zeb leaned forward to get a closer look at the small bundle before it was concealed in the soft brown dirt. As he did, he accidentally snapped a branch that resonated loudly, disrupting the surrounding silence. Simultaneously, a bolt of lightning lit up the sky. It struck a nearby pine tree, shattering bark down the entirety of the main trunk, exposing the tender pulp beneath. Unprotected. The Goatman spun around, staring at Zeb with hollow, lifeless, deep green eyes illuminated by the flash of lightning.

Zeb was too frightened to move between the crashing of splintering bark and the deadly stare. But he quickly regained focus as the threatening Goatman stood up, heading in his direction. Everything after that was a blur.

Zeb managed to run the entire trail through the pouring rain back to his motorcycle at the abandoned barn. Not once did he look back. Despite the creature's ancient appearance, he was certain the Goatman was only a few steps behind him. Zeb was hyperventilating. Only when he pulled his motorcycle into the main Courthouse Square of Hobbleton did he stop to slow his breathing. The rain and lightning had ceased.

From a distance, he could see Sheriff Hudlow, Chief Bullock, and Joe Scully talking on the Courthouse steps. Zeb excitedly approached them with what he had seen. While he was speaking, Bullock looked at him suspiciously.

After Zeb finished relaying the flurry of events at the Mill, Bullock said, "You sure do spend a lot of time down there, son. And you know more than you should. I'd suggest you stay around town or at home so we know where you are. We'll look into what you thought you saw."

Zeb wasn't sure what that fool meant. Was Zeb a suspect? They had become very quiet when he first approached, apparently not wanting to be overheard. No, that made no sense. What were they hiding from him? As Bullock spoke with a smile undercut with something different than Zeb had seen before, the left side of Zeb's head began to tighten. The rumbling in his head insidiously crept in. Maybe Joe was pointing fingers and sidling up to Sheriff Hudlow and Bullock to keep their attention elsewhere. To make himself look innocent. Zeb refused to believe this. Joe had always been good to him. Like a reflex, Zeb pressed his temple and attempted to walk away from all the voices:

Maybe it was You all along. CLICKITY. You know too much.

CLACK. You could have stopped it. Stopped yourself. CLACK.

Zeb refused to listen to the accusatory, nonsensical clatter that clanged around in his head. It was time to get some answers from Ike. At least from what he'd overheard when Ike and Thelka were arguing, Ike was the most likely to know more about the Goatman. And he'd ask Ike about the package he was sneaking out of the office too.

Starting up the motorcycle, Zeb spoke as though he were someone else. He heard himself saying, "*Goatman looked familiar. Too familiar.*" He visualized the masklike, rutted-out, weathered face he had seen flash out of the shadows by a bolt of lightning. The deep green, hollow eyes piercing through him. Malevolent. Both unknown and knowing.

Chapter Twenty-Three

Butcher in the Jungle

Ike was in the pasture repairing the barbed wire horse fence when Zeb pulled up. Methodically, Ike drove a post-hole digger into the ground to either set new posts where the old ones had rotted out or where one of the half-tamed horses had run through them. Often, Zeb or one of his brothers were riding bareback during this inauspicious event. Zeb watched while Ike lined up the new posts evenly spaced and set them in the ground with concrete. Precisely. Perfectly. Zeb knew Ike could not be disturbed once he initiated a task. And Ike would reveal what he and Thelka were talking about in his own time. Ike was not one to be rushed. But when he spoke, he was thorough and straightforward.

When Ike set the last post, he acknowledged Zeb's presence by nodding in Zeb's direction. This was Zeb's cue to speak, and he wasted no time.

"Ike, I tracked down the Goatman this morning. Found him at the Confederate Graveyard by the Mill burying something. It was wrapped in cloth, and I suspect it could be parts of that boy they found a couple of days ago. The one missing a hand and his head. Bullock says he'll investigate, but I think he and Sheriff Hudlow are convinced he has nothing to do with the murders. And I think they have been told to leave the Goatman alone. Possibly by my dad."

Zeb seemed to draw pictures of what he had seen by gesticulating wildly in the hot, stale summer air as he spoke.

Zeb continued, "He was awful to look at. A storm came up. Lightning everywhere. He saw me and started after me, but I took off. I don't see how he'd know who I am, but if he does, I'm worried he may come after me in the night."

"He knows who you are all right," Ike said in a monotone as he brushed away a pesky horsefly.

Zeb clenched his hands and looked at Ike in disbelief, questioning, "He knows who I am? How could that be? I've never even seen him before."

"Doesn't mean he hasn't seen you," Ike replied, wiping a dry cloth across his forehead to stop the sweat from clouding his vision. "He's likely been watching you around here for years. You and your friend Jake. All you boys."

"What are you talking about, Ike? I've never heard any of this. How do you know so much about the Goatman? And if that's true, why did everyone tell me it's all just a fairy tale, a made-up ghost story?" inquired Zeb with a puzzled look on his face.

"Boy, I guess it is about time you found out. Ole Doc was wanting to hold off telling you because of what the Goatman did years ago. Has to do with your friend, Jake Stubblefield. Plus, Doc and the Goatman knew each other since a ways back," Ike continued, reluctantly.

"Now sit down, because this ain't no short tale. And pieces of it are complicated. Some of it doesn't bear repeating," began Ike. Zeb was mesmerized, looking into the dense, vexing air for answers.

"I was startin' to tell you a few weeks ago before you toppled over from that snippet of a snake bite and interrupted me," Ike began. "You know your pa and I was stationed in the Pacific during

World War II. I told you that part. We was primarily support for the initial waves of assault troops. Our Marines launched attacks from island to island against them murderous Japanese. We was mowed down like a sickle cutting through dry wheat at harvestin'."

Ike looked away at the distant fading clouds evaporating to nothingness. The gruesome task of retrieving unrecognizable flesh and body parts of Marines continued to haunt him.

Ike continued, "Like I was tellin' you before you got delirious from the venom, we had been stationed in the Pacific for several weeks when a medic arrived as a late replacement for the assault on the Mariana Islands. He was younger than us. Probably gave a fake age to join the fray supposedly there to save the world for good. I thought I recognized him."

Ike had long since given up on the illusion of saving much of anything. He joined the Navy because there was nothing in Maysville for him other than bigotry and the risk of being lynched for looking a White person directly in the eye. The Navy seemed the least racist branch of service. There were a few good people of all colors in the military, but they were the exception. Ike's service years only accentuated his disillusionment with the human race.

Ike knew most medics were quick to give in to the despair and senselessness of war. There was little they could do on the battlefield itself. Most major injuries were fatal or worse. Intolerable pain. Very few survived. Medics primarily comforted the dying, often purposely overdosing them with morphine to ease the pain.

Ike methodically continued, trancelike, "This fellow's name was Jim Shepherd. Jim differed from the other medics though. Funny and not a Bible-banger like most medics came to be. He had a belief in a master plan not strangled by any specific religion. He could quote scripture from the Bible as easy as passages from the Koran. Usually twistin' words for fun rather than salvation. He saw religion as man's childlike attempt to understand things that can't be explained. At best a pathetic exercise, at worst an organized excuse for hatred. Despite his youth, even blank-faced soldiers who had long given up hope of surviving the war were drawn to him. Also, women found his shock of dark hair, steel dark green eyes, and good looks, as well as his honesty, beyond appealing."

Ike became still and quiet staring into the Oak trees nearby and listening to a single distant Mockingbird. The coppery, rich smell of red clay beneath his feet seemed to creep into the air as it was baked by the relentless sun. He envisioned Jim before *IT* happened.

Jim was aware that the enemy shot medics second only to officers. Consequently, officers wore no insignias. Jim was one of the Japanese' primary targets. Kill him, and many more with manageable wounds die from lack of medical attention.

Despite this, Ike had seen him during horrendous enemy fire attempting to keep the slightest spark of a man's soul alight when the time for this had long passed. Jim seemed to be peacefully tending this year's crop in the field, brushing aside severed limbs like weeds strangling his harvest. Oddly, he would also treat the Japanese soldiers, who were generally despised, with equal fervor. Ike stared blankly across the horizon recalling Jim's heroics. Fragile memories came into view.

Zeb, who to this point had been listening intently, startled Ike from thoughts of Jim Shepherd, saying, "Ike, you went traveling again. Don't always know where your mind takes you, but you're not here. Being as I might be at risk from the Goatman, I would appreciate your acting like you were worried. I don't know what this story or this Jim guy has to do with anything."

Remaining placid, Ike responded, "Now, boy, don't you start with me again. Like I've told you more than once, that may work with Thelka but not with me. Listen up. I am getting there." He resumed. "Jim was smart, but like I said before, it seemed he couldn't tell the difference between Japs and us. Couldn't see the colors, weaknesses, flaws. Couldn't even see my scars best I could tell."

The Mockingbird began a different chorus.

"Well, turns out I recognized him because he was from around Maysville where we was raised. Up in Rabun County. Had family here in Hobbleton as I found out later. Me and him hit it off real well. I worried 'bout him. I fully expected him to be killed each time he went into the field. Somehow, though, he stayed invisible to the bullets, but something much worse got him."

Ike became more animated now, remembering the past in details that he had dodged for years to maintain his own sanity. Zeb watched Ike's every movement as he choreographed his tale in the air as if driven by some overwhelming power. Almost as if he were reciting words from a script that hung before him. Or that were being spoken to him, channeled through him.

Ike continued, "Like I was saying, Jim saved 'bout as many Japs as he did our own — seemed that way anyways. One of 'em had been taught before the war in a university in the U.S. and spoke English like one of them professors. Seemed real nice, and Jim took a likin' to him. Probably kept the Jap from gettin' shot, 'cause from time to time somebody'd get mad at the Japs for killing a buddy or worse and just grab a prisoner. Shot him on the spot."

The Mockingbird's melody began to fade.

Zeb could only imagine what 'got' Jim Shepherd. What Ike was about to reveal. The torture of Jim Shepherd must have been horrid for Ike to have such a difficult time pulling up the memory. Torture at the hands of an enemy he had saved at tremendous risk.

While Zeb found the story increasingly compelling, he wondered what in the world this could have to do with the Goatman.

"What did they do to him, Ike? Musta' been awful. Does he still have family around here in Hobbleton?" questioned Zeb in rapid fire.

The Mockingbird faded into silence.

Ike took a deep breath as if to purge himself from what he was about to tell Zeb. "Turned out that Jap was a special-trained field medic. Maybe why Jim took an interest in him and taught him about ways of savin' the injured. Anyways, that Jap escaped during a night assault. Some thought Jim may a had something to do with it, but no questions was asked. Jim would do anything to get an injured U.S. soldier home, and no one know'd when he was next to need Jim's skills.

"Anyways, them Japs didn't torture him. Much worse," Ike said, shaking his head.

Ike hesitated, unsure whether to continue, but now he was back in the island village experiencing the horror where they found the small Chamorro girl, a native islander whose tribe resisted the

Japanese. And who now held sway in one of Ike's recurring nightmares.

He told Zeb that several weeks after the Jap medic escaped, Marines who had been stationed in a Chamorro village befriended its inhabitants. The innocents trapped in this conflict. A gift of a cheap glass bead bracelet was given to one of the smallest villagers, a girl who shyly smiled at the Marines. The cost of this gesture — horrific. The Japs captured her, and Jim Shepherd was called to the scene.

Ike continued, "She was very much alive when we found her. Staked to the ground, her arms and legs had been severed with a sharp knife — all clean like. Her main blood vessels had been surgically tied off at short stumps preventing her from mercifully bleedin' to death. As soon as Jim arrived, he knew she would die. But with the way she was, he knew real quick this might take days of suffering. To make it worse, the girl was completely aware and somehow only cried quietly to herself while a woman — probably her ma — held her head, stroking her hair as if trying to put her to sleep after a long day of playin' children's games."

Ike was sweating now. His eyes held a piercing, distant, nightmarish look. He didn't notice that Zeb's eyes clouded over and continued, "Coarsely sewn in her neck, Jim saw the beaded bracelet. He gave the small girl a deadly dose of morphine. Jim struggled with what he was doing. He looked at the woman holdin' the small girl. She put a hand on the girl's forehead and held the shy little girl as she gasped for her last breath like a fish tryin' to breathe human air. What happened next changed Jim forever far as I know."

The Mockingbird took to silent wings.

Eyes wildly darting from side to side as if trying to eradicate the image, Ike lowered his head and said, "Next to the child, Jim noticed somethin' on the ground. All the life in him seemed to bleed out, mixin' with the tortured girl's blood and cut off limbs. A piece of paper with handwriting about tying off the vessels meant to save a man with a blowed up leg lay at Jim's feet. In Jim's handwriting. Given to the Jap prisoner by Jim, we finds out later."

Ike stared ahead and mumbled, "Jim's face changed from that moment on. Darkened. Within a week he was transferring out. Never made it back. I never spoke again about it but once. That was to ole Doc years ago when he asked me if I recognized the strange, bearded man who carted around those goats. He'd gotten hurt and wouldn't let Doc take care of him. You kids don't know him as Jim Shepherd. You got your own name for him."

Looking around, trying futilely to erase the indelible, mutating images, Ike returned to the present, focusing on Zeb's astounded face. And the Mockingbird rejoined them more loudly than before with notes Zeb had never heard. The Goatman is not only real, as he already had believed, but he has a name.

Chapter Twenty-Four

Suspect

Silence was all that seemed necessary as Ike walked away from Zeb. Zeb stood looking beyond the horses grazing in the pasture into the horizon, trying to reconcile Ike's story with what Zeb knew to be true. If not the Goatman, then who committed the murders? Or did the event in the Pacific transform Jim Shepherd into an unrecognizable monster hiding even from himself? Transform him from a savior into the Goatman, a gruesome serial killer, some perverse twist of insanity to preserve a modicum of sanity. And what did Ike mean when he said the Goatman had been watching him and Jake Stubblefield for years? Zeb hadn't thought to ask. This might explain the package Ike had concealed in the alley. He'd ask about that later.

It was getting late in the day, but Zeb wanted to share what he'd heard with Wanda and Jake. Maybe they knew more than they were telling him as well. He jumped on his motorcycle, reaching the edge of town just as Wanda started down the Courthouse steps in his direction. She lit up with a smile upon seeing Zeb. She rushed down the sidewalk and, hidden in the shadows, gave Zeb a long embrace. Zeb could feel the tension in her thighs as they touched his.

Wanda stepped back. "You're okay! I was worried when I saw Jake in town earlier. He said you went to track the Goatman by yourself. I almost told my dad to go make certain you were okay, but Jake said not to trust anyone until the killer was found. He said my dad might discuss details of what we find with someone who knows the Goatman. I didn't know anyone knew him. I thought he roamed about hidden to avoid contact with everyone."

"Apparently, you were wrong, Wanda. That's what I had believed, as well, until Ike just enlightened me. Looks like Ike, Thelka, and even my dad have known the Goatman for years," said Zeb, struggling to keep himself from reaching out and touching Wanda's sparkling, raven-colored hair.

Zeb added, "I am at a loss to fully understand who is responsible for the murders. I still think it is the Goatman. Jim Shepherd died in the Marianas years ago."

"Who is Jim Shepherd? I've never heard that name," declared Wanda, who looked even prettier chewing her lower lip, now half facing Zeb.

Zeb proceeded to tell Wanda about Ike's revelation. He finished by saying, "Jim Shepherd is the Goatman's given name. I don't think anyone really knows what goes on in the Goatman's mind after what Jim Shepherd went through."

Zeb couldn't stop thinking about how beautiful Wanda's translucent tear-filled eyes appeared when she cried in reaction to the Chamorro girl's demise.

"I don't know what to say," responded Wanda, wiping the tears from her eyes. She refused to let an emotional reaction to this monstrous story cloud the clarity needed to stop these murders. "That revelation definitely adds to the complexity of the case."

Zeb almost laughed at Wanda's precise wording but restrained himself. Wanda, like most girls, could be sweet until they weren't. Taking her lightly would probably not be in his best interest. She was not one to be taken lightly.

Wanda continued, "You are getting much closer to the truth than I am. I can hardly find out anything right now. Seems like I am being watched as well. Every time I get close to old records, someone from the Chief of Police staff needs me to run an errand. I did note something I found interesting when they weren't watching. Something you hadn't mentioned," said Wanda.

Zeb looked away from the curvature of Wanda's hips just as she noticed his gaze. She smiled through her tears knowingly. Though her face slightly reddened, she didn't seem to mind this attention.

"Go on. What was it?" Zeb asked.

"Did you know who heard the screaming from the Copperhead-bit boy or who pulled him from the Alcovy River that morning?" Wanda inquired.

"No," responded Zeb tersely, pushing his long, curly, tangled hair out of his eyes only to have it spring back. "I figured someone that happened to be passing by the Mill. I remember he kept muttering something about the Goatman. Sounded like the Goatman was trying to drown him. Who was it?"

"It was Joe Scully that used the two-way radio he keeps in his mail delivery car who called in. Who pulled him from the Alcovy. Didn't he mention this when you and Jake were at the Mill showing Joe the Confederate Graveyard? Where you found the newly dug graves?" Wanda asked, frown lines forming on her forehead.

"No. Not a word about that. It was Joe that flagged me down that morning of the snake bites. All he said was that my dad was looking for me. That I was needed at the office right away," said Zeb, pushing against his left temple in an attempt to quiet the nascent, fractured murmurings stirring in his head. Uncontrollable voices disrupting his thoughts.

CLICK. Should have been there. Should have stopped it. CLACK. Should have been you. Joe's wife killed? By Joe. Not Joe. Maybe. CLICKITY CLACK.

"Are you okay?" asked Wanda. "You don't look so good. I know you see things no one else sees. What no one else understands.

And you are ridiculously smart, but I think there's more that you are having to face that you don't have to take on alone. Maybe I can help."

"Too many surprises today. Too many unknowns. I don't know what to think. Sure seems like Joe would have told us that. All these secrets everybody keeps. Joe was acting very strangely the day we found the Confederate Graveyard. For a moment, I was concerned that he might have something to do with the murders. Ike showed up looking for me as a lightning storm blew in. Before that, I had a feeling Jake and I were in danger. I didn't know why, but I had a feeling. Sometimes I just have feelings," muttered Zeb.

"Not Joe!" exclaimed Wanda. "He is one of the nicest, funniest men around. He'd help anyone with anything. Anytime a car breaks down, Joe shows up and helps out."

"Not what I am saying, Wanda. Maybe I was spooked from being at the Mill. Death seems to find that place. As it darkened with the storm blowing in, it felt like we were being watched is all," defended Zeb, before adding, "And Thelka and Ike keep saying how people who are good can go through stuff that turns them."

He didn't want Wanda to be mad at him, so he continued, "I'm going to fill Jake in on what Ike told me this morning. Ike mentioned something about how the Goatman, or Jim Shepherd, or whatever you call him, has watched Jake and me for years. If I can figure out why, work out that connection, it may all start to make more sense. I'd like to see what my dad knows, but he told me to let go of all of this fairy tale stuff about the Goatman and stay out of this. Ike probably didn't tell him anything about me tracking the Goatman. My dad can be unpredictable. I'll have to time asking him. When his patients are doing well and when he's had a little sleep. Doesn't happen very often."

"Doc has always been nice to me. Keeps trying to get me to become a nurse. But I have seen him mix it up with my dad. He can be a handful," she said, with a sparkling smile.

Wanda continued, "I'll keep trying to look at some older reports. We do get shared information in higher profile crimes, especially with something like the possibility of a serial killer in multiple counties. Maybe I can find something more about the family in Chatsworth over in Coweta County that was slaughtered a few months back. From what little I've overheard about the scene, it is likely the killer in Chatsworth is the one that murdered Dollbaby as well as the boy they found a couple of days ago."

"Be careful," said Zeb. "It could be almost anyone at this point. Don't let them see you going through files. If the killer knows anyone at the Courthouse, he could be getting information that could put you in danger. Jake gets all kinds of information hanging out by Edge's Cafe. That stupid Hank Bullock talks about most everything trying to sound important. If it weren't for him, I think these cases could have been solved already."

Zeb was correct on both counts. Wanda could be in danger and Bullock was in the way of solving the murders.

As she turned to go, Wanda leaned back and gave Zeb a soft, fleeting kiss on the lips. Zeb didn't see this coming and stood flat-footed, not knowing how to respond. His awkward stance seemed to delight Wanda, who spun her head back, flipping her hair so that it partially concealed her impish face. She was the one who was ridiculously smart. Maybe she could help him face the demons. Then off she went while a stunned Zeb cranked up the motorcycle to go

see what Jake had heard.

Chapter Twenty-Five

Images

When Zeb arrived at Jake's shack, Jake was nowhere to be found. The door was ajar which was not unusual. Jake frequently left it open to get some cool air. Zeb walked inside and noticed an old picture frame turned face down. From the disturbed dust pattern beneath the frame, it appeared to have been moved recently. Looking around to be sure no one could see him, Zeb turned the simple, hand-carved, wooden picture frame over. It was carved from Oak into the shape of tiny wild roses running along the sides. Above and below were exotic flowers Zeb had never seen. The work was meticulous and very exact with the Oak of the frame appearing to have weathered for several years.

The inside of the shack seemed darker with the single lamp used to illuminate it being of little help today. Zeb peered at the picture and saw the shapes of a man and a woman holding a small child. As his eyes adjusted, the images became clearer. The woman was very attractive in appearance but was in no way familiar. The images of the man and child had faded over time obscuring their faces. The background was indecipherable.

Zeb recognized that the man was wearing an army coat similar to one that he had seen Jake wear. Army/Navy stores sold surplus WWII clothing cheaply, so teenagers often ended up wearing these coats. Also, servicemen kept clothing and some of the equipment they were supplied during the war. It frequently ended up with the children. That's how Clayton got the old, dented Army motorcycle Zeb now rode. Jake's owning a WWII jacket didn't surprise Zeb, but he found the resemblance curious.

He continued to study the picture, wiping some dust away. As his eyes acclimated to the darkness, Zeb tried to make out the letters on the man's name tag. He could not see the smaller letters, though he could discern the capital letters clearly: *JS*.

Not possible, thought Zeb. Not possible that the man in the picture was Jim Shepherd, the Goatman. That he was in some way connected to Jake. Zeb looked closer at the image. The feeling Zeb had when he got a good look at the Goatman in the lightning storm that morning at the Mill returned. He imagined the essence of the underlying bony structure of the Goatman without the horrifying distorted skin draped over it. Concealing it. The familiarity in the Goatman's appearance had been to Jake Stubblefield, Zeb's best friend. *How is this even possible?* wondered Zeb. His thoughts began whirling around, becoming intermixed with an incoherent echoing. Voices he would not acknowledge. Not now.

At that moment, Jake burst into the room surprising Zeb. Zeb accidentally dropped the picture to the floor. The frame shattered, sending sharp glass fragments to all four corners of the shed. Zeb scrambled to pick it up, trying to avoid being cut by the shards.

"What are you doing?" exclaimed Jake, as the scar on his neck flamed a crimson red. "You got no business snooping around in here. Put that down!" he yelled, pointing to the picture Zeb had retrieved from the floor.

"Jake. Sorry. I came over to tell you I found the Goatman this morning. You were right. He is a scary character. I ran when he saw me, but I got a good look at him. Unfortunately, he got a good look at me too."

As Zeb spoke, he watched Jake's now-contorted face. Zeb tried to decide whether to share what Ike had told him earlier. What did Jake already know? It made no sense to Zeb that Jake would know Jim Shepherd or know that Jim Shepherd was the Goatman. But could he? Could he even have been protecting the Goatman all this time? Zeb had seen Jake angry, but this was different. Had Zeb discovered something Jake wanted to keep hidden? Zeb decided best not to divulge Ike's revelation just yet.

Looking around the shack, Zeb noticed several meticulously carved figurines scattered about. Some were old and gray. Others had visible patterns in the wood suggesting they had recently been carved. Odd that he had not noticed all these before. Had they been there all along, or were they new?

Jake had calmed down as Zeb spoke. Sensing this, Zeb continued, "It seemed like I had seen the Goatman before. Like I knew him from somewhere, but that's not possible. I've never laid eyes on him."

Zeb hoped this might get a response — no, a revelation — from Jake. Who were the images in the picture?

Jake simply shook his head, saying, "I have no idea why you thought he was familiar. When I saw him from the bus, he was too far away for me to make out much of anything." The scar lightened. Jake had never deceived Zeb, and Zeb wanted to believe Jake was telling the truth. Jake probably had no idea who the Goatman was.

"Jake, you're pretty good with your whittling," said Zeb, changing the subject to further calm Jake. Zeb picked up a wood-carved coyote lying on the dusty table in front of him. "How did you learn to make these?"

Jake's face softened somewhat as he spoke, "When I was little, my grandad taught me some before he died. He said I had my dad's hands. I guess I was born with some natural ability. 'Bout the only one I got other than fighting. And you know I'm pretty good at that."

Zeb thought about how little he knew about Jake's upbringing other than he'd been alone since his grandad died. There was the rumor he lived with his mother, but there was still the fact that Zeb had never seen her, and there were other stories saying she had died. Zeb guessed Jake was only ten or so when his grandad died, but he didn't really know. He had often wondered how Jake survived out here alone at such a young age, but they had never talked about it. Some things you just don't ask. But now Zeb could not contain his curiosity.

"Did your grandad say anything more about your father?" inquired Zeb, hoping Jake would fill in the blanks regarding his parents. Maybe this would explain the picture he'd found.

"No. He only said they passed in a car accident when I was little. That my pa had been drinking. I don't hardly remember them. I think I got this scar in the crash, but I don't remember any of that. I think Doc may have patched me up, but I could have dreamt that or imagined it."

This would explain some of my crazy dreams, thought Zeb to himself. Zeb often wondered if he had seen things that he had either forgotten or was too young to remember. Things he shouldn't have seen or events that had not yet occurred. Even though there was so much he didn't know, sometimes he knew too much but wasn't sure how. Almost always, these imprinted memories and dreams of past and future were later confirmed. They had evolved into a harsh reality.

CLICKITY CLACK.

Zeb's curiosity overtook his judgment as he blurted out, "Who raised you after your granddad died?"

Surprisingly, Jake responded calmly. "No one that I know of. Joe Scully would drop off food and clothes from time to time. Said it was from Pastor Arp and members of the First Baptist Church. I'd get lunch at school and store up whatever I could. I told people that I lived with my mom, because I didn't want to go to the orphanage in Atlanta. I had already known that was not a good place. Bad things happen there. And later it would have been reformatory school because I do like a good fight."

At this point, Jake assumed a boxer's stance and began shadow-boxing an invisible foe. Zeb stared at Jake's quick hands and feet, amazed, as always, by his agility. Laughing, Jake began, "Like I said, I'm pretty good at it too. It's about the only thing that came natural to me. That and whittling these miniature animals."

Zeb looked around and saw more carvings, which seemed to multiply as his eyes continued to acclimate to the darkness inside the shed. *How have I never noticed these before?* he wondered. His vision locked onto one carving. It was that of a goat and its kid sculpted from a single piece of Oak. This one was weathered and appeared smoother than most all the others, likely from being handled frequently over time.

Zeb questioned Jake, "I never asked you this, but aren't you frightened out here all by yourself? Nobody lives within a mile or so and the Mill is close by. Between the stories of ghosts of Confederate soldiers haunting the Mill, people drowning in the Alcovy, and the Goatman, I don't think I'd ever be able to sleep."

Jake replied, "At first, I couldn't sleep well, but I was used to being alone. My grandfather had to work up until the day he died. Plus, he told me someone was always watching over me. That just because I couldn't see them didn't mean they weren't there. I was little, so I believed him for the most part. Wanted to believe him. As I got older, I liked being on my own. I didn't want anybody tellin' me what to do. That did lead to some fighting with older guys that wanted to boss me around."

Jake paused then asked, "Why are you suddenly so interested in all that? Let's get out of here. I say we go get a closeup look at the Goatman."

Zeb listened, wondering if Jake had more than an imaginary guardian. Maybe the image in the photo was in fact related and watched over Jake. From what Ike had said, this would make sense. But why would the image in the picture stay in the shadows hidden? Was the image the Goatman? Or maybe some relative protecting Jake from the Goatman? Clearly, Jake didn't know or, at least, didn't want to talk about it. Zeb knew Jake well enough to back off questioning him at this point.

He decided to tell Jake a limited version of what Ike had said about the Goatman. About him being a medic from Maysville. Zeb was evasive about the Goatman's real name — Jim Shepherd — and what caused him to become a recluse. And possibly a serial killer.

Jake stared at Zeb, shocked that Ike wouldn't have said something earlier.

He stammered, "Wha..? Well, well, why didn't Ike say something sooner? He must have known we thought the Goatman was the killer. I don't understand."

"I don't either," Zeb answered. "But Ike has his own way of thinking."

"I say we put this to rest. We go find the Goatman and confront him. Find the truth!" exclaimed Jake, anxious to learn more.

"Okay. I agree, but we need to be careful. I last saw the Goatman at the graveyard burying something or someone. He was digging with a WWII shovel that had sharp edges. Plenty sharp enough to cut up someone. I doubt he is still there, but it is a place to start."

"I think I'll bring a little something myself," said Jake, in a voice that seemed older. Jake lifted a plank in the flooring and reached far under it. Pulling out a recently sharpened WWII machete, he smiled. "This should do the trick."

Jake turned his back so Zeb couldn't see a stack of carefully hidden old letters further under the plank.

Zeb nodded his head in agreement but was too busy studying the razor-sharp machete edge to say more. He became motionless watching Jake skillfully holster the blade before he followed Jake out of the darkness, careful to remain behind him. Clearly, there was a lot about Jake he had yet to learn.

As they walked out the door, voices seeped into Zeb's thoughts and began to argue incoherently. Zeb tightened his hands. Then he clenched a fist behind Jake. He could only discern a few frozen words.

Be careful. CLICK. Careful of Jake. For Jake. CLACK. For the Goatman. Of yourself. CLICK CLACK.

Chapter Twenty-Six

Confusion Reigns

When Zeb was four years old, Thelka would grow tired of his shenanigans and mop him into a corner of the kitchen before he recognized what she was doing. Once contained, she would proclaim, "Now you're stuck, boy. Iffen ya step on the floor where it's wet, you'll fall through to China, and nobody's comin' back from that. Ya best jus' sit here 'til it dries. Call me if ya needs somethin'. I'll be cleanin' up 'round the house."

Zeb did as told, not wanting to end up in a foreign place unable to understand what was going on around him. Between Ike's revelations about the Goatman, his feeling of uneasiness at the Courthouse, and Jake pulling out a single blade machete, Zeb felt like he was cornered in the kitchen. He couldn't piece together the uncertainties and unknowns to find his way out. The discrepancies. What was real? What should be his next move? The pressure in his left temple hindered logical thought. Confusion weakened Zeb. Again, the voices started to chant:

Could be Jake. Could be you are Jake. Or Jake is you. Or Jake isn't real. Maybe you need to kill Jake. Yes. CLICK.

Zeb pushed these obtrusive, disturbing, irrational thoughts aside as he followed Jake out the door. He reassured himself Jake was his friend. He could not envision Jake having anything to do with the murders any more than he would suspect Thelka, Ike, or himself for that matter. If only Clayton was here. He'd know what to do.

After taking a breath, he asked, "Jake, where did you get the machete?"

"Funny thing. A few years ago, I was clearing kudzu that was growing up on the back of the shed. I was trying to pull out the weeds but gave up because they were so dense. Next morning, I stepped outside and this machete was lying there on the porch. Almost like someone knew that I needed it, which made no sense. Nobody 'round here but me. It came in mighty handy, though. Very sharp. I keep it that way with the file I use to keep my whittling knife sharp," responded Jake.

The shiny, dangerous machete blade reflected a contorted image of Jake's admiring face.

They decided to hike to the Mill, concealing themselves in the underbrush as they tracked the Goatman. Zeb remembered the hidden trail Joe Scully had shown them. They quickly arrived at the edge of the Confederate gravesite. The Goatman was nowhere to be seen. In fact, it looked like no one had been there for days. No hoof prints or shoe prints.

"Zeb, didn't you see him early this morning before the storm came?" questioned Jake, as he cradled the handle of the machete. "I don't see a sign that anyone was here."

Zeb was confused. He had certainly seen the Goatman and goats. It couldn't have been a dream. Could it? His night terrors seemed real, but this was different. He had seen the Goatman in the flash of lightning that illuminated that horrid visage. Zeb would never forget that. Plus, in his dreams noise was muted and colors less vivid.

"Jake, I saw him all right. He must have smoothed off his tracks. The rain would have obscured signs of the grave he was digging. Come over here," said Zeb, as he pointed to the site where the Goatman had been digging. Before them was a plot of dirt with a soil texture that subtly differed from the surrounding area.

"I bet he buried the right hand and head of the boy they recently found further down the Alcovy near Bramblett Shoals right here. We shouldn't disturb this spot. I need to tell my dad what I saw. Maybe the police will listen to him. Maybe I can convince him to consider that the Goatman may be dangerous despite whatever my dad knows about him," explained Zeb.

Jake scratched his head while looking at the site, imagining a head buried in the dirt before him. Then he realized what Zeb had said.

Jake looked up at Zeb and wondered aloud, "Your dad? What could your dad know? How would he know the Goatman?"

"Jake, it's a long story. Like I told you earlier, Ike knew him during the war before he went crazy. Ike said the Goatman was changed by the war. Apparently, my dad knew him from the war as well. Has since seen him as a patient here in Hobbleton. The Goatman, whose real name is Jim Shepherd, wouldn't let my dad help him much though," explained Zeb, unintentionally giving away the Goatman's given name.

Jake's neck veins began to rise as he shouted, "When the hell were you going to tell me all of this?! Don't you think I'd need to know?! What else are you hiding from me?!" Jake unknowingly began to swing the machete from side to side in front of himself as if slicing through the jungle.

"Jake, I was going to tell you more later. Ike told me this morning. Somehow there is a connection between you and the Goatman. Ike wouldn't go into that. Like he didn't want me to know. I was going to circle back and talk to Ike to figure that out before I told you!" exclaimed Zeb.

"Me and the Goatman! What does that mean? I saw him for the first time ever just a day ago. You've gotten a better look at him than me," responded Jake, dropping the machete after he realized he'd been swinging it around menacingly. But then he took out the carving knife that he kept in his pocket and nervously cradled it.

"I don't know what it means. Ike said the Goatman or Jim Shepherd or whatever you want to call him had something to do with me as well. He implied the Goatman's been watching us for years," explained Zeb. While Zeb was talking, Jake flipped open the blade of the knife and began repeatedly tossing it into the ground next to his own shoes. The knife stuck in the ground, blade first, getting ever closer to Jake's feet with each toss.

Watching this, Zeb demanded, "Jake, stop that! You're going to stab your foot, then we'll have one more problem to worry about. The Goatman is clearly hiding. He's covered his tracks well, and the rain has washed away whatever he missed. We'll not be finding him today. I think I'll ask my dad what he knows. He won't be pleased, but maybe I'll catch him in a good humor today. Some days he can be all right. Some days he becomes an almost childlike trickster. He'll disguise his voice on the phone and act like he is anything from a farmer to an IRS agent. Call up a friend and pull his leg. Pretty good at it too. Doesn't happen very often," he said, both thinking out loud and trying to distract Jake so he wouldn't stab himself.

Zeb's strategy worked. Folding up his knife, Jake said, "I can't even imagine that with Doc. He's always been good to me, but I've seen him be real stern with others. Sometimes downright mean. Scary, like he's out of control. Then a second later he'll be fine. Crazy stuff."

"Yes, I know," said Zeb. "Once he brought a brown paper bag home supposedly containing a cake that a patient had given him. Put it in the middle of the table during Thanksgiving dinner as we all sat down. When we started eating, the bag moved. At first, we thought it was just the bag settling. When the contents moved again, it clearly was no cake. Out pops the head of a very alive snake — tongue slithering."

Jake smiled imagining the scene.

"Thelka ran screaming out the screen door saying, 'Hep me, Jesus! Hep me!' Fastest we ever saw her move. My dad was laughing like a kid who'd pulled his first trick on someone. But that night he was raising the devil at some nurse who had not followed his orders."

Jake grinned as he secured the knife into his pocket. Then he proceeded to question Zeb about Ike's story regarding Jim Shepherd. Once satisfied he had as much information as Zeb, Jake agreed the next step would be for Zeb to find out what Doc knew.

This would be a challenge on the best of days. Unfortunately, Zeb would not find Doc in a good mood. This was not a good day for Doc or anyone in his proximity.

Chapter Twenty-Seven

Rampage

Zeb left Jake at his shack and went to town looking for his dad. When he reached the office, he walked up the back-alley entranceway. Coming out the back door was a younger physician, Dr. Weems, who shared the office and some of the staff with Doc Barton. Dr. Weems was in his early forties. He was pasty-faced, stooped at the shoulders, and rarely made eye contact. He always seemed to have a nervous, confused look on his face, but he was kind to Zeb. He would introduce himself as Dr. Theodore Tecumseh Weems. Zeb liked him, though he felt a bit sorry for him.

"Zeb, I'd stop there if I were you. Your dad is in one of his moods. He was already wired up yesterday. I made things a lot worse last night, but I didn't know what else to do," he said, with a slight tremor in his voice which accompanied him whenever he spoke.

"What happened?" inquired Zeb, stopping in his tracks so abruptly that he almost tripped over his own feet.

"I made the mistake of firing one of the staff yesterday without asking your dad first. We'd talked about firing Chris before. I think Chris was coming in drunk up, but your dad defended him. I'm not sure why. Doc had hired him years before. Something to do with a debt your dad felt he owed the family. Anyways, Chris was drunk again yesterday, and I fired him on the spot without thinking," explained Dr. Weems.

He continued, "When your dad got to the office and found out I fired this fellow, he was enraged. He called me at home. Told me he was going to whip my ass. That I needed to come back to my office before he finished seeing patients last night and wait for him."

Zeb listened quietly. He had witnessed these outbursts many times. They never turned out well. Zeb hoped no one had been physically injured. The explosive aspect of his dad's personality was just part of the equation. A way of life.

Dr. Weems added, "I didn't know what to do. I didn't want to get beaten to death. I considered shooting him with my Colt .45 as he walked into my office, but I figured one of you boys would retaliate and kill me."

Zeb was surprised by Dr. Weems honesty as much as his planned ambush. Zeb stopped him to emphasize that he was correct, for future reference, responding, "Yes. One of us would have killed you."

Dr. Weems continued, "I thought so. Like I said, I was scared. Not knowing what else to do, I called Chief Bullock and Sheriff Hudlow. I asked them to come protect me. They promptly joined me in my office, and we waited on Doc. He didn't disappoint. He walked in my door as promised when he finished seeing his last patient. We were ready. I had Bullock on my left and Hudlow on my right. Their guns were holstered. I was sitting behind the desk concealing my .45 pistol which was pointed at the door."

Dr. Weems was visibly shaking as he relived the moment.

Rubbing his sweating hands together, Dr. Weems uttered, "Your dad was none too pleased. He started raising hell. You can imagine what he said. This was bad enough, but he got two inches from my face and started thumping me on the chest with his finger to make sure I was 'getting this into [my] goddamn head.' At this point, that stupid Bullock intervened and told your dad he needed to calm down. Gasoline on the flame. Your dad started thumping on Bullock's chest with his index finger and told him to 'Shut. The. Hell. Up!' and to 'Shut. [His]. Goddamn. Mouth'!" Weems quoted each word slowly, emphatically as he precisely re-enacted the scene.

Dr. Weems stopped and attempted to swallow through a dry throat, which smothered his words, though Zeb heard him say, "At that moment, I figured we were all going to die. Your dad would shoot me first, and as tough as he is, I figured he'd kill the other two before he died."

Weems forehead dripped sweat. He took a breath before finishing, "I can't recall exactly what happened next. I'm here, so I guess your dad finished up what he had to say and left. That part is a blur. Now I'm going to dodge him for a few days until this storm passes over. You might want to do the same." With that, Dr. Weems hobbled down the back alley as if he'd been mauled by a mountain lion.

Zeb didn't need long to reverse his direction. He'd seen his dad this way many times before. While in his mid-sixties, Dr. Barton once challenged a much younger Hobbleton policeman to a fist fight. It was after a long day and night of work. Zeb and he were driving home around midnight through town.

Dr. Barton had his usual shot of Jack Daniels to smooth off the sharp edges of the day prior to driving home. Not enough to impair his judgment, but enough to be noticed by a young, brash officer. He pulled over Dr. Barton as Doc weaved down the lane coursing through the only yellow blinking light that dotted Hobbleton at that late hour. The weaving was from lack of attention to what he considered artificial boundaries of the paved road. Dirt roads had no lanes. Doc's house calls did not demand attention to speed or the constricting painted stripes.

Zeb had remained in the car. There were several unflattering words directed at the officer, who was obnoxious in his own right. Both men had pistols on them. Fortunately, when Dr. Barton told the police to take off his "goddamn pistol" and how he'd "whip [his] ass," an older officer who knew Doc well arrived. Doc had treated his family for years. Had delivered his children and stayed up all night saving his son after a bad car accident. Sanity prevailed. They drove home without bloodshed or consequence.

Yes, Zeb heard himself think, *best to take the Goatman topic up another day with Doc.* He hurried down the alley hoping to catch Wanda as she left the Courthouse. The shadows in the alleyway were getting longer and darker. Suddenly, a large figure appeared before him. *This cannot be good,* thought Zeb as he considered reversing his course. Zeb wished Clayton was here.

Chapter Twenty-Eight

Obstruction

Before Zeb stood the obese Chief of Police, Hank Bullock. Even though Zeb had no respect for Hank, the man still carried a Colt .45 pistol and a badge. This was not a good combination in the possession of a buffoon.

"Son, what are you up to down this dark alley?" asked Hank, trying to sound important as he straightened his coat in an attempt to cover his bulging belly.

"I was coming over to help my dad in the office," said Zeb, concealing his true purpose. Not feeling the need to respond to Hank with any more than a perfunctory answer.

"You sure reversed course mighty fast. Weren't there more than a few minutes. I didn't even see the back door open," Officer Bullock said with suspicion. In the past, Bullock had always been at least superficially pleasant to Zeb. Something had changed. He was clearly not pleased with Zeb.

Bullock had either been watching Zeb or watching for his dad to exit into the alley. Zeb began to worry about this lowly sycophant. He could potentially be dangerous if cornered, and Doc had insulted Hank the night before in a way he probably had never been insulted. Zeb would protect his dad regardless of consequence and began questioning Hank, "What were you doing back here? Not many cars speeding down this alley. Between Ike, me, and the office help, someone is almost always coming and going. We've never had any problems back here."

Zeb wanted to make it clear that anything Hank Bullock intended to do down this alley would most likely be witnessed. Doc kept his .38 in his right front pants pocket — as he did have enemies — but Zeb worried that a cowardly fool like Bullock would shoot his father in the back.

Noticing Bullock's nervous eye begin to twitch, Zeb felt more confident and continued, "I left the keys in my motorcycle and was going back to get them. Ike was supposed to meet me. He wasn't here yet, so I figured I'd meet him at the cycle."

Zeb wanted to be certain Bullock understood his presence would be known should there be any misunderstandings in the alley saying, "Now if you'll move, I can get some work done. I'd not stay back here. It's hard to see in the dark. Who knows? You might be mistaken for a burglar. I'll let my dad know you patrol around here so he doesn't shoot you by mistake. And I imagine Sheriff Hudlow could probably use your services more to solve these murders rather than roaming around empty alleys."

The Chief of Police began picking at his dirty fingernails as if they would betray him, saying, "Get on along then. No need to say anything to anyone. You won't see me back here again. I don't think Sheriff Hudlow would like to hear that you've been sneaking around seeing his daughter. If he was to call me in about being back here that would probably come up. She's a looker, I'll admit. May be too pretty for her own good."

Hank smirked as he saw Zeb blush and added, "And if you know what is good for you, best if you stayed away from that girl and any of the murder scenes. I'll solve them. You and Jake only muddy the waters. Especially stay away from the Goatman!"

Zeb thought best not to respond. Turning the corner of the alley, he saw Wanda coming down the Courthouse steps leaving work. Even though he ached to see her, he slipped back into the shadows before she could see him.

Bullock had been watching them. Almost certainly, he was the presence in the Courthouse Zeb had sensed. Zeb would need to avoid Wanda for a while. At least until Hank Bullock had other things to do than spy on them. And he knew Wanda thought it was creepy how often Bullock passed her desk when she was in the office. With the frequency of the murders increasing, Zeb thought it odd that Bullock wasn't busy doing more to handle the multiple ongoing investigations. And why did Hank want Zeb to stay away from the Goatman?

Zeb reminded himself that Ike had more information about the Goatman. He'd said something about the Goatman watching Jake and him for years. Ike didn't seem at all concerned about this. For some reason, Ike felt they were safe in the Goatman's presence. Now was the time to find out why. Zeb would tell his dad about the encounter later. Zeb was convinced that the more he knew about the Goatman, the closer he would be to stopping the killer. When Zeb arrived at the motorcycle, he cranked it up and headed out to find Ike. Zeb sensed he was getting closer to answers as the wind plastered his face on the speeding cycle.

Chapter Twenty-Nine

Kindred

Pulling up to his home, Zeb could see Thelka ironing. She had a loud hall fan on and hadn't noticed Zeb. Questioning Ike could wait a minute. He had dealt with Thelka locking doors years before, but he knew it would be unlocked this time. Zeb quietly opened the screen door, then the glass door. He crept down the creaky pine-floored hallway. Looking around the door entrance to the ironing room, he saw Thelka humming to herself. She had no idea he was there. Zeb imagined he was a leopard stealthily stalking prey.

Thelka was afraid of no living man, but haints and ghosts were a different matter. Next to snakes, haints were the worst. Zeb hovered over Thelka's back knowing she would sense his presence. She would feel a haint was returning to grab her. To get his revenge.

Thelka held a dip of snuff inside her lower lip while she recited hymns from church in an indecipherable language that only she understood. While looking out the window, she simultaneously felt and saw the reflection of the past hovering over her. Her past shook her. She screeched. Gasping in, Thelka swallowed her snuff. Then she realized the apparition was only Zeb.

"Fool boy, what is ya doin' here? Iffen I'da had ma' pistol you'da been dead. Yo' crazy little self is in enough trouble 'round here anyways. Ike done told ya to stay away from the Goatman. Yo' pa gonna be mighty mad that ya ain't listenin' 'bout that!" Thelka exclaimed. She put the iron upright on the ironing table, having fortunately avoided the impulse to swing it around and crush the skull of her initially unknown intruder.

Zeb sat on the cool floor knowing Thelka was about to begin one of her tirades.

"You'd not been able to sneak up iffen I had the doors locked. Yo' fool self stopped that when ya put yo' little fist through the window to git in after I locked ya out. Bled all ova' the house. I had to chase ya down to wrap up yo' hand. You wuz jus' laughin' away. Couldn't been no older than six. That wuz crazy enough, but then ya up and did it again a few weeks later. Second time, Doc told me to quit lockin' them damn doors. Like I wuz the problem," she said, rolling her eyes like they were about to fall out of her head.

"The both of ya is plumb crazy. Now I'se gonna git sick from swallowin' that snuff," Thelka finished, as she held her stomach trying to quell the rumbling beneath.

Thelka was rarely quiet. And this day was no different. Zeb initially thought to ask her Ike's whereabouts, but he remembered Thelka telling Ike that he needed to let Zeb know more about the Goatman. About Jim Shepherd. Maybe she knew more.

"I got you this time, ya ole bat. You thought that husband you killed years ago had come back to get you," laughed Zeb.

"Ya don't knows that boy. He deserved it iffen he is dead. Beatin' me wuz bad enough, but when he started headin' to beat my little chilluns all drunk up like he wuz. Well, that wuz when ma' pistol did the beatin'. Prob'lee is dead seein' how I ain't seen him since that night 'bout twenty years ago now. Back then, nobody cared 'bout a Black man dead in a field in the middle of nowhere.

Bleached out bones in that field down in Tacula prob'lee. I did what I hadta and would do it again."

Thelka was not saddened by much of anything. But recalling that night caused the sparkle in her eyes to become dull and opaque. Upon witnessing this, Zeb regretted having brought up that night. A mistake he wouldn't make again. To get her out of that memory, out of that shanty of a house, Zeb asked, "Where did you go that night?"

"I didn't have no place ta go. Yo' pa had doctored ma' kids a time or two. We didn't have no money. He took care of us anyways. When he wuz drivin' home late that night, he see'd us sittin' on a bench outside the Greyhound bus stop in the dark. He stopped. He figured out we had no place ta go and took us in 'til we got a home in the projects at Hooper-Renwick. Been livin' there eva' since," Thelka responded.

"Been helpin' out ole Doc too. Don't know where we'd be iffen he hadn't showed up. I guess we wuz like them stray dogs he picks up. Thinkin' somebody gotta do somethin'," she continued, as her eyes began to soften.

Then, smiling, she added, "Iffen I'd know'd Doc had little devils like yo'self, I mighta' just sat at the bus station 'til I couldn't sit no more." They both laughed.

That explains Thelka's loyalty to my dad, thought Zeb. Seeing the light coming back into Thelka's eyes, Zeb decided it was a good time to see what else she knew about the Goatman. How did the Goatman know Jake? Who was the couple and infant in the picture at Jake's house?

Zeb started, "Thelka, I found a picture at Jake's house. It was old. Had a weathered border whittled from Oak into flowers I'd never seen. There was a couple with a child. The woman, I didn't recognize. The man's image was too faded to see any clear features. From what little I could make out, he resembled the Goatman."

"Boy, ya ain't neva' see'd no Goatman," Thelka responded.

"I did this morning. Got a good look at his face during the storm. Lightning flashed right as he turned in my direction. Almost scared me to death. I took off and didn't look back. I think he was chasing me," Zeb explained.

"Now I done told ya to leave that alone. Yo' fool self don't know what's good for ya. I'll tell ya what I knowz. Then ya leave it alone," reprimanded Thelka. Zeb nodded his head in affirmation despite knowing he would not stop until he proved the Goatman was either guilty or innocent.

Thelka took a deep breath as she reached in her pocket and pulled out a round tin can of snuff. After opening the can, she scooped out a plug with her fingers and deftly placed it in her left lower lip. She began, "Sounds like Ike done told ya some. I don't know nuthin' bout the war. But I wuz here when the car crashed. His name wuz Jim Shepherd then. Nice fellow. Quiet. Kept to hisself. Married a purty girl he'd been seein' before the war, I guess. She more married him 'cause he wuz broke up after the war. Drank a good bit. Lots of them did."

Thelka looked down the driveway which meandered into the pines as she recalled the accident. "As I heard, it wuz a bad crash. He'd been drinkin'. Got goin' too fast around Hog Mountain and crashed down a hill. I guess no one found them for two days. He was trapped under tha' car. Couldn't move. It wuz bad, him bein' a medic and all. Watchin' helpless-like as she bled to death. The child, a boy, was cut across the throat pretty bad. Ole Doc patched him up though. He lived."

"Jake!" exclaimed Zeb. "The boy was Jake! In the picture was Jake and his parents! Jake is the son of the Goatman! I can't believe that!"

"Believe what ya want, but that's tha' truth of it as I knows it. Mr. Shepherd disappeared for a few years after that. Some said he died of grief. Others thought he done kilt' hisself," responded Thelka.

"Where did he go? He left Jake without parents. And Jake's last name is Stubblefield not Shepherd," Zeb objected.

Thelka rolled her snuff around her lower lip. "First I knew he wuz around wuz right after Jake's Grandpa Stubblefield died. Grandpa Stubblefield took care of Jake afta' the accident. Afta' Mr. Shepherd disappeared. Ike thinks Grandpa Stubblefield changed Jake's last name. Nobody knows for sho' why. I'm guessin' he hated Mr. Shepherd for gittin' drunk up and killin' his daughter. Almost killin' Jake too."

"That would explain what Ike said about the Goatman watching Jake and me for years. He was protecting Jake but didn't want Jake to see him. Probably he was ashamed for killing Jake's mom and didn't want Jake to know he was alive. Jim Shepherd thought it best if Jake thought he died when Jake's mom died. That doesn't explain how my dad knew Jim Shepherd before," said Zeb.

"Not sho' 'bout that piece. Ike know'd him from the war. Iffen ya got the nerve to ask yo' pa, maybe he'll tell ya. Or maybe Ike knows. Don't much matter anyways. Point is, yo' pa don't think Jim Shepherd would hurt anyone. Me, I ain't so sho'. That stinkin' war did bad things even to good men. Changed 'em," answered Thelka, her voice trailing off.

"If the Goatman is not the killer, then who? That fool, Hank Bullock, says it is a drug dealer from Atlanta who killed Dollbaby. I think he is lazy, and blaming the death of a Black woman on a Black drug dealer is a convenient way to close a case. It is too similar to some of the other murder scenes I heard about, though Bullock's report is missing some key details," said Zeb, wondering what his next step would be.

"How'd you know all that? Heard about that from that pretty girl, Sheriff Hudlow's daughter, I bet. Oh, you're goin' to git yo'self into all kinds of trouble. Ya got no business messin' with a girl like that, boy," chuckled Thelka.

"That's about the only thing you and I agree on," said Zeb, as he turned to walk away. But he didn't want to think about Wanda since he couldn't see her just yet. And it was Ike he was looking for anyway.

Zeb asked, "Where is Ike? I didn't see him as I came up the drive."

Thelka had resumed ironing and responded perfunctorily, "If I knows where all ya'll is all the time that'd be somethin'. He ain't been 'round here all mornin'."

"One last thing. Have the police been out here bothering you anymore?" asked Zeb.

"Nope, ain't seen none of 'em," she replied.

"Good. Let me know if they do," said Zeb as his face toughened.

Zeb had obtained most of what he needed from Thelka. He needed to find Jake to see what he really knew. Could he have been covering for his pa all these years? Or is Jake totally unaware of Jim Shepherd being his father, which seemed to be the case when they last spoke? Zeb thought it might be best to speak to Wanda first to see if she had any more information from the files. She might also have a good idea about how to approach Jake about his father without appearing as a threat. Wanda was very clever.

And there was the matter about Bullock watching her. Wanda needed to be warned. *What is that about anyway*? thought Zeb. The man is a bit strange and spends too much time around her instead of doing his job. Was Wanda in danger? And where would Jake be this time of day?

Jake would not be found. And Thelka would soon be imprisoned for the murder of Dollbaby.

Chapter Thirty

Files and Bumpers

Zeb had to be careful that Hank Bullock was not following him as he watched the Courthouse steps for Wanda. Hank had made a not-so-veiled threat to inform Sheriff Hudlow of his daughter's meeting up with Zeb. Given the recent explosive episode in Dr. Weem's office with Dr. Barton, Wanda's dad was probably not going to approve of any type of relationship that involved one of Doc's sons. Zeb couldn't understand why Hank had such an interest in either Wanda or himself, but Hank did. That was all he knew at this point.

Wanda opened the door right at five o'clock as the Courthouse closed. This was good, as all the other employees and staff, including Bullock, would be gone. Only the janitor remained. Wanda was radiant. Her long athletic legs were graceful. As she skipped down the steps her dress floated up, exposing the contour of her upper thighs. Another tan line. Zeb held his breath momentarily, trying once again not to stare. This was a difficult task given Wanda's allure.

"Wanda, over here," whispered Zeb when she ambled by close enough to hear him. At first, she stepped back, startled. Then, recognizing Zeb, she raced over, giving him a hug, pressing her breasts against his chest. Zeb didn't know what to make of this but felt warmth running up his neck, grabbing his throat, and making it difficult to speak.

"I didn't think I would be seeing you for a while," Wanda began. "Seems your dad had one of his moments. Unfortunately, my dad was in the group on the receiving end. He had nothing to do with the conflict between Doc Barton and Dr. Weems. He was there as Sheriff in a peacemaker role. But sounds like the scatter effect was significant," she said grinning, watching Zeb's expression intensely.

"Yep. I guess things got out of control. Lucky no one was hurt. Too many guns in too small a space," responded Zeb. Though the feeling of warmth up his neck had diminished enough to let him speak, the rapid thudding of his heart continued.

"How have you been?" asked Zeb. "You look great!" he blurted out without thinking.

Wanda flipped her black hair over one shoulder. Looking at Zeb with one eye now partially covered by her long tresses, she answered, "I've been doing well. Just hoped to see you sooner."

Zeb said, "I've been busy trying to see what more I could find out about the Goatman and the murders. I guess it's conceivable he's not a serial killer, but he remains my main suspect regardless of what anyone else thinks. He was a medic in WWII. Went through some bad times not only in the war, but also when he returned." Zeb retold the details about Jim Shepherd. When he revealed that the Goatman was Jake's father, Wanda's deep brown eyes widened in surprise.

"The Goatman? Not possible," she responded. "That is unbelievable he'd be Jake's father, but like you said, even if that's so, doesn't mean he is not the killer. Who knows what demons dance in his head after all he has been through? Clearly, he is not right, given his reclusive lifestyle and the threatening appearance you described. I want to see him."

Zeb smiled. "That's probably not going to happen. I think your dad has Chief Bullock keeping his eye on your whereabouts. And we don't know how dangerous the Goatman is."

Wanda was having none of that. She exclaimed, "First, Bullock needs to spend more time watching the Goatman and less time around my desk watching me. Second, I am no more in danger than you are. Sounds like the Goatman knows who you are and where you live. He could grab you pretty much anytime. Probably would have already if he was going to. That's why I am not worried to the point that I would stop you right now from looking for him."

Zeb glanced around making certain they had not been followed. He couldn't help but give her a brief kiss on the cheek saying, "Thanks for worrying, but I'll be fine. You are the one that needs to be careful. If it's not the Goatman, it could be anyone."

Wanda seemed to blush. Zeb couldn't tell for certain as she had such dark, tanned skin in contrast to his fair complexion.

She continued, without missing a step, "Looking at the past files, the killer is mostly in nearby counties. Usually does his deeds near a river. Found remains along the Ogeechee, Oconee, and

Ocmulgee in Coweta County. The Alcovy you know about. Probably because of the isolation. Also, to help conceal evidence.

"The three known cases in the county here, if you include the Copperhead-boy, may have been more spur-of-the-moment situations. The other eight cases I found in the files were not discovered for days after the butchering. Left a cold trail. Much harder to solve. They may be random but appear to have been planned. The killer purposely preyed on individuals or families that were isolated and had no nearby families. He is smart. Leaves no fingerprints, tire tracks, shoe prints, or other evidence. Too smart."

"Interesting," replied Zeb, considering all that Wanda had discovered.

"One consistent trait of the killer is he cuts off the right hand of his victims and usually decapitates them too. He takes these parts away from the site. No one has found what he does with them.

"I'd have found out more, but one of the patrol cars had a beat-up bumper from running into a ditch. I had to do the paperwork to have the repair done."

Zeb remembered that Jake told him about two men arguing down by the Mill a couple of nights before. Shortly after they stopped arguing, a car had raced up the hill, running into the ditch briefly. Jake couldn't see more because the headlights were off. The driver was driving by the moonlight. Must have driven the road many times before to have memorized the sharp curves it held hidden in the darkness. Not many people had that ability.

"Do you know who was driving the police car?" asked Zeb, wondering if there was a connection to that night knowing that fender benders were so common that a connection was unlikely.

"No, which is a bit unusual. Typically, the officer driving the car has the accident tagged to his record. Nobody ever does anything about it though. I don't know why they even bother to make note. Maybe they have figured that out. Probably stopped keeping up with the driver unless it is a major accident," Wanda responded. She finished by sharing random thoughts about the patrol car.

Then she thought for a moment before continuing. "By the way, you mentioned my dad was having Bullock keep his eye on me. I had noticed him over my shoulder even more than his usual — and that was too much already. That's going to stop. He creeps me out anyway."

Zeb hesitated, then responded, "I guess I should have told you. Bullock cornered me in the alley and threatened to tell your dad if I kept seeing you. I'm sure he is just trying to impress your dad by keeping you safe, but it almost felt like he was jealous of me, which makes no sense."

Now Wanda's eyes darkened as if a brief cloud had passed over blocking the sun. Zeb hadn't seen this happen often through the years. But he knew she meant business by the clarity of those piercing brown eyes.

"I'm going to tell my dad to put a stop to that. If he weren't so busy with his women friends, he could make sure I was okay himself. He could spend more time chasing down leads than chasing tail. He relies on Bullock to investigate, and Hank Bullock is a waste of time," Wanda finished in a huff.

Zeb was quiet. Though he didn't know a lot about girls, he was sure Wanda was best not challenged when she got this way. Zeb took a step back, surprised by her earthy language. He had heard 'chasing tail' from older friends. He sort of understood what this meant. Coming from Wanda, he didn't know what she knew about it. He suspected she knew more than him. This simultaneously worried and excited him.

"I want you to get me next time you see the Goatman," Wanda commanded. "I want to see for myself if he is capable of these crimes. In the meantime, I'll check on the driver of that car if you think that is important. And I'll put a stop to being followed by that idiot Bullock! Now I need to get going," she finished, stomping off abruptly without a kiss, her perfect silhouette enhanced by the setting sun. She snapped a low-lying branch off a nearby pine tree and threw it on the ground as she started up the Courthouse steps. Zeb had never seen her this angry.

Zeb wondered if Wanda was angry with him but couldn't imagine why she would be. Collateral damage? *Clayton would know. He knows everything about girls.* She got agitated when she referred to her father and his escapades as well as the mention of Hank Bullock's name. Zeb had nothing to do with either. He'd remained silent — a fortuitous approach he figured he would utilize in these situations in the future. Girls would continue to confuse him well beyond this day's events. He was already thinking about something Wanda had said. About the bumper. He had more questions for Jake. It was getting late. He'd head home and check it out in the morning. He waved in Wanda's direction, but she had already rounded the street corner.

Chapter Thirty-One

Heart Attack

Walking into the back door at home later that evening, Zeb noticed an unsettling quiet. Thelka and Ike had left for the day. His father was seated at his usual spot at the kitchen table, but he didn't even move when Zeb entered. No one else was around. A couple of his bird dogs were beside him. They barked briefly. Realizing it was Zeb, they lay back down. Dr. Barton was not much of one for social graces. "Yes, sir. No, sir" was not deemed important. Rarely was there even recognition upon greeting at moments like this, but something was different.

Unexpectedly, Doc swung around looking at Zeb and said, "Thought it was you." Doc was sweating even though the night breeze had cooled the kitchen.

"Are you all right?" questioned Zeb, looking at a man appearing much older than Zeb had realized.

"Damn it. Do I look all right? I'm having a damn heart attack," Dr. Clyde Barton responded, like he was objectively reporting the medical history on one of his patients.

Zeb knew Doc was not worried about dying at this stage. He'd had a good life. He took a peculiar morbid delight in feigning a heart attack from time to time as if to mock the grim reaper. His staged final gasp was convincing. This time was different.

Like his father and brothers before him, Doc was good with this exit strategy. However, he'd lost a brother in WWII. This next to oldest brother was a fighter pilot. A golden gloves boxer. He'd been killed over Germany and was buried in England. Doc wanted to follow his lead. He would rather die a violent, rapid death while fighting a nefarious foe. He had no desire to age and no longer be of use to anyone, including himself. He had watched his mother in declining health dwindle to a hollow, mindless mockery of her prior robust self.

"I was sitting here thinking about my kids. They're not so different from my bird dogs. I treat them all the same, and they turn out so damn different. That I don't understand," he said, leaning over the table in front of him taking slow deep breaths. Each possibly his last. "Hell, all my pa ever told me was that I wasn't worth a damn and was never going to amount to anything," he finished.

"Don't you think we should head to the hospital?" anxiously inquired Zeb, knowing this was real.

"Hell no. Just shouldn't have to hurt so damn much to die," Dr. Barton responded, his angry, though diminished, voice trailing off.

"I ever tell you about my roommate at Grady during residency? One who came in drunk up all the time? One night he stumbled into a lamp next to my bed and it landed on my head. Deep cut on my head. Had to go to the ER and sew it up. I got him back good. Next night he came in drunk and passed out on the bed. I crumpled up newspapers all around his bed and lit them up. Then I yelled, 'Fire, fire!' That drunken SOB fell all over himself running out of the room. I never laughed so hard. He never came into the dorm room drunk up again," finished Doc, wincing and smiling simultaneously.

Zeb stood motionless for several minutes as Doc closed his eyes. It was only after his father became delirious from hypotension that Zeb was able to convince him to go to the County Hospital. Zeb helped Doc down the steps into the car and started out. Since Thelka and Ike had left for the day, there was no one else around. As they drove through Hobbleton, Zeb was castigated for driving in the left lane around the Courthouse Square even though the road had been a one-way street for years.

"Damn it, Zeb, I know I'm dying, but you don't have to kill us all," reprimanded Dr. Barton, leaning against the passenger door. Zeb nodded in agreement, moving to the right lane to appease his dad, knowing this was not the time to correct him. Not that there ever was.

Zeb had no idea who the "all" was. Only the two of them were in the car. *Is it possible Doc has similar intrusive visitors like I see?* Zeb wondered. *Maybe like the ones Ike imagines when he talks about his past and the war?*

On arrival, they went straight to the Intensive Care Unit. Doc's pulse was racing, irregular, and hardly discernable. His blood pressure was extremely low. The cardiologist, Chet Hunter, a tall, quiet man with close-trimmed, black hair and a stiff gait arrived immediately. He initiated pressor agents, telling Zeb his dad would probably not make it through the night and almost certainly not survive so massive a heart attack. Doc would prove him wrong, which didn't surprise Zeb. Zeb felt his dad was invincible. Or maybe Zeb couldn't imagine his world without his father, thus making him, by necessity, invincible.

Regardless, two days later when Zeb walked into the ICU, Doc was back to his usual shenanigans. Upon seeing Zeb enter, Doc stopped breathing and rolled his eyes back, slumping in the bed and feigning a cardiac arrest. The attractive, buxom ICU nurse knew Dr. Barton well. She simultaneously noticed Zeb's arrival and Doc's apparent sudden cardiac arrest. She panicked. Instead of checking for a pulse and breathing, she reached over Dr. Barton to press the red code button on the wall. This would initiate a barrage of staff for resuscitation purposes. As she reached over, Dr. Barton reached up and pinched her on the breast.

"Damn you, Dr. Barton!" she exclaimed, recoiling from the unexpected sharp pain. "If this heart attack doesn't kill you, I will!"

Doc laughed hard until he became short of breath. This was followed by a violent, habitual smoker's hack. Zeb felt in the moment that nurse might have followed through with her threat, but a few seconds later she and the ICU staff who witnessed the incident couldn't help laughing uncontrollably. Most folks couldn't stay mad at Doc for long.

Dr. Barton escaped Death on this occasion, but before summer's end he would willingly succumb. Next time on his terms.

Chapter Thirty-Two

Disappearance

Zeb's focus for the next several days was assisting in his dad's recovery. He was worried about Jake and his whereabouts, but there was little he could do about that now. Dr. Barton was not an easy patient — to no one's surprise. He attempted to smoke in the ICU after he determined which position in the ICU bed eluded the visual monitors. This was foiled after a diligent older ICU nurse noted the cigarette smell in the room. As soon as Doc returned home, he lit up a cigarette followed by a shot of Jack Daniel's whiskey. So much for a gradual recovery.

Zeb had asked his father why he didn't retire. Working seven days a week for countless hours at all hours would have been tough even for a young man. Doc's cursory response was, "And what the hell would I do?"

Zeb never brought it up again.

Once Zeb felt his dad was stable, he took off in search of Jake. It was time to get Jake up to date on the events that had occurred prior to his dad's heart attack. This included getting the courage to confront Jake. Ask if he knew that the vile, unkempt Goatman was his father all along. Ask if he'd known, before Zeb had let it out, that the Goatman's given name was Jim Shepherd. And, most difficult of all, ask him if he knew that his father had killed his mother while driving incapacitated by alcohol. Zeb had further learned from Thelka that Jim Shepherd had beaten Jake's mother once while in a drunken rage. Zeb had decided not to press Dr. Barton for further information about Jim just yet. Too soon after the heart attack. Best to see what Jake knew first.

The summer was passing quickly. But still no Clayton. Though Zeb missed him every day, he had stopped asking about him when no one else seemed to be concerned. Clayton could hold his own. The morning sun rose later as Zeb cranked up the cycle revving the motor to warm the engine. He shifted gears and began to roll forward.

"Zeb! Hold up," shouted Ike. He was coming out of the pasture. His six-foot-tall frame effortlessly jumped over the barbed wire fence despite his age. His agility never ceased to amaze Zeb, who eased back on the throttle.

"Where is you headed? It is getting more dangerous out there. That last boy that was slaughtered, his head was found by someone fishin' downstream in the Alcovy. Close to Bramblett Shoals. Never would have been found otherwise. Some people I know said he resembled you. Now that's two boys about your age looking similar. May be nothing to it, but it has me and your pa worried," said Ike.

"That may be so," responded Zeb, as he had heard a rumor noting the marked resemblance of two of the recent victims to him. "But I certainly don't resemble Dollbaby. Probably just a coincidence. Anyway, I was headed to see Jake. He needs to hear the whole truth about his father."

"That's the other thing I was about to tell you. Joe Scully said he hasn't seen Jake for several days. Said he usually sees him three or four times a week on his delivery route. Joe was starting to worry about him with all that's been going on," added Ike.

"Why didn't you tell me sooner?" asked Zeb, turning off the ignition. "I don't have any reason to think the Goatman would hurt Jake after all these years. Probably protected Jake while he stayed concealed in the brush after Jake's grandfather died. But someone is out there killing and more frequently. Either that or the killer is becoming more careless and, in some ways, more unpredictably dangerous."

Ike shook his head in agreement, his facial scars glimmering in the bright sun. He said, "I was thinking the same thing. That's why I am worried about Jake. That boy is tough and street smart but not a match for a serial killer. Your dad had me tell Sheriff Hudlow about Joe Scully's concern for Jake. He said he'd personally get over there to check out Jake's shack. Doc didn't want him to send Hank. He never has liked Hank. Said something about him isn't right. And Doc can read folks pretty well."

"Ike, I'll be careful. I'm going into town to ask around. To see what else has happened since my dad's heart attack. Is there anything else you know of that would help solve these murders?" Zeb diverted his eyes away from Ike's, knowing full well that he was going to look for his friend, Jake. Sheriff Hudlow didn't like Jake. Zeb doubted that he would go out of his way to check on him.

Zeb didn't like to lie, but technically he told a good part of the truth. He did plan to see Wanda in town if he could catch her leaving the Courthouse. First, though, he would make sure Jake was all right. He had a pretty good idea about where Jake would be. After Ike reassured Zeb that he didn't have any other information, Zeb cranked up the motorcycle, making it impossible to hear Ike's last words of warning. Zeb knew Ike would try to stop him if given the chance, but as fast as Ike could run, he couldn't catch up to the motorcycle as it lunged forward with a twist of the throttle.

Zeb noticed the air was cooler speeding along the back road to Jake's shed. The impending fall had begun shortening the days of summer. He would go to Jake's first. If Jake wasn't there hiding out from some enemy past or present, Zeb had a second place in mind. A place where Jake would go when things got bad.

"Jake, are you here?" called out Zeb, first cautiously then loudly — both times to no response. His voice echoed over the hills and faded away. The tree frogs quieted momentarily only to resume their clatter as soon as Zeb stopped fracturing the silence. He stepped into the shed. The door had been partially closed. It was never locked. No purpose to that, as the windows and door could easily be pushed in.

The usual clutter remained undisturbed. But Zeb noticed the picture of Jake's parents was gone and the false floor where Jake kept the sharp machete was open. The machete was gone. Jake must have left hastily. "Why would he take the machete?" wondered Zeb out loud, rethinking Jake's whereabouts. Turning to leave, Zeb noticed a single, small hoof print in the dirt under the overhanging roof line that had not been washed away by the summer afternoon thunderstorms. *The Goatman…* thought Zeb. *What was he doing here?* Next to the footprint lay a small, fractured piece of wood. It was the weathered head of the goat Zeb had seen days earlier that had been carved years ago.

Suddenly, the muffled grumblings began. Relentless. Unforgiving:

Jake is dead. Gone. CLACK. Invisible. Too late. CLICK. Always too late.

Zeb pressed his fingers hard against both temples to shut out the noise. He thought the worst of what he'd seen at the shed. Still, if Jake was safe, he'd probably be only a mile or so down the road. He sped away.

Pulling up to the vacant Antioch First Baptist Church, Zeb stepped off the motorcycle onto the packed dirt. No one was around. Zeb walked through the creaky wrought-iron cemetery gates down the uneven path that led to the back of the graveyard. Before him lay the headstone of Hiram Stubblefield, Jake's grandfather, amongst several other gravesites. Some were marked. Others were not. This was where Jake would go when he needed to disappear. Next to Jake's grandfather was a grave Zeb had not noticed previously. Engraved on the headstone:

Debra Stubblefield Shepherd
Entered this World August 8, 1927
Departed February 17, 1948

Jake's mother had been here all along. Buried here after intoxicated Jim Shepherd's car crash had killed her. Upon recognizing her name, Zeb wondered how much Jake knew.

"Jake, are you here?" called out Zeb several times, each time louder and more frantic. Jake was his friend. A friend who had more than once stepped in front of Zeb when older bullies around town had confronted Zeb.

While listening for a response and met only by the murmur of a summer breeze through the pines, Zeb recalled the first time he met Jake several years prior. Zeb was outside the town movie theatre waiting to go in. There was only one movie per week, and the Saturday matinee cost twenty-five cents. A town bully, Donnie Elrod, three or four years older than Zeb, started pushing him, trying to start a fight after Zeb wouldn't let him break in line. Zeb was scared but tried to act otherwise and stood his ground.

Donnie was smaller than Zeb, despite the age difference, but he was intimidating. When Donnie realized Zeb would not back down, he sneered menacingly, threatening, "I'll cut you up a little. Then we'll see if you don't move out of my way."

Zeb watched in fear as Donnie reached into his back pocket and pulled out a knife. In retrospect, it was a small pocketknife, but in the moment, Zeb imagined a six-inch switchblade was about to be unleashed on him. Zeb stood panicked. Frozen. Jake had been nonchalantly watching with his hands in his pockets. He didn't know Zeb at the time but had enough of Donnie's antics.

"Put that knife back in your pocket, or I'll ram it up your ass," Jake said matter-of-factly. There was no anger or excitement in his voice. Jake meant what he said and had no doubt about the outcome should Donnie refuse to listen. Apparently, Donnie had no doubt either, as he collapsed the blade and slid the knife into his back pocket. Then he slinked away. He gave Zeb a threatening stare as he silently slithered down the back alley.

In that moment, Jake Stubblefield became Zeb's best friend. There was something about Jake that drew Zeb to him. It was more than what had occurred. Jake had a quiet confidence and self-reliance that Zeb immediately admired. In other ways Zeb would later envy. Jake was fair-minded and, while not looking for a fight, was quick to step in when he sensed someone was being intimidated. The thought of Jake being in danger trumped all other concerns in this moment.

Jake would have responded by now, thought Zeb as he rushed up the hill by the church. Rounding the corner of the church, he tripped over the roots at the base of an enormous Oak. Zeb landed sprawled out on the downtrodden earth. He started to stand up, but before him, obscured by the bright sun in his eyes, was the outline of a man who seemed to materialize from nowhere. This couldn't be good.

Chapter Thirty-Three

Illumination

"What's the hurry, son?" resonated a voice familiar to Zeb. It was Pastor Paul Arp. Zeb had last seen him when he came to speak to the grieving family of the snake-bit boy who died. The Pastor had known Zeb for years through his office visits to Dr. Barton as well as the occasional sermon that Zeb was unable to escape. Pastor Paul had spent hours talking to Zeb during weekly visits last spring, but Zeb never quite understood why the man had taken a sudden interest in him. Maybe it was the pastor's attempt to put some sense into him.

Zeb liked Pastor Paul. Everyone did. He was a tall, affable, elderly man with an unassuming smile that seemingly never left his face surrounded by a shock of graying hair. Zeb was immediately at ease in his presence. Pastor Arp never had anything bad to say about anyone.

"Pastor Arp, I didn't think anyone was here. I was looking for Jake. He's been missing for a couple of days according to Joe Scully. He's not at the shack or here," responded Zeb as he scurried to his feet, regrouping his lanky legs.

"I noticed he hasn't been around here for a week or so, which is unusual. He generally visits his grandfather's grave two or three times a week. We leave the back door to the church open so he can get to the refrigerator. The congregation has been feeding him since Grandpa Stubblefield died," said Pastor Arp, shielding his eyes from the sun.

"I wondered how Jake made out after his grandfather died. They must have helped watch over him at the shed as well then?" Zeb inquired.

Pastor Arp straightened his loosely fitting collar, responding, "Yes. Several members watched over him until his father showed up out of nowhere. His father is reclusive, but always has an eye on Jake. I believe you kids know him as the Goatman."

This response surprised Zeb.

"Pastor, how did you know about the Goatman? I mean about his father. About Jim Shepherd. Does Jake know? What about his mother, does he know what happened? How the Goatman killed her driving drunk? I noticed her grave beside Jake's grandfather for the first time just now," said Zeb.

"Well, I knew you boys were tracking Jim as a suspect for the recent murders. Seems he gets accused of everything that people don't understand or fear. I didn't know he was being blamed for Debra Shepherd's death as well. I can tell you that Jim drank heavily right after the war. He told me so, but he stopped entirely soon after he married Debra. Stubblefield was her maiden name. Beautiful girl. Jim stopped after he struck Debra one night in a drunken, stuporous rage. Never touched the stuff again. And certainly, never struck her again. He adored her and their son."

Pastor Arp picked up a wheat straw broom and swept the front porch steps of the church as he continued.

"She was the one who couldn't stop drinking. She took the loss of her three brothers on Christmas Day during the Battle of the Bulge hard. Debra was actually the one driving that night according to Sheriff Hudlow. That was not common knowledge. No one talked about it, with Grandfather Stubblefield being inconsolable at the death of his only daughter. He would not listen to reason. He ran Jim off, threatening to kill him and the child, Jake. He demanded that Jim leave the infant with him and get out of his sight. Mr. Stubblefield had a mean side. He meant every word of it," explained Pastor Arp.

"Knowing Jim, he probably took the blame to comfort Debra's father, despite the way he was being treated. And, of course, to protect Jake. That was Jim," finished the Pastor.

"So the Goatman HAS been a myth all this time," mused Zeb, more to himself than to the Pastor.

Pastor Paul laughed. "Oh no, the Goatman is very real in the imagination of pretty much every kid in the county. And Jim certainly looks the part, but I can't believe he'd hurt anyone. He even treats those goats like they are his family. I know he is afraid to get too close to Jake because Jim feels as if he's cursed. Bad things seem to happen wherever he goes. Unless I'm way off, Jim is not the murderer."

"But I saw him burying something down at a Confederate Graveyard next to Freeman's Mill the day after the second boy was found. He gave me an awful, terrifying stare when he saw me hidden behind a tree. I took off, certain he was chasing me to stop me from revealing what I'd seen. I am convinced he was hiding missing body parts from the crime scene. I told the police, but with Hank Bullock doing the investigation, they won't find anything. And the Goatman probably moved the parts elsewhere after I saw him," continued Zeb, brushing off the dirt from his pants.

"Anything is possible, Zeb. People change in unpredictable ways when their life becomes untenable. The human mind is not built to withstand such dreadful trauma. The irrational becomes rational. Jim Shepherd was a changed man on returning from the war. It is conceivable that the tragic death of his beautiful wife and the accusations that followed may have altered his mental state even more. His outward appearance is indicative of something concerning, but I just can't fathom Jim Shepherd being the killer," surmised Pastor Arp, watching Zeb move toward his motorcycle.

"You boys do need to be careful. It is a dangerous time. Two of the recent deaths were boys about your age. I know both their families. Good kids who did nothing wrong. They were both adventuresome and independent, which was a good thing until this evil began," warned the Pastor as he looked around the church grounds to make certain everything was orderly and safe.

"Thanks, Pastor. I'll be off. Something happened at the shed. The Goatman was there. I saw small hoof prints and Jake took a sharp machete with him. I don't know what all that means and really don't care. I just hope Jake is okay. I need to find him," responded Zeb as he straddled the motorcycle.

"How are you doing Zeb? With Clayton being gone and all?" Pastor Arp asked, trying to minimize the question.

Zeb ignored him as he started the motorcycle. He didn't want to be thinking about Clayton and how much he missed him right now. But he also didn't want to be rude, so, looking back over his shoulder, Zeb added, "Thanks, Pastor. I've gotta go find Jake."

Jake would not be able to answer.

Chapter Thirty-Four

The Search

Zeb spent the remainder of the day looking for Jake. He carefully searched the Mill area first, as well as the path the Goatman had used between the old farmhouse and the Mill. Nothing. No prints. No tracks. The old barn at the collapsed farmhouse was empty as well. He came across Joe Scully delivering the mail after exhausting the places he knew Jake would have likely gone.

"Joe, have you seen Jake today? Pastor Arp said you hadn't seen him for a few days. That you were concerned," said Zeb, pulling up beside Joe's car.

Joe, with a crooked smile, responded, "Nope, I haven't seen him. He up and disappeared. I generally see him somewhere while I deliver the mail. He'll show up."

Zeb found it odd that Joe was smiling as he spoke about Jake being missing. But Joe was always smiling. Even so, this seemed an inappropriate response given the fates of two other boys recently found. *Does Joe know more than he is letting on?* wondered Zeb. *How could Joe be so sure that Jake would show up? The other boys showed up, but not alive.*

"How did Jake seem the last time you saw him? Did he give a hint about what he was up to?" asked Zeb.

Joe Scully responded, "You know Jake. He keeps to himself. I saw him at the shed. He appeared preoccupied about something. Mumbled something about a picture. Said something like he couldn't believe it was true. He seemed angry. You know the look. Like he was ready for a fight. He threw a wooden carving he held concealed in his palm against the wall of the shed, shattering it into several pieces. He looked like he was on a mission of some sort."

That explained the goat head from the carving that Zeb had found in the dirt by the shed. It didn't explain why Jake was so angry. This worried Zeb even more, as Jake was not rational when he got worked up. That was effective with his contemporaries. But if the source of Jake's anger is a cold-blooded killer, he may not fare so well. Also, the sharpened machete is a formidable weapon. Jake could injure or even kill someone without intending to. Someone who may be innocent.

"If you see him, Joe, get me word or have him come find me. Tell him to calm down. I don't know what got him going, but his anger may be pointed in the wrong direction. I'm going to town to see if anyone there knows anything more," said Zeb, carefully watching Joe's preoccupied expression, trying to decipher its meaning.

Joe chuckled, "And I bet you'll be seeing Sheriff Hudlow's daughter. She is a looker." Then Joe became more serious, "I don't think the Sheriff much cares if you are with her some, but I've seen Bullock eyeing her in a way that concerned me. Both of you need to be wary of him."

Zeb nodded in agreement, though he had seen Bullock as a blunderer who spent most of his time tripping over his own feet, an outcast seeking attention and approval. But he also knew Bullock made Wanda feel uncomfortable.

Arriving at the Courthouse around lunch time, Zeb decided to wait at Edge's Cafe where he could watch for Wanda while listening to the local gossip. Invariably, this led to a discussion of the latest theories regarding the identity of the serial murderer. Zeb sat in a corner partially concealed by a support column as the regulars took their seats.

The Mayor, Ray Jordan, sat at the head of the table as the lunch club convened. A polished, graying country trial attorney with a slight lisp to his voice, Ray enjoyed the company of men who were back scratchers. This allowed him to pontificate unabated day after day during court recess on a variety of topics most of which he had only cursory knowledge. As Zeb anticipated, the discussion landed upon theories about the identity of the killer running loose in the area.

The Mayor started up, saying, "I just don't buy the idea that some Black man from Atlanta killed ole Dollbaby. I like my nephew, Hank Bullock, but I think he is mistaken by closing the case with this theory. From what I hear, the scene was too similar to the last boy that was mutilated as well as that family from over in Chatsworth. Who knows how many more?"

Ray Jordan took a puff from his well-rounded cigar. He looked pleased at his attentive, pasty audience and continued, "I don't know what to make of the snake-bit boy. Apparently, he kept repeating something about the Goatman, but all these kids think the Goatman is after them. I'm a little surprised no one has lynched the Goatman based on suspicion and gossip alone. Wouldn't be the first time that was enough. If it weren't for Doc, I suspect we'd have had a good many more lynchings. He watches over the Goatman like he does Ike, Thelka, and all their type — like they mean something."

What Zeb was about to hear shook him as he huddled deeper in the corner of the Cafe, better concealing himself.

The Mayor liked to hear himself talk. This didn't slow him from eating as he took an oversized bite from his daily tomato, mayonnaise sandwich before continuing, "I've heard some say they saw Jake Stubblefield with a large sharp machete stomping around looking for someone. That boy has always been trouble. Lives out in that shack close by the Mill with no supervision. You can't help but wonder if the answer to the identity of the killer isn't so obvious that we just can't see it. Now I'm not saying Jake's done anything. That would be slander. I'm just saying it could be anybody. Could even be me," he laughed, finishing up his sandwich and wiping away mayonnaise from his ruddy jowls as he spoke.

The cafe crowd laughed in response as if on cue. No one seemed to take the Mayor's comments seriously, but Zeb understood the seed had been planted. Remaining in the shadows while everyone left, Zeb tried to fight back thoughts that Jake could have anything to do with the killings. It just wasn't possible. Yet, thinking back, Jake could have been at any of these sites undetected. He had the means and the physical ability to carry out the butchering. *Did he have a motive?* wondered Zeb. *Do any serial killers have a rational motive? When asked, don't people who knew them say they couldn't believe the serial killer would be that person?*

Zeb felt as if the irrational, taunting voices in his head that he had attempted to mute most of the summer, were beginning to mock him:

Could be anyone. CLICKITY. Anyone at all. Maybe even you. You know too much. Maybe you are the killer. CLACK. Yes, you are the killer! CLACK.

Zeb refused to acknowledge this thought. It made no sense. He fought back images he'd seen in his dreams. Maybe they were nightmares that had been brought on by daily events. Car crashes and injuries as well as deaths were common in Dr. Barton's medical practice. Zeb had witnessed these his whole life. But sometimes the images in his head were all too real.

Then Zeb saw Wanda making her way out of the large wooden Courthouse door in the distance. He crept away from the cafe undetected. She looked around as if she thought she was being followed. Zeb watched her move in his direction. He, too, made certain no one was watching, as he motioned to her while partially hidden in underbrush near the Courthouse.

"Have you heard?" Wanda asked, before Zeb could speak. Wanda looked serious, with her eyes narrowing as she looked around suspiciously.

"No. I haven't heard anything. Is it about Jake? He went missing a few days ago," said Zeb.

"I hope not. They have found another young male down by the Ocmulgee River. Same findings as with the others. I only saw the report come across the desk this morning. I think almost certainly they are related. No one is talking about it, which seems strange. No head or right hand on the scene again, which will make identification difficult," finished Wanda.

"A scar! Did he have a scar? A scar like Jake?!" blurted out Zeb, feeling as if he was watching himself, from a distance, ask the unthinkable.

Wanda responded, matter-of-factly, "There was no mention of a scar. I'm certain it is not Jake." Wanda said this despite knowing that details were often omitted in a preliminary report. She would not allow this possibility to incapacitate them.

"One other thing, Zeb. And you're not going to like this. Now don't get angry. She's all right, but Bullock arrested Thelka. Claims a drug dealer he arrested in the projects said he saw Thelka fighting with Dollbaby. Claims it was the afternoon after Thelka was released from jail. Takes away her alibi."

Zeb stood paralyzed in disbelief. Not Thelka. She couldn't survive in jail. She was terrified of being caged alone in the dark. She was convinced there were haints there. Bad ones. And to her they were as real as the wind. This time they wouldn't leave the cell lock off so she could walk around.

"I need to see her now!" Zeb exclaimed, his voice a pitch higher than usual. "I know she didn't do this! Bullock could threaten a druggy with life imprisonment or worse, and he'd say anything Bullock wanted. He's just trying to impress your dad who suspected Thelka. He never has liked Thelka."

"Calm down. My dad's got nothing to do with this. He didn't even know she was being arrested. Your father is trying to get her out on bail as we speak. Won't be easy this time though. They are holding her for the murder of Dollbaby. Best thing you can do now is go home and wait on them," said Wanda firmly, not pleased Zeb had accused her father of anything.

Zeb spun away without another word. He had no one to turn to now. No Jake. No Thelka. No Wanda. No Clayton. He was alone.

Neither Wanda nor Jake knew at the time, but she had information to share with Zeb that would determine more than their next step. It would determine who closest to them would live or die.

Chapter Thirty-Five

Trapped

Miles away and far beneath the surface, Jake rolled over, semiconscious, in a deep cavernous hole. In a haze before him stood the Goatman. Though weak and dazed, Jake tried to stand. He fell, as he was shackled to a rusted metal hook anchored into the ground. Jake felt the back of his head with his free hand where he noticed a constant throbbing. A large, jagged gash ran diagonally across his head separating dense hair with clumps of dried, thickened, blood.

The Goatman was slumped from the shoulders and covered in tattered cloaks layered like the years that had beaten him down. These coverings seemed heavy with grief and pain. The Goatman, though untethered, was to the point he could hardly move as he pulled rocks down from the walls in this damp enclosure. He stacked them in a pile next to Jake. Jake could not recall what had happened, but it appeared the Goatman was going to bury him alive under rocks. Silence him for good. The Goatman's arms hung menacingly by his side.

Blurred images appeared on the dark walls of this cavernous place. Jake gradually focused on one wall in particular. There were flat objects tacked to the wall. Round objects in jars were lined up on a ledge on the wall beside them. Jake tried to get a better look at the Goatman to see if he had any weapons. He felt his only chance for survival would be to kill this monster regardless of who he might be. As he lay in the cold, he tried to remember how he had gotten here.

A few days earlier, Jake had intensified his search for the Goatman. Angered by the suspicion that the Goatman had killed his mother while driving drunk, Jake had not been careful in his pursuit for the man beneath the cloaks. Jake didn't know who this strange man that lived with the goats could be: his uncle, a distant relative, his father? But Grandpa Stubblefield said both his parents died. Who was the man in the picture? If he were a relative, why had he left Jake alone? The thoughts sickened him. Enraged him. He had rambled around Hobbleton visibly angry, demanding information from anyone who could possibly have known anything about the Goatman.

Everyone was evasive in their responses, and all Jake heard was that he needed to calm down. To get control of himself. Jake thought Dr. Barton and Sheriff Hudlow knew more than anyone else, but Doc was busy in surgery and couldn't be disturbed. Sheriff Hudlow was nowhere to be found. Jake had returned to his shack to look through old belongings and see if there were any clues that might explain what had occurred the night of the car accident that left him scarred for life.

Jake kept a bundle of letters hidden in the false floor where he stored his machete. He had never opened them, preferring to imagine that whoever had written them would return one day. He felt that by opening them, his past and future would merge. Be fused. Immutable. Now he had to read them, as the past would not remain silent. The photograph, the old carvings, and Zeb's revelation from Ike regarding the Goatman had forced Jake back into the darkness of the shack for answers.

He had picked up the stack of yellow envelopes from under the loose boards and began opening them. Most of them were letters to Debra Stubblefield from islands in the Pacific Ocean during WWII. They were signed by Jim Shepherd. The tone in the initial letters was optimistic, almost cheerful, as Jim described the beauty of the islands and atolls. Even after he was entrenched with the Marines during amphibious landings from Guadalcanal in the Solomon Islands up to the Gilbert Islands. Even after experiencing the horrors of war, Jim Shepherd's letters indicated that he remained in good spirits.

Something changed after the U.S. Marines liberated the Marianas from the Japanese. The last letter was postmarked from Guam. Jim had befriended the native Chamorros, indigenous people of Guam who fought alongside the Marines. All seemed well. Then the letters stopped. The next bundle was of letters that Jim Shepherd had sent to his parents after WWII. Jake assumed the letters must have come back into Jim's possession after his parents died. Jake was not yet aware of Jim's traumatic experience with the Chamorro child tortured by the Japanese.

While looking at the letters, Jake noticed a car rolling by the shack. *It is probably Joe Scully*, thought Jake, choosing to ignore it. He was entranced by a letter to Jim's parents shortly after Jake was born. As Jake read the first sentences, he heard a slight creaking of the worn-down wooden floor behind him. Turning to find the source, Jake felt the force of a blunt object to the back of his head.

Then he felt nothing until he regained semi-consciousness in the darkened cavern days later. With his head aching, he strained to remember something, anything. A throw of a punch. The reverberation of jaw meeting fist. Ringing, then silence. Were there goats?

Jake tried repeatedly to stand only to collapse, restrained by the chains binding him. Before he lost consciousness again, his mind registered an image like a still black and white picture —from the wall of objects in the cave. Horrified at the sight, he lapsed into nightmares.

The Goatman had briefly turned to look at Jake but resumed his task as if driven by some horrid, evil force out of his control. In a frenzy, he pulled rock after rock down, each landing haphazardly beside Jake. Abruptly, the Goatman froze upon hearing heavy steps on dried, brittle pine needles — steps that threatened to halt the Goatman from his task.

Chapter Thirty-Six

The Letter

Zeb was angry at himself. He had upset Wanda when he accused her dad of being complicit in Thelka's arrest. Bullock could have acted without first discussing his decision with Sheriff Hudlow. Regardless, Wanda was only trying to help him, but his rage and concern for Thelka clouded clear thoughts. Moreso now than ever, he needed to catch the Goatman. Put a stop to all of this. Save Jake if he was still alive. Get Thelka out of prison. He could apologize to Wanda later.

Zeb didn't know what to make of Wanda's suspicions as he rushed over to Jake's shed again. Wanda had gone through the police collision files as he'd asked. She confirmed that this was the only crashed police car without a driver having signed it out or filing a report about the incident. It was an unmarked police car that was seldom used, making it even more unusual. Wanda had checked the only two collision repair shops in the county. There were no other cars that had crashed and needed repair of an extensively damaged left bumper for the past several weeks. This didn't seem like much to Zeb, but he was beginning to trust Wanda's instincts. If this car was the same one Jake had seen crash by the Mill the night the second boy was murdered, then at a minimum, someone in the police department was hiding something.

Zeb futilely called out for Jake as he rushed back into the shack. Had he missed something? He'd been so focused on the goat prints and shattered carving that he hadn't seen the stack of old letters strewn on the floor. The envelopes were discolored and graying, but the pages inside looked as if they'd just been written. Also discarded on the floor was a letter that had been ripped in two. Zeb picked it up and pieced it together. He began reading. It was dated November 13, 1947.

Dear Mom and Dad,

All is well here. I occasionally see some relatives. I had forgotten it was Aunt Elise and Uncle Tyler that had introduced me to Debra when I was visiting them before the war. Debra is even more beautiful now, though I don't know how that is possible with what she has been through.

Debra is taking great care of Jake. He is the joy we both lost during the war. As you know, Debra took the deaths of her three brothers hard. We were both drinking heavily when I returned from Taiwan, but I have stopped altogether since Jake's birth. Debra has almost stopped as well, but I fear she is drinking when I'm at work. I think with time she'll be fine. We have a temporary home in a structure that Debra's family owns. Some would call it a shack, but it serves our needs.

You may remember Clyde Barton from up around Maysville. Turns out he settled here in Hobbleton. He started a surgery practice after he finished residency training at Emory following the war. He is encouraging me to return to the medical field, and I plan to do just that. Clyde's classmates, who now oversee the surgery program at Emory, have offered me a position as an incoming surgical resident this fall to finish what I started years ago. I look forward to this and seeing you over the upcoming holidays.

Your loving son, Jim

Pastor Arp was right. Jake was definitely Jim Shepherd's son. Debra Stubblefield Shepherd was almost certainly the one drinking that night of the car accident. She had been the one who crashed. Not Jim. This didn't stop Jim from taking responsibility, though a younger Sheriff Hudlow and Doc Barton knew otherwise. Jim, trapped under the car, had watched her slowly die, unable to reach her. This, on top of the horror Jim experienced with the young, innocent Chamorro girl butchered by the Japanese medic he had mentored, was more than Jim could take. If not for Jake, Jim would have ended it all.

Just like the Pastor said, Jim must have thought he was cursed. Unless he left Jake for his grandfather to raise, he would have worried his presence would somehow further injure the boy. Jim had disappeared immediately after his wife's funeral, leaving Jake in Grandpa Stubblefield's arms. He returned years later as a recluse when he heard of Jake's grandpa's death. He decided to watch over Jake from the shadows. Even after all those years, Jim feared getting too close. This twisted narrative all made perfect sense to Zeb now.

What it didn't explain was why Jake had left in such a hurry and so angry. Nor did it explain the goat tracks at the shack around the time of Jake's disappearance. *The answers must lie at the Mill,* thought Zeb. He'd missed clues from the shack. Maybe there were answers to Jake's disappearance that were in plain sight around the Mill. It was getting dark earlier, as fall was approaching, but his search would not wait. He needed to get answers to save Jake from whatever danger he was in and to keep Thelka from imprisonment in the dark cage she feared. He was sure she wouldn't survive there for long, and he couldn't imagine his life without her.

Zeb wished Clayton would turn up. Clayton would know what to do to guide Zeb through all of this and make things all right again. Where was he? Why hadn't he come home?

Zeb jumped on the cycle. At the same time, he could hear the rumble of an approaching thunderstorm with heat lightning flashing in the distance. A Blood Moon was creeping over the pine trees dotting the horizon. Zeb had a bad feeling. He'd been here before, and it had ended badly.

CLICK CLACK.

Chapter Thirty-Seven

Clarity

This time, Zeb didn't stop at the top of the hill to Freeman's Mill to think about the descent and perils of crossing the bridge over the Alcovy River. He didn't even slow as he approached the crest of the hill, recklessly flying down. It was as if he had become someone else. He felt fearless. Any uncertainty was silenced by his only thoughts of saving his friend Jake and protecting Thelka. Though the voices began murmuring in his head, he quieted them by focusing intently on each curvature of the dirt road. If he could make it across the bridge, he knew that, somehow, he'd be able to save his friends.

A jagged tree line, the cutting kind, slashed the darkening, flaming, crimson sky overhead. Each subtle rut and scattered rock came into full view. Magnified. All in slow motion. Tangled briars reached out to gouge him. Clawed at him as he approached the rickety bridge. Vines seemed to twist around his ankles trying to ensnare him. Zeb didn't notice any of this. Instead, he pushed forward, accelerating down into the waiting jaws of the old wooden bridge over the Alcovy, intent only on achieving his goal. Over the menacing, narrow, longitudinal planks. The front wheels of the cycle wobbled wildly, trying to hold their grasp of the narrow line of a board that had chosen them.

CLICK CLACK CLICKITY CLACK, CLICK CLACK CLICKITY CLACK! The ancient timber rattled.

He'd heard that exact sound before. And not only with the voices in his head or in his nightmares. Stolen memories that had lain dormant, like flowers in winter, began to emerge like a train turning the bend from a distance, accelerating as it gets closer. The groaning timber under his motorcycle held the past. Revealed the past in order to portend the future. Frozen for months.

CLICKITY CLACK.

Words again hung before him. Back. They were back. This time, his focus couldn't stop them. The voices. No, not the voices, just one voice: Clayton's.

CLICKITY CLACK.

Clayton's laughter. It surrounded Zeb. Now he couldn't help but remember. He had been here with Clayton in the early spring. Memories, like waves in a storm, came crashing back, flooding in — one after another. Only this time, Zeb didn't feel like he was drowning in it. Instead, he clearly heard Clayton tell him that if he made it across the bridge, he could follow his big brother anywhere. Just as Zeb wanted.

Zeb had been maneuvering the motorcycle full throttle as Clayton howled, hanging on behind Zeb. Laughing away. The memories stumbled in, one after the other, no way to stifle them anymore. Clayton encouraging him, yelling "You can do this, Zeb! Go for it!"

CLICK.

Suddenly the front wheel got hooked in a gap between the boards.

CLACK.

Then Zeb remembered fighting the handlebar to pull the wheel out. The rush of air as he and Clayton went over the flimsy rusted railing into the Alcovy. Hard.

CLICKITY CLACK.

The cold rush of the current stealing breath. Sinking. Sinking. Then two hands lifting him up. Not playfully in the air like he remembered. Desperate.

Clayton's hands battling the current, pushing Zeb up to the light with all of his strength. To the surface where Zeb could breathe. Zeb clinging to a log that kept him afloat.

Frantically searching. Searching. Searching. "Clayton? Clayton! Where are you?!" Only finding silence. Clayton gone. Never to surface again.

As Ike had said: The Alcovy does not give up her dead.

The images flew at Zeb like delicate shards of glass, shattering, splintering, reflecting sunlight in convulsing colors. Fleeting images of past and present. Converging. Then Omitted. Then back again. Fluttering mocking, beautiful horror. Coalescing. Commingled. Assimilated into the tragedy that stood before him frame by frame. Seamless. No longer concealed in the corners, in his nightmares. He felt lost in his weakness, never so alone.

CLICKITY CLACK.

And then it was over.

Zeb had made it. As he crossed the Alcovy on Clayton's motorcycle, he finally understood the demons that had held him hostage, the voices that had plagued him for months. He faced them when he remembered what had happened and understood Clayton would not be coming back. His body would never be found. They had searched for weeks. The guilt had overwhelmed Zeb. He had killed Clayton. Created the murmuring, chanting voices slicing through his head. Cutting. Unpredictable. Unforgiving.

CLICKITY CLACK.

Zeb looked back at the bridge and the perpetually moving river below. Tears filled Zeb's eyes.

CLICKITY.

He let out a primordial scream.

CLACK.

This time, it was a crystalline image that emerged from the relentless, distorted, shadows concealed in the corners of Zeb's thoughts and dreams. It forged into Zeb's memory, as if fearing the slightest movement would destroy it. Cause it to disappear without a trace. The image — the knowing — was one of forgiveness. Peace. Silencing the guilt. The oppressive voices. It was an image of Clayton.

"The chanting was not Clayton!" Zeb shouted out loud, to the melting shadows. "Clayton would have forgiven me!"

The image enabled more memories to pour forth. Zeb recalled the moment that Clayton had told him that he had lived more in eighteen years than most live in a lifetime. Clayton said he had only one fear. This was right before he had disappeared below the shimmering water. *CLICKITY CLACK. CLICKITY.*

Before they started down the hill that day, he had said, "What a ride we're gonna have. I've already had. I just don't want to get old. No use to anybody. Anything ever happens to me, throw me on a mountain top or toss me in a river. I got no use for a box stuck in the ground. I'm not meant to be a decrepit old man anyways. I'll be taken up soon enough. I'll always be here behind you regardless. No regrets, Zeb. Let's go!" With that, Clayton tipped his cap — a sign between brothers that all would be okay.

Zeb shut off the motorcycle as he slid into the gravel on the far side of the bridge. He had confronted the past that smothered him. He couldn't save Clayton. Clayton would never come back. But maybe he could save Jake. He would have time to mourn Clayton without avoiding the past any longer, but now he needed to go if he was going to be able to find his friend. NOW.

Hiding the cycle in the brush to avoid detection, Zeb silently slipped through the thickets wiping his tear-stained eyes while attempting to let go of all but the image of Clayton backing him up. Watching over him. Things felt different now.

Before he stepped into the opening around the Mill, Zeb heard a clank of metal against rock in the direction of the graveyard. Remaining concealed, he crawled along the path that Joe Scully had shown Jake and him weeks earlier. A lightning storm approached, darkening the sky. Before him, he saw a picture that had been part of the visions he'd imagined repeatedly.

It was the Goatman digging a gravesite. Even from a distance, he looked and smelled horrid. His beard dragged across the ground as he hunched over the hole, digging deeper with every shovel full of dirt. An apparition personifying evil. Zeb was close enough that he could see the dark, hollowed out, empty eyes that had long since given up any sense of hope or promise. The Goatman's scent reminded Zeb of the disturbingly sweet smell of death in decaying animals killed by the roadside. Fear devoured this place.

Previously, the sites of disturbed dirt at the Confederate gravesite were small, but this one was large enough to accommodate a full-grown man. *Is this somehow related to the recent murder by Bramblett Shoals? Was he burying the boy's head and right hand? If so, why the large hole?* Zeb wondered. How emotionally damaged was the Goatman? Could he be the killer of Dollbaby and the snake-bit boy, the mutilated boy, and the Chatsworth family, among others? Had he killed Jake? Zeb was frozen in terror as he watched.

Jake was nowhere to be seen. Zeb decided that he needed more help. He'd have to find Ike or his dad. Just as Zeb was about to make a run for it, he saw headlights coming across the bridge over the Alcovy River. The car briefly stopped in the hidden spot Joe Scully had shown them weeks before, as if the driver was searching for something or someone. Then it came to a full halt in the clearing in front of the Mill. The driver stepped out. He left the motor idling with the headlights on. At first, Zeb thought he saw Joe Scully come around in front of the headlights. When he saw a much larger outline, he knew this wasn't Joe. Then he heard an unmistakable voice that sounded deeper and more in control than Zeb had ever heard.

"Jim! Goatman! Whatever you call yourself these days. Good, you did as told. Come on down here. I got your boy still alive as promised. Had to rough him up a bit. He's a fighter. Always has been. Come on down and see him. Neither one of you will be around much longer. Don't try anything, or I promise you'll have to watch him die slowly and painfully. I can make another promise. You won't want to have that as the last thing you see. I'll make it quick for both of you if you continue to listen and do as I tell you.

"Hell, your boy has had the perfect course across his neck for my knife to follow. I've been admiring it for years. It's a shame I don't have time to do a proper job slicing him up, but I've stepped up my work some lately, and it looks like it's getting folks riled up. Even Sheriff Hudlow is starting to ask questions. Shoot, if he ever takes time to even get off of one of them whores of his, he'd probably be likely to figure things out and join us down here. No time for dawdling. Let's finish this quick. I see you did as told and dug that hole deep enough for the two of you. You can thank Jake for bringing this ending upon you. This is all his fault. He was just starting to ask too many questions. Him and Zeb. That Zeb will be next," he rambled, as he adjusted the Chief of Police hat that he now wore tilted to one side.

Lightning flashed across the sky, and, in disbelief, Zeb could see the sickening yellow eyes of Hank Bullock. *How could it be?* Thought Zeb. *It is not possible.*

Jim Shepherd did as commanded, moving down the hill to the clearing with pain in every step. He'd been beaten and starved. Each step looked like his last. His beloved goats followed close behind as if they sensed his pain. It almost looked to Zeb like a goat funeral procession. One after the other, they emerged, materializing from the thick underbrush.

Bullock opened the door of his unmarked police car, pulling Jake out backwards by his cuffed hands. Jake toppled to the ground barely conscious. He, too, had clearly been beaten. There was a mixture of dried old blood and new, the latter forming rivulets that seemed to fracture Jake's face into shattered fragments.

"Come on over here and get him, Goatman. Your boy is a stubborn brawler. I keep thinking he's done, and he'll still try to fight me. But I will prevail. I want both of you over by the grave. There's a storm coming. That's good. It will wash away the evidence. And there won't be much this time if you continue to do as told. I'll finish you in the grave and cover you up. Since I'll be the one looking for you, I'll be sure not to look here," laughed Bullock. As he aimed his six-chamber revolver at Jim Shepherd, the Goatman leaned over Jake trying to support him.

Zeb remained still, frozen. Afraid to think. Uncertain what to do. The voices were gone, but Zeb's mind was blank. Then he forced himself to imagine what Clayton would do. If he rushed Bullock, he had no chance. The clearing was too big for any surprise attack. Bullock was larger and held a gun. As he considered options, he watched Jim futilely trying to lift Jake. He was too worn down and clearly did not want to bring his son to his death.

"Jim. Get him up or I'll finish it here and now. Damn it, I don't want to be dragging both of you through the brush!" Bullock exclaimed, poking Jim sharply in the ribs with the revolver.

He aimed his pistol at a Billy goat that had quietly positioned itself between Bullock and the Goatman. "I think I'll start in on killing these damn old goats. Not quick, mind you. Gut shots so they'll linger. Now, get Jake up."

Zeb became angry as he listened to Bullock's abusive language. He had to do something. Had to at least give them more time. He couldn't simply hope someone would miss him and show up. That was unlikely anyway. He quietly gathered nearby rocks, planning to throw them in different directions. Bullock would be distracted, realize he was not alone, and seek Zeb out rather than immediately kill Jake and his father. Zeb knew he could crawl through the low brush faster than Bullock. Dodging bullets was another concern. Bullock, for all his weaknesses, was known as a good shot. But it would be worth the risk to save his friend.

Before Zeb could throw the first stone, the Billy goat raised up and rammed Bullock, jarring him. Simultaneously, Jake's father mustered his last bit of strength and lunged at Bullock, but it was not enough, as Bullock shot Jim Shepherd in the mid-section. Then he shot the Billy goat in the head, instantly killing it. Jim wheeled around as he staggered. He fell backwards, sweeping the surviving goats into the thick brush as he tumbled down the adjacent hillside. There he lay, motionless.

No way will I let him kill Jake, thought Zeb. *I need to be brave like Clayton would be.* Without delay, he began throwing stones in different directions. One landed on the roof of the Mill. Two others crashed through the brush behind Bullock. When Bullock spun around, reacting to the noise, Zeb threw a larger stone directly at him, which struck the back of his head. Unfortunately, this did little damage. Bullock quickly turned toward Zeb, eyes glaring. The lightning intensified, illuminating the brush, as Bullock shook his head and stumbled in Zeb's direction.

"There you are, you little bastard. Why am I not surprised? Get out here before I kill you and leave you for the rats!" yelled Bullock, pointing his revolver directly at Zeb's forehead.

As Zeb emerged, Bullock added, "This is even better than I planned. Three for the price of one. You can put them in the grave and join them. I'll pay back ole Doc for humiliating me the other night. This will probably kill the old SOB. Now you won't be between that girl and me."

Zeb started in the direction of Jake, dragging his feet trying to think of his next desperate move. Bullock was the watcher. The murderer. The torturer. How could he not have known? Anger mixed with despair began to creep in. He had to protect Wanda. Protect all the people he cared for. Zeb moved forward as if in a dream. He would rush Bullock. Maybe go for the gun. Then he sensed silent motion nearby.

Out of nowhere, the brush behind Bullock exploded, as a bolt of lightning coursed across the naked sky. Zeb watched as Ike hurdled through the brush like Zeb had seen him do over barbed wire fences time and again. Like a panther, he pounced, knocking over

Bullock before he could take aim at anyone. Ike easily took the obese man down, but before he could find Bullock's gun, two shots were fired. One struck Ike in the right arm. The other grazed him in the head, knocking him out. Zeb jumped forward to help only to find Bullock's gun once again aimed at his forehead.

"Enough!" snarled Bullock. "I don't know who else knows you were sneaking around here again. Couldn't be Thelka. I got her locked away for good. I warned you to stay away from the Mill and to stay away from that girl! This will solve both those problems. I got to finish this up quick. There's a change of plans. Get Jake up the hill to his grave. I'll leave that nasty old Goatman where he lies. I'll tell them I caught the Goatman burying the two of you. Ike was his accomplice. I had no choice but to kill them on the spot. They'll believe me. A Black man and a "nightmare" have no chance to tell the truth. No one is listening. Dead men don't talk. And when she hears that I attempted to protect you, Wanda will see me as the savior."

Bullock sneered with blood-shot, monstrous, jaundiced eyes as he motioned with his pistol for Zeb to move in Jake's direction. A dirty finger was wrapped around the trigger.

All hope lost, Zeb struggled in vain to lift Jake. Then he thought he heard a familiar cough rounding the still idling police car. Out of the shadows stepped Doc with his 44 Magnum rifle aimed at Hank Bullock. He was out of breath and coughing sporadically from having run the few steps across the bridge. The idling car and commotion had masked his detection.

"Hank, drop the gun. I got no problem killing you, but I'd rather watch you hang. I suspected you had something to do with these slaughters. I told Hudlow so, but he wouldn't half listen. Said I just didn't like you, which is also true," ordered Dr. Barton, like he was directing a surgical procedure under battlefield conditions.

As Bullock leaned in Zeb's direction, Doc sternly commanded, "Next move, Hank, and you won't have another! I'm not much good with a pistol but with a rifle from fifteen feet I won't miss. Zeb move away from that monster."

"Now, Doc, this is a misunderstanding," replied Hank. "The Goatman was up to no good. I caught him… He would have killed your boy and his friend. I was just trying to save them."

"Don't even start, you cowardly bastard. I know the truth. Ike beat me down here after I called him. Wanda told her dad she discovered it was you who was driving the patrol car the night the second boy was killed. The one Jake had seen crash. You who altered the records. She found another unmarked car was missing when closing the office. She told the Sheriff and ran to my office to let me know Zeb was in danger. Hudlow will be here shortly. If Ike is dead, I'll strangle you to death with my bare hands," finished Dr. Barton, calmly tightening the trigger on his rifle.

In the distance, police sirens could be heard over the rumbling skies. Their red and blue lights twirled into view as they coursed down the hill.

Thunder exploded across the sky as Doc began coughing just long enough for Bullock to level his gun, firing without aim. Doc responded in kind. Shots were fired in rapid succession. Bullock was hit in the left shoulder, feeling the full force of the 44 Magnum rifle spinning him around. Bullock's first shot zipped past Dr. Barton's ear. Doc's second shot would finish the murderous monster called Hank Bullock. A head shot ripped through the side of Bullock's skull, exploding as it exited Bullock's face leaving no recognizable structures. No yellow eyes. No mouth. No nose or tongue. Nothing but gurgling flesh.

When the gunshots ended, there was only silence. Even the skies had stopped rumbling. Dr. Barton stepped back like someone was pushing him out of the way. He sat on the fender of the police car with a quizzical look on his face. Then he slumped to the ground.

He mused in astonishment, "Well I'll be damned. This is one helluva note."

Zeb rushed over thinking the strain had caused his father to have another heart attack. Grabbing Clyde Barton to help sit him up, Zeb recognized he was wrong. He felt the crimson fluid oozing out of Doc's chest.

"Zeb, get me a cigarette. They're in my front pocket unless the dirty bastard shot them too. Hope Ike is okay. Fearless Son of a Gun. He ran through those hedge bushes like nothing I've ever seen.

He would have been a hell of a running back. I never saw anyone like him. Don't know how he thought he could take on a coward with a gun. Zeb, you take care of him.

"Thelka's fine. I bailed her out earlier. But you watch over her too." Dr. Barton instructed, as his eyes began to wander. Suddenly, the sky exploded with crisscrossing thunderbolts.

Zeb nodded his head as tears crept down his face. Zeb was not aware of this until he felt a soft hand brushing them away. It was Wanda, who had refused to exit the patrol car when Sheriff Hudlow sped out of the Courthouse to the Mill. She clung to Zeb's back as he held his father, neither wanting to let go.

"Zeb, it's okay. He's ready," Wanda whispered.

Doc coughed, then resumed speaking, "Life's been good to me. I've done it all and then some. It's a fine night to die. This old body is worn out. Funny..." Doc stopped mid-sentence. Then added, "I don't feel anything."

He took a final, long drag on the Chesterfield and exhaled slowly. As he did, he muttered, "It is getting darker earlier this year.

I can hardly see a thing. Stars are getting brighter." His voice trailed off as he slumped further forward. There were no stars.

Zeb held him with all the strength he had, keeping Doc from falling face forward, pleading, "Don't leave! We can fix this!"

Wanda held Zeb even more tightly.

"Son. Sometimes you got to let go. We killed the bastard, didn't we?" His father then kept repeating as in a whisper, "You're ready for this.

"Is it dawn now? Things are getting even brighter. There on the hilltop. Can you see them?" Doc was slurring his words, so Zeb leaned closer to listen.

"On the hilltop. My brothers are waving for me to come. They look young. Zeb, Clayton is tipping his hat looking at you. Smiling. Turning away with the others. Waving me to follow. Sun is coming up behind them. Bright. Ike. Ike's here. No more scars. Peaceful. No, Ike, come back."

With a final breath, Doc gasped, "Zeb, I'll see you soon enough. Take care of Thelka. Take care of Ike."

Then Doc was gone.

Chapter Thirty-Eight

The Loss

"Zeb, is you in there?" asked Thelka, to no response, as she stood outside Zeb's bedroom. Zeb had left early in the morning to check up on Jake. Seeing Ike out by the pasture, she called out to him, "Ike have you seen Zeb? Eva' since he lost ole Doc, he ain't eatin' much a nuthin'. He don't have much meat on his bones anyway. That boy's gonna shrivel away to nuthin' from a months-long diet of grief."

Ike yelled back as he walked in her direction favoring his right shoulder. The sun was at his back, and rays split through the clouds around him. The air was cool with autumn at the doorstep.

"What is it you want now, woman? I got work to do."

Thelka responded, "I'm worried about Zeb. He ain't his self no more."

Ike pulled up his long sleeves and drew in a breath saying, "I don't know whose self he is then. Ain't none of us the same no more. You didn't take a liking to that jail cell before Doc bailed you out. Ain't been quite your usual, ornery self, neither. Zeb's going to be fine. He's tougher than you think. Ole Doc made sure he could take care of himself. Never held him back from doing anything. I'm guessing Doc treated his boys that way 'cause he knew his health was failing with all those cigarettes and sleepless nights. Figured he wouldn't be around forever. Toughen them up. Losing Clayton was rough on all of us, but especially Zeb. Grief treats us all differently. It works in strange ways."

Ike kicked a rock off to the ditch, watching it roll until it stopped, and continued, "Doc didn't take a break in the last several years. He considered Sunday a day off. Only worked about six hours that day unless someone was having a baby or broke their leg. He was tough. Zeb's got a lot of Doc in him. All his kids do — or did. Zeb just needs a little time."

Thelka pulled down the ironing board as she considered what Ike said, asking, "Ike, what happened down there? Would ya tell me?"

Ike told her the events of that stormy evening. After he finished, he added, "Thelka, I seen Doc after I was shot. Well, more kinda' sensed him. Like a dream, only different. Him and his brothers, but not like now. Like when we were young. Them boys were always good to me. Doc loved his brothers. They were joking around. The oldest brother was the troublemaker back then. Blew the windows out of the Courthouse in Maysville with dynamite once. Never got caught. Clayton was on the hilltop in the distance smiling and waving. Seemed like he tipped his cap, tellin' Zeb he'd be waiting and then they could travel across the Alcovy together."

I remember knowing these scars were gone," Ike said, as he touched his face lightly. "It seemed quiet and safe. We could look back and see all the death at the Mill, but it didn't seem to matter anymore. Like we were where we were meant to be with who we were meant to be. I was overjoyed. Then, I was tumbling back, lying on the ground all shot up. I didn't want to leave them," Ike finished, peering into cottony clouds drifting nearby.

"Probably just a dream from the concussion," he finished.

Thelka looked puzzled and stared at Ike, asking, "Ike, you weren't afraid?"

Ike smiled and answered, "Wasn't like that. I guess I been worried about dying like most folks. Not anymore. Seems like the rumblings in my head done calmed themselves. This here place ain't all that important. I am ready whenever my time comes. Like I said, I didn't want to come back. Doc and his brothers wanted me to stay with you and Zeb for now."

Thelka turned away. She started humming church hymns as her eyes glistened, relieved by the image Ike had described. She sprayed starch on one of Doc's stained, worn-out shirts. Tested the iron with a moistened finger. Listened for the anticipated *hiss* and started ironing them for the last time. Refusing to believe he was gone. Holding on to him with this last ritual.

Chapter Thirty-Nine

Back Roads

Zeb rumbled up to Jake's shack feeling as if he were arriving for the first time. Nothing felt right. Time didn't feel like time. People seemed to be different. They looked pretty much the same, but their voices sounded like they belonged to someone else. The only ones that he recognized were Ike, Thelka, Jake, and Wanda. Zeb didn't know what to make of this.

Jake was on the front steps whittling an indecipherable object. Most of his bruises and cuts had resolved. This was the first time Zeb had seen him alone and healed enough to ask about what had led up to the confrontation at the Mill.

Jake looked up and managed a smile, saying, "I wasn't so sure we'd make it out of there, Zeb. Was looking grim. I don't half remember, but I know if it weren't for the rest of you, I'd be a goner. Sorry about your dad. But I think he went out like he wanted. More than once he had told me there's nuthin' good about getting old. He put an end to that monster Bullock on the way out. Went out battling, just like he wanted.

"Sorry about Clayton too. I know you miss him something fierce and it's tough accepting he is gone for good. I tried telling you back in the spring when he drowned, but you couldn't hear it then. Not from anyone."

Zeb shuffled slowly to the shack, dragging his feet before responding. "Thanks. I wish both of them were still here." He paused then continued, "I was sure it was the Goatman. I didn't even consider Bullock as the killer, but he had the perfect situation to hide what he was up to. As Coroner, he was doing the autopsies and forensics. As Chief of Police, he did the investigations and reports. No one questioned him. Makes me wonder if he had something to do with the previous Coroner's disappearance. I thought he was just incompetent. A bumbler, same as you thought. Didn't occur to me that he could pull off something like this.

"If it hadn't been for Wanda, we'd all be goners. I didn't even know it at the time, but she was patiently there for me as I worked through the loss of Clayton. She knew all along but also knew it was too soon for me to face. That I'd get there on my own time. Same as you. I was on the edge. She's the one who identified Bullock as the killer. Set off the alarm."

Jake's hands rubbed over the smoothness of the wood he was carving. He looked at Zeb squinting in the sunlight and responded, "I understand what you are saying. I hardly remember being hit from behind at the shack. I kind of remember the Goatman, my pa, was there struggling with someone. I first thought the Goatman was attacking me. Turns out he had been watching over me. As the search for the killer heated up, he sensed I was in danger. That you and me both were.

"My pa was also the one fighting Bullock at the Mill the night the police car ran into the ditch. He tried to save the Copperhead boy. He tried to save me. I thought he was trying to bury me under rocks at one point when he was trying to help me escape Bullock. He could hardly lift them."

"Ike told me your pa had been sick," Zeb said. That's why he was too weak to do much. I had seen Ike sneaking bags down the alley behind the office and wondered what he was up to. Ike was bringing medical supplies, since he said your pa had pneumonia and wouldn't come to the office to be treated. That your pa said he was ready to die, but my pa wouldn't let him, not with you here."

Zeb buried his bare feet in the soft red dirt. "I saw the Goatman digging a grave at the Confederate gravesite and, like you, I figured the worst of him. I figured he was burying body parts from his recent kill. I was terrified it was you. We'd heard that nursery rhyme and talked about the Goatman for so long that I didn't even stop to question for more than a minute if it was him."

Jake abruptly stopped carving. He stared at the wood he was transforming into a definable object in his hands and said, "Zeb, I got to tell you something I hadn't told anyone else. Too awful."

Silence took the place of words, and Zeb looked at Jake staring into an invisible horror. Zeb had never seen Jake like this. *What could it be?* thought Zeb. They'd been friends for years and talked about pretty much everything. Zeb would accept — without judgement — whatever Jake was about to reveal. They both knew that. Especially now, after all they had just been through.

"They haven't found where Bullock had us yet. I hope they never do. I was going in and out of consciousness chained to the floor, but for a moment I could see clearly."

Jake stopped. He took in a deep breath, speaking as he exhaled as if to purge himself of some evil thing. "I could see shapes on the wall of the cave. Round ones in jars on a ledge. Flat ones tacked to the walls. Couldn't make them out at first, then they came into full focus. On the wall were hands, tacked and shriveled up. In the jars, floating in some kind of liquid, were heads. A lot of them. It was terrifying what that monster did," said Jake, his voice trailing off. His hands began trembling and he dropped the imperfectly carved object to the ground.

Zeb reluctantly reached over and touched Jake's shoulder saying, "It's okay. He's gone. You helped stop him for good."

Zeb thought about adding that Bullock had died as he deserved. He had suffered for several days. His yellow-eyed face was blown away by the 44 Magnum rifle Dr. Barton had fired. However, his brain was intact, and he seemed fully aware of his horrible injuries and pain. He had struggled with every breath and suffered up until the very end.

Looking at Jake, Zeb felt that image may trigger even more angst for his friend. He knew what it was like to deal with haunting images and demons. *Maybe in this instance, it will be better to spend time for healing, not hatred*, thought Zeb. *Not vindictiveness.* Bullock was dead, so there'd be no more jars with body parts other than the ones Jake had already seen. Zeb reached down and carefully handed the dropped carving back to Jake. Then, understanding that some distance and time from the trauma was necessary to get through it, he changed the subject.

"Jake, I meant to ask you. Who do you think that wild-eyed Black man you saw running up from the Mill through the thicket the day they found Dollbaby might be?"

Jake shook his head. "I have no idea. Maybe he was with Dollbaby when Bullock nabbed her, and he escaped. Bullock couldn't have caught up to him and probably wasn't too concerned about a Black man's accusing the Chief of Police of anything."

Zeb thought for a minute. "Maybe so. I doubt he was an accomplice. Could be Bullock came up with the idea that a Black drug dealer identified Dollbaby at the morgue to give himself a fall guy. No one else saw that Black man at the morgue. Bullock said he disappeared. If a Black man showed up later and accused Bullock of anything, Bullock would ultimately have had him convicted for all the murders and have him hanged."

Jake stared blankly into the sky, mumbling, "Guess we'll never know. Hope we never see him again."

Zeb warily smiled, lightly jabbing Jake in the ribs and agreed. "Me too. Could have been the haint of Thelka's first husband come back to nab her!"

Looking around at the Oak trees and silent hills of softening pine against the pale blue sky, Zeb continued, "I see the Goa… your pa is recovering well. Looks like he is starting up building a barn down the end of the drive. I was sure he was dead when Bullock shot him and he fell back into the brush. He's lucky he survived. He was doing everything he could to save you."

Jake responded, "Yeah, he did. He's got his own demons though. I hear his nightmares. Most have something to do with the War. Something about a little girl. Some from the car crash that killed my mom, as best I can tell. Preacher Arp told me he wasn't even the one driving the car that night. Life's not been so great to him. I know now that he's a good and decent man."

Both boys watched as a blue-green striped caterpillar crawled up a light green leaf illuminated to transparency by the filtered sun. Then Jake continued, "He hardly speaks to me even now. Keeps his distance. I guess he still thinks there is some curse on him that injures people around him. That's what Preacher Arp thinks anyways. I talked to the preacher about it a couple of days ago. I hope my pa stays here. Says he'll live in the barn with the goats when he finishes it. At least for now."

Jake stretched his neck, which flattened and seemingly erased the now fading, colorless scar. He then resumed his meticulous creation carving the fine patterns in the Oak wood to life. He looked around for the Goatman but only saw Jim Shepherd emerging from the dense brush surrounded by his congregation of goats.

Jim almost seemed to smile as he glanced over at Jake and Zeb from a distance. The two of them together seemed to remind Jim of his youth and friendship with Clyde Barton.

"Good. I bet those nightmares start to fade once he's faced those demons and is around you for a while, Jake. I know mine have, even though I'll always miss my pa and Clayton," said Zeb as he turned to go, imagining the beginning notes of Beethoven's *Moonlight Sonata* whispering through the Oaks.

As the light splintered, reflected through the pines, Zeb envisioned Clayton running up the hill before him. His face breaking into a smile. Tipping his cap and motioning Zeb to join him when he is ready. *Clayton is waiting. There is nothing to fear.*

The sweet smell of jasmine floating on a light breeze pulled Zeb back. It was a scent Zeb had not previously noticed.

"Where are you headed now, Zeb?" asked Jake. He continued and grinned as he tossed a pebble at Zeb, "Let me guess.

Brown eyes, long tan legs, dark hair, and great smile. Can't say I blame ya."

Zeb confidently straddled the motorcycle, playfully rocking it side to side. He looked back at Jake and nodded in affirmation as he kick-started the cycle.

Wanda was anxiously waiting for a ride to explore mysteries hidden in back roads. Somewhere across the railroad tracks, entwined on the motorcycle as they rambled across the tracks into a flaming crimson sky.

Just the two of them. Places the Goatman had left behind trying to find his way home. Places Zeb had only just begun to understand.

~ The End ~

Postscript: Author's Reflections

Coming of Age in the 60s meant going nowhere. No cell phones. No texts or Facebook or Twitter or X. Older siblings held the keys to mysteries, and adults locked the spaces tightly. Out of fear for our future. Out of the knowledge that age comes quickly.

We discovered our own keys. And none too soon. We were mostly bored intermixed with momentary fleeting fascinations.

Young love. A sport. A musical instrument. For many of us, alcohol and, later, drugs. Some dangerous adventures. All addictions. All wonders.

Putting together uneven fragments. Reshaping them with little notion whether they would even come together. The marvelous anticipation. Like a glacier moving ever so slowly, then — without warning — a sudden crash melting into a sea of mysteries. And no manners. That futility came later.

The Goatman was written to explore the mysteries entrapping us in that time. An amorphous skeleton key to unlock the uncertainties that held us in fixed frame. And, for a moment, give a hint of what drove a generation of post WWII graduates. They were "The Greatest Generation," or so it will always seem. Damaged, sometimes deranged, but tough. Tougher than the horrors many had lived. Not on a screen, but up close — a buddy, a teacher, an enemy — still human. And the murderous guilt that all too often follows war.

It was, by nature, different for each human form. As different as the perspectives. And that could be confusing for our young minds, especially because the communion of elders rarely spoke of it. The death. The pain. Never acknowledged. As if silence would erase the thoughts. The suicides — the deformities, some visible. Some unchained.

Uncles who never returned from WWII. Those that did only to succumb later by their own hand. A vacuum pulling inward only to find that untouchable silence. Why? How? And another who disappears. Still, the silence. No mention of them. Melted into a history of unknowns. But we knew to respect the shrouded silence. Idolize the living and, more so, the dead.

The Goatman attempts to sense a moment. The mystery is not always the same. To define it is to deny it. Fleeting mists that disappear as light pierces their protective mantle. Maybe the experience of one fictional frame is all it should be. Scattered fragments of fascination. More sensed than seen. Like The Goatman himself. And so it was written.

Book Club Questions for Wallace Martin's *The Goatman*

1. The author has stated that much of the narrative, while fiction, was drawn from his childhood. Which characters did you find most credible? Were there any characters that did not seem credible or appeared to be too stereotypical? If so, why/why not?

2. Expanding on the previous question, which scenes did you find most credible? What about them felt most real?

3. Which characters did you find most interesting and why?

4. Did you identify with any of the characters, or did they remind you of someone you know? If so, in what ways?

5. While darkness, shadows, and fear are prominent in the narrative, did you sense redemption, courage, and hope throughout as well? Where did you find symbolism or examples of each aspect?

6. Which was your favorite moment, and why did that stand out for you?

7. Were there any scenes that made you anxious? Made you laugh or cry? Frustrate you?

8. Did you find the dream sequences revealing or distracting?

9. Did you feel any scenes could have been deleted or expanded? If so, which one(s) and how would you have written it (them) differently?

10. Were you surprised by the ending? The revelation of the identity of the killer? Other revelations?

11. Publishing today (2024) is a genre-driven phenomenon. Which readers do you think would find this story most appealing? Young adult? Nostalgic mature? Murder mystery fans?

12. If a movie or mini-series were to be made of *The Goatman*, who would you want to see playing the lead characters?

13. Were there any lines in the book that stayed with you or which you wanted to tweet or share with your friends?

14. The title is inspired by an individual who roamed through rural Georgia during the post-WWII era. He was called "The Goatman" because he traveled with a cart pulled by twenty or so goats. Interestingly, he may have known the author Flannery O'Connor and influenced some of her short stories. Can you see elements of Flannery O'Connor's approach to narrative in *The Goatman*? What other classical authors do you think influenced the writing of this book?

15. If you could ask the author, Doc Martin, any question about his experiences, writing process, or *The Goatman* book, what would it be?

The Goatman author, Wallace Martin, can be contacted with comments, questions, or media inquiries/interview requests at Goatman1953@yahoo.com or TheGoatmanBook.com

www.ingramcontent.com/pod-product-compliance
Lightning Source LLC
Chambersburg PA
CBHW051940240626

47153CB00005B/1561